Bloodline

Brian O'Connor

Published 2011
by Poolbeg Press Ltd
123 Grange Hill, Baldoyle
Dublin 13, Ireland
E-mail: poolbeg@poolbeg.com
www.poolbeg.com

A catalogue record for this book is available from the British Library.

ISBN 978-1-84223-486-0

About the Author

Brian O'Connor is the award-winning racing correspondent of the *Irish Times* and author of *Add a Zero* and *Kings of the Saddle*. This is his first novel. He lives in Wicklow with his wife and children.

Acknowledgements

When this book really needed help fighting its corner, Gaye Shortland came out swinging. No one could have done more. Thanks to her and everyone at Poolbeg, especially Paula Campbell. Thanks also to Vanessa O'Loughlin for including that short story in *The Big Book of Hope*, which kicked things off. And to Neil Mount for being cool.

There are a lot of O'Connors to thank, too many to list here, but you all know who you are. Special mention though to my parents, Dolly and Seán, and to Sinead and Ann. As for the wife and kids, I got lucky.

To Niamh, and our two fine boys,
Peter and Johnny.

1

I was trying so hard not to think of milk chocolate crumbling in my mouth that the skid was a shock. For the entire hour's drive from Dublin, the damn radio ad had played at every break and my husky-voiced tormentor had at last made my concentration slip. Just the slightest touch on the brake was enough. The wheels lost grip and no amount of leaning back in the seat stopped the car from careering towards the old railway bridge. Instinct took over: years of hitting the ground at thirty miles an hour had been a painful but useful education. I brought my arms up in front of my face and willed myself not to tense.

There was only ever going to be one winner in a battle of metal and stone and sure enough the ancient humpback bridge came off best. Automatically, I went through the checklist: twisted my neck around, moved every limb and wiggled toes in a voodoo ritual against dreaded paralysis. Everything was still intact and in much better shape than the car.

I got out, cursing stupidity and chocolate. Existing on

1

minute portions of boiled chicken, large doses of vitamin pills and huge amounts of fresh air had long meant that my stomach no longer rumbled in protest at the starvation diet it had to exist on. But every so often my mouth would rebel and start to water at even the idea of something with sugar in it. On bad days it was almost unendurable. Dreams didn't consist of beautiful women or great horses or winning big races, but of being left alone with a burger, fries and a medium shake. Medium would do. I wasn't greedy.

But those dreams had been costly. The front of the car was caved in. There was no steam, no dramatics. A turn of the key didn't yield so much as a turn-over. It was almost like the engine didn't want to impinge on a deathly quiet night. The stars were startlingly bright in the black sky and a half-moon helped throw every shape on the flat Curragh plain into stark definition. Less than half a mile away, huge banks of the green, prickly gorse that thrived throughout the hundreds of acres of Irish horse-racing's headquarters were clearly visible in their new icy-white coat.

It was my own fault, driving in the early hours during a freeze-up. I'd given myself loads of time for the familiar trip from Dublin to the Curragh to ride out at Bailey McFarlane's stables. It wasn't particularly important, just a normal morning's exercise, but the cold weather had brought racing to a standstill for a while and boredom could provoke any amount of silly behaviour. Totalling the car was a heavy punishment though.

I was dressed to ride out so I pulled my jacket tight, retrieved a whip and a helmet from the boot and started to gingerly jog the mile or so to the yard. Road conditions weren't that bad: just my luck to have encountered a rogue piece of ice. The vast expanse of grass to the side of the road was white and crunchy-hard underfoot and I made good progress. Within minutes I was turning into the avenue leading to Bailey's yard. It was then I saw a figure in the distance, to the left of the avenue, walking quickly towards a huge clump of gorse.

What was anybody else doing around the Curragh in such weather before six in the morning? Nothing sinister crossed my mind. That would have been too incongruous on the peaceful night that was in it. And there was something familiar about the rolling gait as the man – it was clearly a man – disappeared behind the bushes. Upping the pace, I left the avenue and made for the clump of gorse, rounding it just as he was getting on a big tracker motorcycle.

"Everything alright?" I asked.

The figure started, then viciously kick-started the bike. He had the visor down on his helmet so I couldn't see his face. Even then I wasn't particularly alarmed. But he gunned the engine and came right at me. A hefty boot caught me on the side of the head as I tucked my body to roll on the hard ground. After a few tumbles, I jumped to my feet and watched the bike career southwards towards the lights of Kildare town.

Even then the most I suspected was that the guy had been trying to break into the tack room. There was a constant demand for cheap saddles and riding equipment and plenty were none too scrupulous about which lorry it might have fallen off the back of. It was a constant irritant but nothing serious.

Except now the cold darkness was suddenly interrupted by lights coming on in the yard, quickly followed by the sound of a man swearing. I recognised Rocky's voice and the unaccustomed panic in it. The stables' night-time security was a seventy-something ex-stable-lad whose habit of nodding off in the tack room was tolerated because of the general assumption that that would be the target for any intruder anyway. There was also a worldly shrewdness to the old man that made him far from a soft touch.

Running back to the main stables entrance, and vaulting the big iron gate into the yard, I made for Rocky's usual lair. All around me, the sixty horses of Bailey McFarlane's string were still cosily lurking behind stable-doors shut up against the cold. It was an old-fashioned yard, almost a hundred years old, rectangular, with boxes facing into a bare cobbled centre that was a nightmare to clean but which resonated with the history of past generations of thoroughbreds and people. I noticed as I ran that a light in Bailey's house next to the yard had also come on.

The tack room door was open but nobody was in there. I ran back out and only then saw Rocky's hunched form emerge from an alley that bisected the long row of boxes on one side. The old man was desperately trying to dial a number on his phone while cursing it at the same time.

"Rocky, what's going on?" I shouted.

"Oh Jesus, who is that?" he asked, backing away, his eyes struggling to focus in the harsh glare of the lights.

"It's Liam Dee, Rocky. Are you okay?"

"He's dead, Liam. He's dead. His head is caved in. Oh, Jesus!"

"What? Who's dead?"

He pointed a trembling finger down the alley that I knew was referred to by everybody as 'the dump'. It was long and dark and mostly full of empty drums and assorted bits of rubbish slyly discarded whenever those in charge weren't looking. A few yards down the alley to the left was a door into a box used for new horses. It had a low roof but it was roomy and was a more relaxed place for new arrivals to settle in because it didn't look directly on to the yard.

Decades before, it had been a room where stable staff could stay and there was still an incongruous glass window facing out to the alley.

Rocky was pointing to its door. I would have given a lot not to have to walk down and look in. Rocky was no shrinking violet and he was badly shook-up.

The door was open and the floor was bare. Years of animals lying down on fresh straw had smoothed the surface so there was a slight sheen to it in the reflected light. Despite the weather it was surprisingly warm, which might have had something to do with the low timber-beamed roof.

He lay in a corner in a pool of dark blood. The slight body might have been asleep. I took a step closer, saw what remained of the back of his skull and struggled not to vomit.

I heard Rocky say something and then a new voice gave me an excuse to back up.

"What do you mean Liam is in there?"

I emerged to be met by the sight of my boss in an incongruous pink dressing-gown and Wellington boots. Her arm was around Rocky's shaking shoulders but her eyes were on me.

"Don't go in there," I said, scrambling in my jacket for a phone. "Rocky, did you ring the police?"

He shook his head. I noticed there were tears in his eyes.

"Okay. I'll do it."

"Would someone tell me what the hell is going on," Bailey thundered before pushing past me.

"Bailey, don't!"

I tried to grab her but it was too late. She turned around quickly, her hands on her face that was white with shock.

"Dear God, it's Anatoly."

2

The only sounds came from crows lazily gliding over the yard to examine flashing blue lights that still had enough power in the morning gloom to make you blink. But there wasn't a murmur where there should have been the snorting clatter of keyed-up horses emerging from their night's sleep and the shouts of frozen lads trying to keep them under control.

After the initial frenzied arrival of police cars and an ambulance, there was an eerily mundane hour where little seemed to happen. The crime scene was sealed off and so was the stable yard. But then things seemed to stand still in the wait for specialists to show up. Rocky, Bailey and myself told a couple of detectives what we'd seen. Rocky said he'd been in the tack room when he thought he heard someone running outside. He figured his ears were playing tricks on him at first but went out to have a look and saw the box door in the alley open. That was when he saw the body, turned on the lights and tried to call the guards. But he'd heard an engine gunning outside the yard as well – like a motorcycle, he said.

I told them how I'd encountered someone on a motorbike who'd tried to run me over.

"What did this person look like, sir?" the detective asked.

"I'd guess he was about my height, but it's only a guess. He was wearing a helmet so I couldn't see his face. Apart from that, nothing really – jeans, a leather jacket, boots. It was all so quick."

"What make of bike was it?"

"It was one of those trackers, like they use for racing on mud."

He asked me what I was doing around the place so early. I explained that I had just driven from Dublin. He asked if anyone could verify what time I had left Dublin. I told him there wasn't but I'd stopped for petrol soon after leaving Sandyford and the people in the station knew me.

"And what were you doing here, sir?"

"I was coming down to ride work. I'm Mrs McFarlane's jockey. My car skidded and hit the railway bridge so I ran the rest of the way here."

"So you work here every day?"

"No. I usually just ride out one morning a week, or come for schooling."

"Schooling?"

"Getting horses to practise their jumping."

The detective told me to stay around and I assured him I wasn't going anywhere. It all felt completely unreal. Such things didn't happen in the middle of the Curragh. The bald, flat plain contained more horses than people, and most of the villains had four legs. Anything to do with horses could be dangerous and sometimes people were killed. But from a flailing leg or a bad fall: this was terribly different.

The staff arriving were met with the full tableau of a crime scene. Bewilderment reigned. I heard someone mention he'd seen Liam Dee's car crashed on the way to work which reminded me I should do something about it. I got permission to return and deal with it. After phoning the insurance company and a recovery vehicle, I retrieved a bag from the boot and walked back.

"Sorry, sir, you can't go any farther."

Even with the peaked cap pulled down over his eyes, the Garda on duty at the stables gates looked very young. Traces of acne peeped painfully over his tight shirt collar. It was true then, I thought. Noticing how young the cops are really is a sign of getting older. Not for the first time recently I wondered how someone else would see me.

It was just bad luck that I was too tall to be automatically nailed as a jockey. Riding over jumps meant the strict Lilliputian demands of the flat game didn't apply but, even so, being half an inch under six feet was simply the wrong shape for my job. The effort of keeping an infuriatingly lengthening body at a weight well below what it desired was hard work that never ended. Not that I deserved sympathy. It was my choice. In fact, it was no sort of choice. There wasn't a time when the idea of riding a racehorse didn't seem like the most exciting thing in the world to do. It still felt like that most of the time. More than enough reason to keep putting my thirty-four-year-old carcass through the wringer.

"My name is Liam Dee. I'm Mrs McFarlane's jockey."

As I spoke, a man dressed in a baggy white jump-suit emerged from the alley and pulled down a face mask. He leaned his head back and breathed out, releasing a long stream of cold, smoky carbon-dioxide towards the sky. He was followed by another similarly dressed man who walked to the back of the ambulance. As I watched, the radio strapped across the Guard's chest crackled to life and he gave my name. A few seconds later it crackled again.

"You can go into the house, sir."

Bailey McFarlane was sitting in the kitchen, back straight, shoulders wide, an untouched cup of tea in front of her. Even then, the depth of my affection at seeing that familiar figure surprised me. I had always been more outwardly friendly with other people in the yard. In fact, the venom of some of our past rows was still raked over with relish by both friends and rivals. It was hard to blame them. We were easy to cast in cartoon roles; we even did it ourselves.

I sometimes regarded Bailey as loud and uncompromising. She considered me too reserved all of the time. My natural inclination was to look inward. Bailey liked being looked at. The little differences had for a time become so magnified that there were a couple of years where we hadn't even spoken. I'd ridden other horses and Bailey employed other jockeys until one day at the races I received a smack on the shoulder and she leaned towards me to whisper: "What you need is a real woman!" That was typical: a big performance hiding all the subtlety underneath.

"Liam. Thank God. Come in," she said now.

The equally familiar figure of Eamon Dunne, the stables' head man, emerged into the kitchen from the big dining room. Through the open door I could hear the sound of people talking quietly. I put my hand on Bailey's arm. She grabbed it and squeezed tightly. Her skin was quite smooth considering how hard she worked in the open air, but the wrinkles still showed all the fifty-seven years she had so defiantly announced on her last birthday. The gesture, though, was enough for me look directly at her. Those vivid

9

blue eyes that could twinkle with mischief and narrow into boiling rage now looked nothing but scared. Our larger-than-life boss was badly rattled.

"Just lying there in the box. Who could have done something like that to Anatoly?"

Anatoly. I didn't even know his surname. Stable staff changed all the time anyway, but the mix of nationalities made remembering names even harder. It was unusual for any sort of yard on the Curragh not to have at least one person in it from Eastern Europe or South America. Bailey liked dealing with an agency that supplied people from Ukraine; "real horse people" she called them approvingly. I calculated there must have been at least six of them working in the yard. Quiet, stoical workers who laughed among themselves in their own language and smiled shyly when dealing with anyone else.

"It's only a few days since he came and told me Bobbie had broken his leg – crying his eyes out, the poor devil."

Small, thin, blond hair. The only real reason his face stuck in my mind was the huge grin that looked faintly comical because of the big gap between his front teeth. It made him look absurdly young. He couldn't have been more than nineteen or twenty anyway, looked fifteen, thousands of miles from home, living in a country he probably hadn't even heard of months before.

Among the four horses he looked after was Bobbie, or Another Rumble as he was known on the racecourse. That was way too much of a mouthful for everyday use, even for those with English as a first language, and 'Bobbie' tripped easily off any tongue. It was hard to affectionately tell a horse called 'Another Rumble' to move his arse while you mucked him out. Every horse has a pet name at home. Bobbie wasn't particularly good, but he tried hard and his willingness to work had resulted in a win at Galway the previous autumn. As we came back to the winner's enclosure, Anatoly had looked up at me with a smile that could have melted an ice-cap as he repeatedly patted the horse's sweating neck.

The tears he'd cried the previous week must have been bitter indeed. Bailey had phoned me for a chat about the horses in general and then, almost as an afterthought, mentioned that Bobbie had had to be put down after breaking a leg. The almost off-hand delivery only emphasised how much she must have felt the loss. But for Anatoly it would have been even worse. He looked after the horse every day, put up with his moods, cared enough to devote his own working life to keeping him happy. Apparently it was just a half-speed canter, the usual morning workout to keep muscles warm and the mind happy. But the kid would have felt the jarring sense of all that powerful rhythm underneath him suddenly turn to shattered bewilderment as Bobbie's leg snapped. There would have been no option but to end it quickly before the horse endured too much pain. Nothing else to do except hold the reins, speak gently to his stricken friend and try not to upset him by crying too much. From what Bailey said, the last part had been impossible.

A surge of unexpected bitterness made my mouth taste bad. Just a vague impression of a funny face and a story of tears at the death of a horse. It wasn't much, was it? That day in Galway had been only another race for me, but it must have been Anatoly's best day since getting off the plane. I found myself hoping desperately that he had made a much bigger impression on everyone else, that the others had taken the time to get to know him, shown more interest than their self-absorbed bloody jockey.

"Who's in the dining room?" I asked Eamon.

11

"The other Ukrainian lads," he said, sipping a cup of tea. "Poor bastards."

Eamon was a short, squat man with thinning hair and a ruddy face that frequently split into a wide grin. Jolly Eamon with his warm heart and kind eyes didn't usually do vehemence but there was a bitter twist to his mouth that spoke volumes for how the stables' head man had got to know poor Anatoly better than me.

"Right, let's do something constructive and try and help them," Bailey announced in her best no-nonsense tone. It was a long time since she had left public school in England, but her accent remained cut-glass clear, as did her desire to get on with things. She paused before going through the door and took a deep breath.

"Liam, can you come with me?" she asked.

I nodded and followed her into the wood-panelled dining room that couldn't have changed much since her grandfather had first arrived on the Curragh from India and decided that this old house, with its forbidding stone and warm interior, was the perfect spot to train racehorses. The long table that dominated the room had also made the journey from the sub-continent. As always, there was a shine to it that reflected like a mirror, despite the nicks, scratches and blotches all over the top and the legs which only added to the feel of solidity that the table radiated. Bailey always joked that the damn thing was too big and one Halloween it was going to end up on the fire. I'd heard that first nearly fifteen years earlier but still the table remained. Bailey's respect for time and place meant that she would have thrown herself on any fire before that table was moved. Right now it was at the centre of a quiet desperation that was palpable as soon as we walked in.

Six figures stood up. One young lad, who couldn't have

been more than twenty, was munching a mouthful of bacon sandwich as quickly as he could so as not to be eating in front of Bailey. They were standing almost to attention, six men ranging from just out of their teens to a hard-eyed thirty-something in the corner.

When Bailey spoke, I noticed a tremble to her voice I hadn't heard before.

"Are you all here?"

"Lara is visiting friends in Dublin," the older man replied. "She worked the last four weekends, so you gave her some days off. She will be back later."

Called Vaz by everyone in the yard, he spoke with a heavy accent, but his English was good and the others clearly deferred to him. He was too big to ride work and usually remained in the yard mucking out. But Eamon had told me his real value was in breaking in the young horses. He said the man was remarkable in how he could almost persuade the nervous youngsters by words alone to permit him on to their backs and to violate their tender mouths with bits of iron and leather. It was a fantastic gift and one that was invaluable to Bailey. A lot of talent in racing had been soured from day one because of a heavy hand.

Vaz spoke again. "We will go back to work now. Anatoly would not like horses to go hungry."

"There is no question of anyone going hungry," Bailey said. "The work will be done. But if anyone wants to go back to town and . . ."

"Thank you, but we will be okay."

They trooped out. Vaz nodded to me. Only after they had closed the kitchen door behind them did I ask Bailey where the local lads were.

"Must be out in the tack room or the feed room. Look, I'm sorry about this but I don't think I'm up to going out there. Eamon will be fine with the yard. Is there any chance you could carry on without me? Just canters. I spoke to one of the police. He understands the horses have to be taken out and fed and all the rest of it. They can't seal off the whole place."

"Yeah, that's no problem. You've had a terrible morning. Why don't you go back to bed for a while?"

"No, it's not that. I guess I'm just shaky about having to deal with all that's going to come now – the police and the papers and everything. God, it'll be terrible."

"It won't be great. But we'll get through it. Everyone will pitch in."

"He was such a lovely young lad, Liam. And some bastard does that to him!" She suddenly sobbed. Her shoulders heaved and grief took over. I put my arm around her.

"And you," she said. "You were lucky. He might have done the same to you. Dear God, what are we dealing with here? Did you get any look at him?"

"No. It's like I told the detective. It was all a bit of blur, just a helmet and a jacket and then a boot. But . . ."

"What?"

"Nothing. You go and lie down."

I gave her a hug. It was weird: we'd probably had more physical contact between us that morning than in all the years we'd known each other. I tried to come up with something appropriate to say but failed. Not that it mattered. What did anything matter with a young boy lying dead outside?

3

It only took one shout and suddenly a yard that had been funereally quiet erupted into mayhem. I was helping Eamon wheel the feed-barrow around to a string of horses anxious to get stuck into a belated breakfast. Lost in our own thoughts, and trying not to get in the way of the police streaming in and out of the cordoned-off murder scene, it needed almost a double-take to register that people were running.

In a corner of the stable block about a hundred yards away two men were fighting. It felt unreal, almost blasphemous. But they were on the ground, clung together, ignoring everyone else and the circumstances around them, to resolutely punch each other.

One of them was Vaz and he was on top of a straw-haired stable lad called Duignan. The younger, Irish guy was getting the worst of it. Powerful punches rained in on his head and he released his grip to pull his arms up to protect his face. It was then that another lad whose name I didn't know rushed in and kicked Vaz in the ribs, knocking him over.

"Get off him!" he roared and turned around to be met

by a couple of Ukrainians, one of whom connected perfectly with a punch to the side of the head. Suddenly it was a free-for-all.

Some of the police barged in to help Eamon and me break it up and thankfully had the size and the weight to make an impression. But it still took a minute to separate the two sides, which ended up facing each other through a line of police.

"Why don't you arrest this man?" Vaz shouted, pointing at Duignan, who was wiping blood from a cut under his eye. "He knows who killed Anatoly! He knows!"

"Fuck off!" Duignan responded. "Don't you fucking start. I'll have you fucking wiped out if you say that shit about me."

"He sell drugs to Anatoly!" Vaz roared. "Him and that other fucker!"

"That's bollocks!" Duignan shouted back. "I didn't go near the little fucker – ever. Why don't you all fuck off home where you came from, you Russian bastards?"

"We are from Ukraine!" another man shouted.

"Yeah, yeah, who cares? It's all the fucking same."

"Well, that's hardly true, now, is it?"

The tones of the new voice in the midst of the clamour ducked and dived like a drunk swallow: a real hornpipe of an accent, from Kerry, or perhaps Cork. From the south anyway. But the face of its owner looked to have hired the sound coming out of it for the day.

Grey was the only word to describe his pallor in the cold air, and it summed up the hair that only just about retained some flecks of mousy brown. The drooping moustache made his narrow mouth look mournfully defeated. A dusty brown suit only added to the impression of middle-aged resignation. But then I noticed the eyes. Whereas the rest of him looked like it was waiting on a pension, there was a liveliness to them that made sense of the voice. There was also an assumption of command in an otherwise unprepossessing figure that made everyone listen.

"I realise that emotions are fraught right now but it would help everyone if we can get through this with as little upset as possible," the grey man said.

"Ask him about the drugs!" Vaz shouted, which provoked more yelling and threats and pointing gestures.

That took a little while to subside but the small man dominating the middle ground allowed things to quieten before continuing.

"When everyone has settled down, we will take statements. If there is anything you wish to say, then that will be the time to say it. Until then, I would suggest everyone get back to work until we come to you. And if that could be done without us having to baby-sit you, then that would be all the better."

Slowly everybody walked away. I hung around for a little while, ready to pre-empt anything kicking off again. But it didn't. Instead it seemed the little policeman's orders were being obeyed. Even more plainclothes detectives poured into the yard and began taking statements. I told one that I'd already given mine and asked if there had been any joy with finding the man on the motorbike.

He said he'd heard nothing and proceeded to take a statement from the sandwich-eating Ukrainian lad who I'd noticed had been well able to stand up for himself in the fight.

"What the hell was that all about?" I asked Eamon who had relentlessly continued his progress with the feed-barrow, opening up the stables' top-doors despite the incongruity of what was going on around him.

"I knew some of them didn't get on but that was shameful," he said.

"But what's all this stuff about drugs?"

"I don't know. All that's like another world to me. But you hear stuff."

"Like?"

"Apparently some of the lads here take . . . things . . ."

Since I was fairly sure that Eamon's recreational substance of choice was a burger on the way home from a few pints, his awkwardness with drug terminology was hardly surprising. The idea of snorting or injecting anything would be alien to him. For almost twenty-five years he had been head man, worked alongside Bailey when the idea of a woman training racehorses was still original enough to provoke scoffing doubt, been there when money was tight and owners scarce. A shoulder for Bailey to cry on when a good-for-nothing husband couldn't cope with being known as Mrs McFarlane's husband. Eamon was even the first person to encounter a shy, city teenager who showed up unannounced one Saturday morning asking to ride out. If Bailey was the flagship of what was now one of the most powerful yards in the country, Eamon was the busy tugboat that kept everything and everyone in line. If he didn't have up-to-date drug slang on the tip of his tongue it only emphasised the quiet integrity that made his rule in the yard more benevolent than dictatorial.

And I was hardly some street-wise dope operator. There had been the usual experiments as a kid, a few smokes, but nothing serious. Certainly nothing to constitute any risk in going through the drug-testing system that all jockeys had to comply with. Anyway, riding and winning and jumping fences was always my number one narcotic of choice.

"There was more to it though," I said. "Did you see the way the locals ganged up on them?"

"Don't be making something out of it, Liam," Eamon said. "People are all over the place."

I let it lie. What was to be gained from pursuing it anyway? And Eamon was right. Everyone was all over the place.

"Anyway," he announced, "there isn't time for that stuff. There are horses here that have to be worked. We have to get on with things."

4

It was a sombre string of horses and riders that pulled out for the gallops. Normally the walk was punctuated with laughter and curses as everyone struggled to control their skittish partners. But although one or two of the horses jig-jogged, more picked up on the mood and plodded quietly from the yard. Perceptive creatures anyway, only the more dense couldn't tell that something was different. The silent, mysterious language that travelled both ways through the reins let them know.

We passed the gates and trotted for five hundred yards until we came to the crossroads. The usual procession of cars filled with harassed parents taking their kids to school or rushing to work had to wait in impatient neutral as we crossed over to the all-weather gallops. Every trainer on the Curragh paid fees to use the facilities, but in the morning it was a case of first come first served and a small group of horses from another yard were already sorting themselves out before they set off up the long narrow straight of wood shavings that was the only thing saving us all from inactivity during the freeze-up.

In the first car a child of no more than six pressed her face against the window and stared out at the police cars and commotion. What kind of horror was waiting for Anatoly's family, I wondered, as we circled. Raising a son to adulthood and then being told that the little boy who had broken your heart with both joy and worry was dead in a place thousands of miles away. Having to cope with the terrible unfairness of it all, and knowing that somebody else's child had inflicted this awfulness. How could anyone's heart recover from having to bury the best part of themselves?

Death had never touched me like that. There had been aunts and uncles and cousins but they had been old or sick. Everyone close, parents and sister, was still around, still well, still allowing me the luxury of believing in some form of permanence. Even the job I had didn't provoke doubts about my own mortality. I couldn't allow it to. Too much thought could bring doubt and from there it was only a short jump to fear.

Only once had the idea even briefly wormed its way from the back of my mind. A fall in a race years before had been as straightforward as these things can be but, as I rolled to a stop, another horse hit the ground behind me. The memory of a flailing leg coming straight for my face as I looked up, winded and unable to move, was still clear. There had been enough time to register what was about to happen and what that steel-tipped hoof would do. It wasn't a life-flashing-before-my-eyes moment. Instead there was only a mild bitterness at dying such a useless death: on my back in a big field at a nondescript racecourse. Except I got away with it. Another horse's legs collided with the revolving half-ton on the ground and the impact moved my attacker only fractionally, but enough to make the hoof sing past my ear. Of course, my equine saviour landed on top of me but that was like a mother's kiss compared to what might have happened. He rolled over and sank me deeper into the ground but came to a halt elsewhere.

Once my breath returned, I actually stood up. Remarkably, nothing had snapped. I was dismissed as just shaken, that all-embracing phrase that covered everything from a headache to bangs that shook to the very soul but which jockey decorum demanded be treated nonchalantly.

For a few nights afterwards, I had dreams about that leg coming towards me but luckily they then disappeared. Whether that was due to luck or some deeper realisation that if they kept coming back I wouldn't be able to do my job, I preferred not to think about. Eventually it became just a distant memory. That is, until recently. There were no nightmares, nothing dramatic. Just the memory slipping back in under the radar, like now. And, hard as I tried, it wouldn't go away. All in all, not a good sign.

"Fucking awful morning, Liam."

Johnno Parle, the stable amateur, had a voice to scatter crows, but even he was keeping the decibel levels low. The burly figure moved his horse alongside as we circled. It was hard not to like Johnno. He was one of the few amateurs riding who was actually an amateur. Most were youngsters trying to make enough of a name for themselves to turn pro. They were full-time in everything but name. I'd done the same myself. But not Johnno. He was a big deal in the finance game and that gave him the time and the money to indulge his love of racing.

"You have no idea how lucky you are to be able to do something so well, and to get paid for it," he was fond of telling me. "I live for the mornings I can come down here and just breathe all this in."

Johnno loved it so much he got down to ride out most mornings before heading back to the real world. Journeys to the racecourse were somehow also fitted in and the man always managed to look as fresh and eager as a child entering a playground. As he said: we had no idea how lucky we were. But even the relentlessly positive Johnno was on a downer this morning.

"He was a sweet kid," he said. "There wasn't a bad bone in his body."

"I hardly knew him."

"You'd have liked him, Liam."

My loss then. Everyone's loss. Such an awful, wasteful loss. The string paired off and started up the gallops at a fast canter. Johnno was riding one of his own horses, a stately old gelding with his best days behind him. He needed a few taps of the whip down the shoulder to maintain the pace and briefly I examined how Johnno crouched low in the saddle and kept clicking his tongue to encourage the old boy forward. We had a mile of this ahead. Johnno would have a sweat on him by the time he finished. Not that he'd mind. Fresh air, horses and physical exertion were what he wanted and what he was getting.

I turned my gaze back to the long stretch of brown wood-shavings ahead and almost guiltily relished the surge of joyful release underneath me. Even at a routine home canter, there was a barely contained power to Patrician which never failed to get my heart beating a little faster. Over the years, and some seasons of being champion jockey, I'd ridden a lot of very good horses. But in the still-maturing frame of Patrician there was the potential for something extra special. He had travelled to Cheltenham the previous year with just three races under his belt and destroyed the best youngsters over hurdles. Now he was doing the same

23

over fences. In four runs he had barely been out of a canter and in my view had only begun to show what he was capable of. Now, with Cheltenham approaching again, it seemed half the country wanted to talk about whether he should go straight for the Gold Cup or wait a year and run instead against his age-group in what would surely be a stroll. The relentless questions had resulted in Bailey's temper reaching frazzle-point more than once. Privately, I had told both her and the owner, a kindly old gentleman from New York, to go for broke and try for the race that mattered the most. After all, who knew where we would all be a year later? Bailey took that to mean the horse's venerable owner, and I let her.

A church spire in the nearby town cut through the top of the gloom and dominated the view as I concentrated on keeping my hands as still as possible. Patrician's gifts included a depth of stamina that no ground seemed able to sap, cat-like jumping, and a liking for passing other horses. But what really distinguished him, even from the couple of Champion Hurdle winners I'd ridden, was his speed. The ability to quicken off any gallop was what on more than one occasion had me grinning as we passed the winning post. It was something that Bailey said would have him winning a really big race if we ran him during the summer flat season. Being able to do it at the end of three miles in sinew-sapping mud was a weapon I couldn't see being beaten.

The trick though was to tap into that speed only when it was needed. Letting him loose on a cold morning at home with no competition but Johnno's old soldier was a thought to get me sweating too. Patrician's rude good health and happiness with the world reverberated through the reins. All it needed was for me to change my grip just a fraction and he would have taken it as green for go. So, instead, I concentrated on sending calm-it signals to my dark-brown partner whose mane I could taste as we parted the air.

It was an unequal battle. If Patrician wanted to go flat out, there was little that ten and a half stone of me could do to stop him. Thankfully he seemed to know that too and didn't feel the need to prove it. We got to the end of the gallop in one piece and with the wild thoroughbred instinct to run like crazy under acceptable control.

I had a silly smile on my face as we pulled up – Patrician usually had that effect. I wasn't one of those jocks who punched the air and waved to the world when they won a race, but even a half-speed feel of all that raw talent made me want to shout out loud. I was still smiling as we trotted back to the yard.

The ambulance had gone, but little else had changed. A pair of uniformed Gardaí stood outside a band of yellow tape that cordoned off the immediate area around the stable box. Inside it, the inch-by-inch search for any kind of helpful fragment of information painstakingly continued. Johnno spoke to one of the policemen, who told him they were waiting for the state pathologist to examine the body. That phrase alone didn't belong in the yard. It was something from television reports where the medium alone divorced much of the reality from the words. Such language belonged to a harsher world than this. Except now it didn't. It all felt very wrong.

Normally the squeak of wheelbarrows as the boxes were mucked out provided a tinny soundtrack to the saddling and unsaddling, but not now. The door to the tack room at the top of the yard was open and I could see Vaz being interviewed by one of the uniformed policemen. Farther into the gloom was another of the bright yellow jackets. As

I led Patrician to a hose to wash down his legs, we passed a box where a statement was being taken from another of the Ukrainians. The guard towered over him but there was a quiet sympathy that seemed to remove any threat and his English was slow and halting through inexperience rather than fear.

Most horses reacted to the water hose with indifference, but big tough Patrician always transformed into a maiden aunt whenever it was turned on him. Whether it was the cold, the splash, or just the feel of it, he skittered around, his feet skidding on the cobbles and his head tossing in resentment. It meant having to keep a tight hold on the reins while pressing a finger on the top of the hose to make the spray as light as possible. I was concentrating so hard on keeping a hold of him that the voice behind made me start.

"Excuse me – I'm looking for the person in charge around here."

I looked up. It was the little policeman from earlier.

"She's inside. I think she might be in bed."

"In bed?"

"She's taken what's happened this morning very hard. I suggested she lie down for a while."

"You suggested? And who are you?"

"Liam Dee. I'm a friend of hers."

The moustache twitched at that one. But he didn't say anything and I started to walk back to the horse's box. Normally Joey, the lucky lad who looked after the stable star, would take over and brush Patrician down while he munched his way through breakfast. This morning Joey was clearly up to his tonsils elsewhere. I slipped off the saddle and bridle and went to work with the combs. Grooming was something I'd always found mildly therapeutic and Patrician regally allowed me to brush him down while he ate. The world could go at whatever speed it liked but this demanded its own tempo.

Then that voice piped up again.

"From the way you said your name, I guess I'm supposed to know who you are?"

"Of course not," I replied. "Should *I* know you?"

"Detective Inspector Diarmuid Yeats. I'm in charge of this investigation."

"I'm the jockey here. Just helping out."

"Ah. Sorry. I don't know anything about racing," he said, glancing at a tiny pocket notebook he'd fished out of a breast pocket.

"Lots of people don't," I said.

"Not from around here."

"I live in Dublin."

"So, you weren't in the area last night then?"

"No. I was at home."

"Anyone able to confirm that?"

"Afraid not. Watched a little TV and went to bed early. Very dull."

"Sounds like a bit of heaven to me."

There was a mild sardonic weariness to Yeats which was easy to like. I combed out Patrician's forelock, ignoring the impatient head tossing at an interrupted meal, and straightened out his blanket to be even on both sides. The policeman watched me throughout, his arms leaning on the half-door as if he had a lot of time to kill and little idea how to do it. Finally he stirred enough to speak.

"So you don't usually work here."

"No, I'm just here to ride out. One morning a week."

"Right."

He said it like it meant something. I put the latch on Patrician's door and walked towards Eamon, who was practically running towards the tack room. The second lot was pulling out to go to the gallops. The last time Eamon had run anywhere was probably on a school sports day. Normally the man didn't come even close to breaking sweat. Time will look after itself, he was fond of saying. But it was needing an awful lot of help now. He practically skidded to a stop and I introduced him to Yeats, who asked if it would be possible to see Mrs McFarlane. Eamon ignored him and directed me to a quiet old mare called Nancy's Delight. He legged me up and Nancy plodded towards her place in the string. There were going to be no fireworks this time. I looked behind and saw the two men walking to the house. Bailey's sleep was about to be cut short. I suspected there was an unlikely adroitness to Yeats which made him get what he wanted.

Johnno was waiting at the gates for me to join him at the head of the string. The two of us started from the stables at the head of the line and were making our way to the gallops when a large green Mercedes emerged from the gloom. Brakes screeched, Johnno swore, and my mare suddenly swerved off the road. The feel of grass underneath her feet only made her more energetic and by the time I had regained some sort of control, our green surprise had driven past the rest of the string and up towards the house.

I waved a quick reassuring hand to Johnno, who shouted back: "What a pair of dickheads! They could have destroyed us."

"They're certainly in a hurry."

"At least *she* should know better."

The "she" was Bailey's daughter Charlotte. The other "dickhead" was her husband Franco. As we re-formed our line towards the gallops, I felt a pang of sympathy for Yeats. He wouldn't know what'd hit him.

5

Bailey was visibly trembling in a kitchen that looked to have shrunk. The vortex of wills and egos that pounded through the room seemed to have sucked the very space away. Normally it was my larger-than-life boss who tended to fill the air. The fact that she now stood on the margins by the sink, white-faced and shaking, said everything about what had been going on.

In the middle, Franco Hoy stood only inches from Yeats, jabbing his finger at the policeman's chest and yelling. Yeats didn't move and was trying to speak calmly, but it was useless. At well over six feet, with a dark, brooding face that glowered under a large mop of black curls, Bailey's son-in-law had the physical presence to put most men on the back foot. He also had the sort of deep, booming voice that testified to an ease at shouting other people down.

Except far from being a bruiser, Franco was in fact a sculptor, a good one too apparently, working on great chunks of rock and marble that were hauled into a back garden shed and later emerged shaped forever by his imagination. I'd seen some of his stuff and even my ignorance couldn't ignore the obvious skill. Not that Franco gave any thought to my opinion. I was just the mother-in-law's help: reasonably well-paid help, but still only providing a service with my hands. He worked with his hands as well, but to express an artistic temperament: to shout to the world what he thought of it. My mitts were only for brute strength. I wondered what he would say if I tried to describe the earlier mental tug-of-war with Patrician but there wouldn't be any point. He would dismiss it as fanciful.

Home for Franco and his wife Charlotte was less than a mile away at a lodge house that Bailey had given them five years earlier when they married. The impression I'd got was that it was supposed to be a temporary arrangement but Charlotte and Franco gave no signs of moving. Far from it. Charlotte regarded herself as her mother's assistant – even if she was often indulged with less-than-strict working hours – and had informed Bailey that the current arrangement was perfect since they were all living so close to each other. The brilliant white smile that accompanied that statement precluded any argument.

Charlotte Hoy had a clear, lightly tanned face that usually beamed with a straightforward good nature which made the idea of any other side to her seem ludicrous. Throw in a relentless blonde cheeriness and it was easy to dismiss Bailey's only daughter as personable froth. Johnno certainly did so, but I suspected that was because he had struck out with her. Years before, I'd tried my own luck, and even gone out with her a couple of times. It had been pleasant enough but neither of us was torn apart when it became obvious that we bored the hell out of each other.

I stepped warily towards Franco and Yeats and waited

for a temporary lull in volume. But before I could speak, Yeats got in first, looking directly at me.

"I had to ask. It's relevant to our investigation."

"Bullshit!" Franco roared. "You're just trying to fit someone up! We all know what you cops can get up to. Bending stuff to make yourselves look good."

Franco was building himself into a sweat. His eyes were bulging with more than just indignation. There was genuine anger there. Charlotte's face was revealing none of its usual friendliness either. Instead, she walked over to her mother and put an arm around her. Bailey hardly seemed to notice.

Again Yeats directed his attention to me. "There was nothing loaded in my question."

"Nothing loaded!" Franco exclaimed. "You say there's nothing loaded in accusing Charlotte's mother of being this guy's lover. And that she had some kind of motive for killing him. Jesus, I'd hate to see you when you're really packing!"

"One of the staff here has given a statement saying that they saw Mrs McFarlane and the deceased embracing. I have to find out if that has any bearing on the circumstances we now find ourselves in."

"You're nothing but a maggot, sifting your way through shit. Can't you see the woman is upset by what you've said? Have you no feelings?"

That sounded harsh to me, but then who knew what emotions could be stirred up by something like this. What I did know was that the idea of Bailey and a kid like Anatoly having a sexual relationship was bizarre. Hiring staff for more than just work wasn't her style. And hitting the hay with a slight youngster like Anatoly was way off beam. Bailey liked her men big and bluff from what I'd seen over the years. There had never been anyone serious since her husband had run off, but there had been a number of fellas she liked to call on when the mood took her. All were of similar age, attitude and class to her and all were capable of enjoying the moment without wanting much else. As with most things, Bailey's attitude to sex was of robust good humour. Jokingly she liked to describe the act as "the grim thing". At a guess, I would say she viewed it as a more enjoyable way of building up a sweat than pounding a road, and little more. But my opinion was of no importance to Yeats right then, so I took him aside under Franco's angry glare.

"When did this embrace take place?"

"Some days ago."

"I think you'll find it happened last week. It's not what you think. One of the horses Anatoly looked after had to be put down."

"Mrs McFarlane mentioned that."

"I know you don't know much about racing, but stable lads view their horses like children. They look after them every day, take a pride in how they run and how they look. The depth of feeling can sometimes be extraordinary. That's why Bailey would have embraced the lad. Purely comforting."

There wasn't much reaction from Yeats, but then I guessed he was probably trained not to show much anyway. The upshot, though, was that he approached Bailey, apologised for any offence in a neutral voice that carried whatever nuance she wanted to take, and said he would be out in the yard for some time if anybody wanted him. In the circumstances it was a pretty stylish retreat but that didn't stop Franco sneering once he'd gone.

"Fucking cop bastard!"

Bailey returned a wan smile and encouraged everyone to

try and get back to some sort of normality. Charlotte wanted to stay and make more tea but there was a hint of exasperation in Bailey's voice when she told her daughter that there were more pressing problems outside. Charlotte eventually took the hint and left. Franco followed, saying he would help in the yard too. Since I was pretty sure Franco didn't know which end bit and which end kicked, it appeared little more than a gesture but he seemed keen to make it. Bailey made no attempt to stop him. I made noises about riding next lot but she cut me short.

"I know it's a lot to ask, Liam, but is there any chance you could stay here tonight?"

She was embarrassed. I was pretty sure the idea of sex with me figured much the same on her radar as it would have with Anatoly. But the actual voicing of any vulnerability was a different matter. For all the up-front heartiness she showed to the world, Bailey didn't like to reveal much of her innermost thoughts. No doubt experience in such a male world as racing had shaped that attitude. So much so that her eyes now blazed defiantly while at the same desperately looking for help.

"Sure, no sweat. I have to wait for the car to be fixed up anyway. And it would be just as easy to get a spare dropped here as anywhere. Probably better, in fact. Thanks."

She cleared her throat and tried to shrug off the uncomfortable emotion, but clearly felt an explanation was necessary.

"Charlotte and Franco mean well, but sometimes they can be a bit overpowering."

The short admission was more than enough. Whatever Bailey really thought about Charlotte and her choice of husband was usually kept very firmly to herself. It was the same with her son, Jamie, who had left to go to college many years previously and who had rarely come home since. I had a hazy memory of blond hair, a slight build, and a quiet nervousness. Families possess their own dynamic, each different, and mostly different to what you might expect. The only certainty was that a typical family doesn't exist.

"It wasn't nice what that detective was suggesting but I suppose he had to ask," Bailey said.

"I don't think there's a problem. Inspector Yeats has probably seen and heard it all before."

"You think?"

"Yeah. My guess is he's okay. He was just going through the motions."

"That's a relief. I thought so too, but so much is happening I wasn't sure," Bailey said before turning to some washing in the sink and laughing slightly with what I supposed was embarrassment. "I guess that's why I'd like you to stay. You're able to see straight, Liam. It's obvious when you're out there racing. The more pressure, the better you are. Never a doubt."

There wasn't much to say to that. She wanted to depend on a man barely able to control himself at the mere mention of a chocolate bar. Bailey needed a stronger shoulder than mine. A lot stronger. It was different out on the track. There it was just me. Sure, there were other horses and other jockeys but ultimately it was about me and getting the most out of the beast underneath. What I relished was the idea of competing against the rest, with each race providing the certainty of finding out who was best. The little red pole at the end never lied. But this was the real world where a young man could get his head caved in before breakfast. No such certainty existed here. It was much too complicated for a simple jockey. Bailey needed more. As it was, all her pressure-loving hero could manage was a fresh pot of tea.

The one useful thing I did was to make her go back to bed. She objected, half-heartedly, but eventually climbed the stairs. That allowed me to hit the phone. The first call as always was to my agent Jack Hobbs. For someone whose house in Dublin I had never been in, and whose family remained just faceless names in occasional anecdotes, Jack was still the person I spoke to more than anyone else.

Quiet, friendly and possessed of a dry wit, Jack first appeared in my life when I was struggling to make an impact as a young jockey. He was well known in the betting ring, employed in one of racing's seemingly innumerable administrative jobs, but really concentrating on some serious punting. The quality of the clothes on his back and the car he drove spoke better than any words about his status as a rare gambler who was making it pay.

When he first approached me about booking rides, I was both flattered and wary. Big-time punters and young green jockeys were a mixture to set bells ringing in the stewards' room. Slowly but surely, however, it became obvious that Jack viewed the job as a theoretical test of his knowledge. The ten-per-cent commission was more than enough to cover his financial interest. In fact, I often thought he would do it for nothing, such was the quiet satisfaction he got from getting me on the back of an obscure winner. Never once had he asked me anything to do with betting or how much he was having on. If I'd asked him to have something on for me, he would have been horrified. With Jack there were readily identifiable boundaries across which nothing should pass. He kept his nose in the form book and I kept my nose out of it. It was an arrangement that had worked seamlessly for a decade – familiar, professional and perfect for both of us.

"I've got you the ride on Knock Abbey in that big

handicap at Leopardstown at the weekend, if the bloody weather ever lets go."

"That's good."

"You sound underwhelmed, young man. What's wrong?"

I told him. Even while talking, I knew it all sounded dreadfully past tense. Surely it was too soon for that. Anatoly was still lying just yards away. But I looked out the window and could see the vet's jeep with its back door open. The living creatures in their boxes demanded attention, no matter what. Later in the day Eamon would re-jig the rota and Anatoly's horses would be assigned to someone else. By the end of the week, the strange new voice grooming them would be familiar and the old one forgotten. Which didn't stop it seeming way too quick.

In his usual imperturbable way Jack said he was sorry and I told him I would be staying put for a day or two until things settled down. A couple of trainers down the country had left me messages and I was calling the second one back when Yeats suddenly appeared at the door. It was a peculiar knack to have, popping out of thin air like that. He turned down the offer of tea and sat down at the table.

"Mr Dee, I have a problem. I have spoken to some of the people working here and I swear I didn't understand fifty per cent of what was said. In fact, I had better luck with most of the foreigners than I had with the locals. For instance, can you tell me what the hell a 'box-walker' is? There's an old man out there who won't give a statement to us until he's cleaned out some, and I quote, 'box-walking bastard'."

That sounded like Jimmy Grimes, a crotchety old-stager who had been at the stables with Bailey's father forty years before and who still looked after his four with a paternal affection that might not be guessed at by those unfamiliar with his rather fruity vocabulary.

"A 'box-walker' is a horse that won't stay still in his stable and is constantly moving. They use up energy and it's hard to keep condition on them. And the lads really hate it because it means the bedding has to be cleaned out more often. Makes more work."

"Alright. Another person said something about the deceased's horse being a 'weaver'. What does that mean?"

"It's like a tic. Some horses move their heads from side to side. Like some people have a squint or whatever. It's not as bad as walking the box."

"Right. I see that I'm in over my head on this, so I'm going to take a chance, Mr Dee. You're not here all the time but you're familiar with the people and the lingo, and I would like to be able to turn to someone for a translation every so often. You also seem to be not completely unintelligent."

"I don't know what to say. Are you waiting for me to blush?"

"Hardly. But I would like your co-operation. If I need to bounce things off you, like an opinion on someone, would you help?"

The man was certainly full of surprises. He sat back, his left hand playing with a teaspoon on the table, keeping any emotion off his face. It was on the tip of my tongue to tell him that squealing on people wasn't really my style, but something made me stop. Who the hell was I to start clambering up a dubious moral mountain when a young man was lying dead?

"I'm not going to hang anyone out to dry," I said.

"No one's asking you to. Don't worry, it's nothing major.

Just a steer, here and there, to save time. I'll have that tea now, if it's still going."

The busy kettle was starting to hiss into life again when a cry came from the yard and Yeats jumped up. I followed him outside to where Eamon had a slim figure wrapped in his arms. Vaz and the other Ukrainians milled around. There wasn't a lot to be said. The only sounds were choking sobs from the girl whose long blonde hair Eamon was smoothing with a rough hand. He looked at Yeats and myself.

"This is Lara. She's just come back from a couple of days off."

Slowly the pair disengaged and the young woman turned around to face us, her hands wiping away tears and strands of hair from her face. As she caught sight of Yeats, there was a perceptible effort to compose herself. Even in the middle of her devastation, it was impossible not to notice how beautiful she was. A golden tan was accompanied by the sort of searing cheekbones that might have looked almost too severe if they hadn't been topped by a pair of spectacular green eyes that seemed to see more than they should.

I was aware of Yeats shuffling next to me. She had achieved in one glance what I presumed many criminals over the years hadn't: put him off balance. Lara was tall but defiance made her appear even taller. She must be used to dealing with men examining her like this, I thought, and looked away to Eamon. He caught my eye and simply shook his head. But the silence was broken by Yeats asking for her full name and where she had been.

"Lara Kuznetsov. I've been in Dublin visiting friends."

Lara's English was good. There was an accent but not much of one.

There was no sense of intimidation as she answered Yeats' questions about names and addresses of the people she had seen in the city. Instead, she appeared almost relieved to be on neutral ground, as if using it to regain equilibrium. I noticed Yeats try to guide her away, presumably to question her more privately, but she was not for moving.

"I have been in this country for eight months. I am from Odessa. I work as a stable-hand and I ride out. Mrs McFarlane also uses me to help with any muscle problems the horses may have. I am a qualified physiotherapist. Sometimes I work on horses with back problems."

"Were you a friend of the deceased?"

"The deceased?"

"The dead man."

There wasn't a flicker at the bald words.

"Anatoly was my friend."

"A boyfriend?"

The suggestion received a stare that suddenly made the air seem colder. I almost looked at Yeats to make sure he hadn't turned to ice. But he persevered.

"I'm sorry, Miss, what was the nature of your relationship?"

"Friends. That is all."

"What about sex?"

"What sex? There was no sex."

"Really? Maybe Mr Ignatieff felt something for you and you weren't even aware of it."

"You are a silly man."

The childish language contrasted so much with the disdain in Lara's voice that Yeats' face was briefly a picture of confusion. He was game enough though.

"I'm sorry you think so, Miss Kuznetsov. But what you

think of me is not really relevant to what I have to do here. And I need to know the nature of the friendship between you and the dead man."

"We were friends. Anatoly was not interested in me like that. He was not interested in any girl. Anatoly was gay."

6

Bailey's fears about the media came true. Within a few hours the phone calls started, quite timid at first, wondering if the story was correct. Just checking, they said. Then a number of television crews in colourful 4x4s appeared at the bottom of the drive. Thankfully Yeats had put a Guard on duty at the main gate and the camera crews had to content themselves with shots of a freezing cold Curragh and some long-range pictures of horses staring out from their stables.

But the Guard couldn't stop the constant phone calls. Nor could he discourage some of the more intrepid newspaper reporters who managed to make it to the front door. Softly voiced apologies for disturbing everyone at such a terrible time emerged from hard-eyed newshounds. All wondered if Bailey could answer just a few questions and all assured they only wanted a minute of her time. Some passed letters through the letterbox containing written evidence of their desire to tell the real story of what had happened but, since no one knew what had really happened anyway, the letters quickly ended up in the bin. Others got a hold of my mobile number but received the answers Yeats had told me to give.

"Just say nobody can comment right now and leave it at that," he'd said before heading back to his office. "Don't get pulled into conversation. You've probably talked to lots of reporters over the years but these guys will be under serious pressure to come up with something. It's inevitable. Horses and racing make something like this a bit special – almost sexy in its own weird way." Yeats had shrugged ruefully, as if to say he had long since given up wondering if the great news-hungry public gets what it wants or what it is offered.

I'd noticed he'd been kindness itself with Bailey when he'd talked to her earlier. I didn't reckon it was snobbishness that made him do that. The same had happened with Vaz and the other Ukrainians; he had questioned them all – even those who'd already given statements. "I like to hear things for myself," he'd said wryly. "Cold paper on its own never provides much flavour." Once more I pondered on how appearances could be so deceptive.

The picture I presented to the press at the door and on the phone was determinedly neutral. Not aggressive, unhelpful or friendly. It wasn't difficult. Over the years there had been any number of disgruntled punters and angry trainers who felt I was a cretinous excuse for a jockey and informed me of such in exotically forceful terms. It quickly became obvious that shouting back only made the situation worse. That presumed they were listening and the last thing anyone who has lost their dough wants to do is listen. So I'd learned to let it wash over, bite my lip, think of the next day. The barbs still cut but it was important not to bleed all over the place. That would have embarrassed me more than any insult.

Somehow the day eventually drew to a close. Almost guiltily, everyone came into the house to watch the main evening news, as if seeing it on television would make it official. Eamon had asked everyone to work late so we could catch up and no one had refused. I'd noticed through the afternoon how Anatoly's countrymen kept to themselves and I presumed they were more comfortable with their own thoughts and language, and it was impossible to ignore the demarcation in the big drawing room as the pictures of our familiar little world were sent to every corner of the country.

A blurred black-and-white photo of Anatoly hovered on the screen as the reporter sombrely relayed the information. At one stage, a couple of local stable lads could be seen grinning towards the camera which provoked a rustle in the room that was cut off by one glare from Eamon. I noticed Lara's eyes flicker at the interruption. She stood at the back – her height meant she was easily able to see over everyone. I found myself looking at her longer than was good. She really was stunning, and serious, and desperately sad. I made myself stare back at the television. Hardly the time, Dee, and hardly the place.

The lead story eventually ended with the reporter saying that a source had informed him that Mrs McFarlane was devastated by what had happened and everyone at the stables hoped that the killer would be brought to justice as soon as possible. So I was now a 'source'. Idly I wondered how I would be described in the papers. '*Unhelpful, smug prick with the personality of a stone*', no doubt. Which meant job done.

Eamon said the van that dropped people home was

waiting and everyone began to move but stopped when Bailey stood up and asked for attention. She cleared her throat and started to speak in that familiar, clear and confident voice. There was also a weariness to it that I hadn't heard before.

"I want to thank everyone. This has not been an easy day. In fact it's been the most awful I can ever remember. I haven't had a chance to speak to everyone individually, but I want to say now how much I appreciate the work you have done today under the most terrible circumstances. It can't have been easy for any of you. Anatoly will be in our prayers and our thoughts. We'll all miss him very much."

As they left, Bailey had a smile, a word or an embrace for everyone. The big woman looked as if she was trying to share her strength, that somehow, by touching, she could transfuse all her energy and passion into the rest of us. In return, she got an embarrassed mixture of goodwill and hesitation. When Lara's turn came, they stood for a while in the embrace, each too proud to cry, but too raw to stand alone.

After everyone had left, I went to boil the kettle. The kitchen was large and more or less the nerve-centre of the whole place. But like the one in my own semi-d in Sandyford, it suffered from its owner's lack of enthusiasm. Bailey had once informed me that the idea of cooking a hot meal put her in a cold sweat.

"It's one of the reasons my good-for-nothing husband pissed off," she said. "He couldn't get a decent dinner. His backbone used to rattle off his stomach!"

I could do the basics, just in small portions. An expedition for cups unearthed a small bottle of brandy. I put a couple of healthy shots into two cups of tea and returned to the drawing room. Despite the cold, both sets of glass doors that led out to the garden were open. Bailey had gone outside. A February wind was blasting but Bailey didn't seem to notice. She took the cup and we drank without tasting. It was some time before she broke the silence.

"I thought of ringing his family, in Ukraine. The agency had their address and phone number, all the details. You know, the farthest he had ever been from home before he came here was to travel two hundred miles to Kiev. First time out of the country, first time on a plane. But what the hell could I have said? They probably don't even speak English. God, they might not even know yet."

Her voice caught at that and I wondered if I should say or do something. Like tell her everything would be alright or give her another hug. Something that might allow her cling to some sort of comfort. But I didn't move. The only sound was a leak from the water-chute striking the stone surface.

"Look at that," she said eventually. "The pipe's dripping. That thing has been iced up for days. Maybe it's starting to thaw out."

"Thank God for that."

"Thanks again for staying, Liam. It'll only be tonight."

"As long as you need."

We returned to silence and thought our own thoughts while listening to the hopeful sound of dripping water. But Bailey suddenly gave a little laugh.

"I was thinking about that time years ago when you were just a kid and that lunatic horse ran away with you up the gallops. What was his name again?"

"Plato's Republic."

"That's right. Plato's Republic." She laughed. "You were this quiet kid who wouldn't say boo to a goose, and you were suddenly insisting that you could ride this mad horse who dumped almost every jockey who ever rode him."

"Eamon said I wasn't good enough to ride him. Not strong enough."

"He was right."

"Yeah, well, I quickly found out."

"Jesus, you went for miles. At one stage you were heading for Cork."

"And after everyone stopped laughing, you gave me the bollocking from hell."

"You took it, though, and the following day you were back for more. Never backed down. It was one of the reasons I started giving you rides. The way you took all the crap and didn't let it grind you down. Just got even quieter and more determined. It was one of my better decisions, I think."

Thank God for Plato's Republic, I thought.

We went back indoors, ordered a Chinese takeaway which Bailey picked at and I mostly tried to ignore. The television was still on but the sound was down, and Bailey didn't seem to be aware of it. Instead, she focussed on the portrait of her grandfather which dominated the room from over the fireplace.

Its faintly musty appearance and dark colours didn't fit in with the rest of the determinedly light and modern furniture but still the old guy looked as if he might strike out at even the suggestion of moving him elsewhere. Apparently he had been a real hard case, a second son who had made his money in India in the 1920s and came back determined to plough his fortune into horses. And what better place to do that than on the Curragh? Millions of dreams had been lost on thousands of horses over hundreds of years in this spot. Not that anyone was likely to have seen Mr McFarlane coming: big bluff whiskers and a stiff-backed dignity couldn't hide the shrewdness in his eyes. Sure enough he'd turned this place into a raging success.

Apparently Mr McFarlane Junior preferred betting on horses to training them, not that I'd heard anything like that from Bailey who idolised her father. It was Eamon who filled me in with stories of debt, worry and charming incompetence. But the place still emerged healthy enough for a McFarlane woman to return it to its former glory, and even a little bit more.

I looked at the portrait again and wondered at the woman sitting opposite me in front of the dwindling fire. Here we were, being monitored by the hundred-year-old memory of a man whose brooding presence still grimly loomed over the place. No one knew better than me how shrewd and gutsy and plain modern Bailey was. But she clung to the past with this quiet determination, as if it justified her in some way, and made sense of what she was. Maybe it was an Anglo thing, like the way she had quietly but resolutely packed two children off to school in Britain so they came back with the accent and attitudes she wanted for them. Different but the same, or, if one wanted to be fanciful, the same coin but different sides. Throw in hundreds of years of history, religion and class and it was a brew that demanded more attention than I was able to give there and then.

The office where Bailey spent hours most days poring over entries and form books was on the other side of the kitchen, but the answer machine in it was purposefully turned to a high volume to allow it be heard from where we were sitting. One ring was followed by a high beep and the voice of the person leaving the message. There were lots of them and they allowed silence between the two of us as we listened and waited for the next one.

Mostly they were from owners, people with horses in the yard, who over the years had also turned into friends. I found myself recognising voices from umpteen pre-race parade-ring conferences. Their concern sounded genuine but Bailey said she would call them back in the morning.

Also in the mix were a couple of late hopefuls from the newspapers. I recognised those voices too, except this time they had the angry impatience of people under pressure. No more imploring: the tone was 'ring us back now'. Obviously the heavy gang worked nights.

After the second one had hung up, Bailey broke our silence with a question she clearly didn't really care about any more.

"What do you think they'll say in the papers?"

"Probably nothing more than was on the news. What else is there to say?"

"It doesn't matter anyway."

"No."

"Look, I know it's not even nine yet, but would you mind if I go to bed?"

"No, of course not."

"I'll show you your room first."

It was the first time I'd ever been upstairs. As we climbed the wide timber steps, it felt like an intrusion and I couldn't help but try to make my steps softer, as if an alarm might go off at any moment. On the first landing there was a wide window that looked out over the lit-up front garden. I knew that the view over the hedge and onto the Curragh must be special, but that would have to wait until a clear morning. Bailey led me up another flight and turned left along a corridor. We walked to the last of three doors and I followed her in.

"It's the main guest room. You should be okay here. The

bathroom is just down the hall. Treat the place like your own. I don't care for shrinking violets sneaking around wondering if they can take something from the fridge."

"The fridge is safe, Bailey, and I'll be fine. So will you."

"You think?"

"I don't think. I know."

Less than twenty-four hours earlier the idea that I might be the one trying to reassure her about anything would have been ridiculous. But the day had changed us all. Bailey's fragility was understandable. Anatoly had been her employee, a kid in a strange place, her responsibility. He had been killed in her care. No one would feel that responsibility more. Her grandfather was probably the same. In a more dutifully paternal way to be sure, but that duty, obvious or not, would count for everything with Mr McFarlane's granddaughter. Why else would she have considered ringing Anatoly's parents? In a world where blame no longer seemed to stick to anyone, Bailey still believed in doing things properly. No wonder, then, that the questions that had hovered over us all day suddenly poured out.

"I know it's a stupid question, Liam, but why? He's too young to be dead. Too bloody green and silly and lovely. What an awful damn waste."

It was no effort to hug her then and tell her everything really would be fine and not to worry. Words were useless, but I figured the tone of them might help in some way; like a nervous young horse being broken in and responding to a reassuring voice.

She left after telling me her room was on the floor below, nearest the stairs. Standing at the door, watching her walk back down, I realised I would do a lot for this tough, hard-edged woman who wasn't nearly as fierce and unyielding as she'd spent her life pretending to be. I might have thanked

God for Plato's Republic but boil it down and everything traced back to Bailey and her generosity. Staying in the house with her for however long would be no hardship.

The room was like something from an Edwardian play. There was a white ornate ceiling high enough to accommodate model aircraft. Towering walls were also brightly coloured and the furniture was a mish-mash of modern and stuff that had accumulated over the years, on top of a carpet so lush it might have moulted earlier in the winter and grown a new coat. But everything was dominated by the four-poster-bed. It was so high it needed a little bunny-hop just to sit up on it. I was almost chuckling at all this over-the-top luxury when a faded black-and-white picture on the wall caught my eye. It was the bed, with a man and a woman posing and laughing in front of it; 1951 was the date written in pencil underneath. The woman was probably Bailey's mother, although there was no obvious physical resemblance. But the man was clearly her father, all size and brio with a big grin on his face as he anticipated diving into the elephantine cot behind them. Lord alone knew how much well-to-do hanky-panky had gone on in this gargantuan bed.

Quickly undressing to my boxers, I peeped out through curtains so thick they might have doubled as duvets. The room faced out on to the yard. No inquisitive eyes stared back at me. All the horses were tucked up inside, top doors closed again against the cold wind. The boxes were as old as the house, made of stone and built to last.

As I looked down, a torch beam flickered. It was Rocky, back working, dutifully patrolling as he did every night, except Sundays when his son took over. I wondered if he had been cured of his habit of nipping into the tack room for a snooze. Quite what seventy-year-old Rocky was supposed to do if someone came raiding was more debatable than ever. He momentarily lingered at the police tape, said something to the Guard on duty, and shone his torch down the alley. I'd seen Yeats talking to him earlier, not surprisingly giving the old man the benefit of his full attention. But Rocky couldn't tell him anything more. Eamon also reported that our aged eyes and ears at night was aggressively pointing out that he couldn't be in different places at the same time. Rocky was definitely not going to be made a scapegoat.

Not that he was one anyway. If the old man could have helped, he would have. We all would. Asking why somebody hadn't done something to stop it was now ultimately as futile as asking why it had happened in the first place. Closing the curtains and climbing into bed, I knew the only question that counted now was who?

7

Joey, Patrician's lad, offered to drive me into Newbridge. The garage looking after my car had got in touch to say a replacement could be picked up at lunchtime. Apparently I'd done such a good job wrecking it that a repair job was all but impossible: annoying but irrelevant. Bent metal – so what.

We were in town within minutes of knocking off for lunch. Joey chatted away about Patrician and said he figured the horse was getting even better and stronger. We'd got to know each other a little since his pride and joy had burst on the scene. He was a likeable, straight-forward young guy who I'd noticed throwing a few shapes with the best of them in the middle of the previous day's ruck.

"What was all that about yesterday," I asked as we joined a traffic-jam. "It could have got really dodgy if the police weren't there."

"You've got to stand up for your mates," he replied.

"And your mates all just happened to be the Irish guys?"

"Are you mates with any of the eastern Europeans?"

"No. But I'm hardly ever here. You guys work alongside each other every day."

"Look, I'm sorry the fella died. He was alright. And the rest of them are good at what they do. Some of them are very good. But there are Irish fellas in this town who're very good too, fellas who've worked for years on the Curragh, and they're now drawing dole because there's no jobs out there for them. And these foreigners are coming in on the cheap."

"I don't believe Bailey's employing anyone on the cheap, Joey," I said.

"Yeah, maybe not her, but some are. And there's Irish people out of work in Ireland at the same time. Surely you look after your own first. Do you think if we went over to their place, we'd get better treatment? Would we hell!"

The traffic crawled on and we stopped talking for a little bit.

"So, Anatoly was okay, was he?"

"Yeah, he was," Joey said. "Sorry about that. I suppose it sounded bad. I don't not like anyone. But things are dog rough in this country at the moment. People are worried."

"Had you much to do with Anatoly?"

"I used to help him out a little bit. He wasn't one of the better ones. I'd say he hadn't had much to do with horses before he came here. But he learned a bit. He'd have been alright, provided he didn't get too into the Bob."

"The what?"

"You know – Bob Hope – dope."

"He liked it, yeah?"

"Ah, sure who doesn't like to get out of things every so often," he grinned, looking sideways at me.

I guessed to a young fella like Joey, I must have looked old. Every generation believed it walked on a wild-side incomprehensible to its elders. It was part of the thrill of being young. I guessed being on the receiving end was as sure a sign of passing time as any grey hair.

"It doesn't mean he was a junkie or anything, Liam. Don't build it up. Everyone likes a smoke sometimes, or a pill. What's the harm, unless you go stupid on it? I just thought he might have been hitting things a bit heavy, that's all. But it wasn't like he was main-lining H or anything."

I was digesting this piece of information, and wondering if Joey had shared this information with the police, when he pulled in to park.

"There you go," he said. "You'll be able to head back yourself, right?"

"Yeah, thanks. Look, Joey, did you tell the cops this stuff about the drugs?"

"No. Of course not."

"Why?"

"Because it's nothing."

"It's nothing? Anatoly was buying drugs and is killed – and that's nothing?"

"You make it sound like some gang thing on the telly. It's just Christy and the lads trying to make a few quid."

Joey wasn't ruffled in the slightest. He even grinned slightly as I got out of his car and leaned down to look at him through the open window.

"Liam, you're getting into a sweat about nothing. It wasn't drugs that got the guy killed."

"Then what did?"

"I don't know – but it wasn't drugs," he said, looking past me. "And if you don't believe me, why don't you ask *him*?" With a nod he indicated someone behind me.

I turned around to see a familiar figure walking fast past a supermarket. His face, usually creased with smiling cynicism towards the world, was baldly exuding the hardness that had always sat just behind the charm. Head down, it was all he could do not to break into a run. A small knitted cap covered his tightly cropped blond hair and I noticed the wispy blond moustache had been shaved off. But there was no doubting who it was. The stride of a man who had spent five years at sea on various merchant ships before settling for dry land still possessed a dancing-the-hornpipe singularity that had jolted my brain just a couple of nights previously. Christy Wolf was always a hard man to ignore.

Bailey's horse-box driver didn't register my face straight away. But then he stopped and looked straight at me. I could see from his pale-grey eyes that he knew I knew. I even glanced at his feet to check if there were big boots there, maybe even the ones that had caught me on the head as he sped past on his bike. There weren't, just a dirty pair of sneakers. And by the time I looked back up, he'd turned around and started to run.

I followed him, with Joey's shouts in my ears, thinking this kind of cops-and-robbers stuff couldn't be happening. What was I going to do if I caught up with him? Christy Wolf was a product of Dublin's inner-city flats, a tough man, just a few years older than me. He'd driven Bailey's runners around the country for some years: always efficient, always on time, and always backed up by an innate horsemanship that was the product of 'jockeying' horses (that distinctive bareback style common to some of Dublin's rougher estates) near his granny's home in Finglas, rather than any riding-school education he might have got.

There was a good twenty yards between us when he ducked into the big supermarket and vaulted over a chain at the checkouts. By the time he had weaved his way to the back of the store the gap was extended to thirty. I wasn't holding back either. As well as strength, he had speed, not to mention having forgotten more about fighting than I would ever know.

Bursting through a heavy piece of flapping plastic into a big empty yard, I looked wildly around. There was no sign of him. I spun around quickly to see if he'd doubled back but the only one there was a man in a suit holding a phone.

"You can't come back here," he said. "I'll call our security man."

"Don't worry. I'm not stealing anything. Did you see a man run through here, just before me? My height, but broader?"

"No."

"Is there a way out of here?"

"Sure, there's a gate just around the corner."

I sprinted over but there was no sign of Wolf. The gate was locked but less than six feet high. He could have got over it easily. I had one final look around and ran back through the shop.

The female voice at the police station informed me that Detective Superintendent Yeats was out of the office. I stood on the street and cursed. There must have been some feeling in the oath because she offered to try and put me through to him. I thanked her profusely and prayed the little man with the moustache would pick up.

"Mr Dee," he said clearly, "I thought the deal was that I'd get in touch with you."

"I know who nearly ran me over," I said quickly. "It was Christy Wolf, the guy who drives the horse box. He sells drugs. I've just seen him here in Newbridge and he took off from me."

"Alright, are you still in Newbridge now?"

"Yes."

"Right, I'm just ten minutes away. Tell me where you are and I'll pick you up."

He pulled up in a nondescript estate car and we drove to the police station in Kildare town. On the way I told him what had happened.

"I thought you said you didn't recognise him?" Yeats asked.

"Not his face. But there was something about the way he moved that night that rang a bell. I just couldn't figure what. And then I saw him and got it. He knew too. Why else would he run off?"

"Yes, but you couldn't positively identify him, could you?"

"I suppose not. But it is him. Don't you believe me?"

"It's not a question of what I believe. I just wonder if he knows you can't positively identify him."

We went straight to an interview room and Yeats had a uniformed policeman take my statement. He then told another pair of detectives to find Christy Wolf and pick him up. Both men smiled when told.

"I can find an address for him from Bailey," I offered.

"Don't worry about that. We know where Christy lives," one of them said.

Yeats waited until they left the room.

"Mr Wolf is not unknown to us," he said. "We've been trying to speak to him since our investigation started."

"You mean you know about him and drugs?" I asked.

"We have had suspicions for some time," he said.

"Then why didn't you pick him up straight away?"

"Because we couldn't locate him," he said. "It also doesn't help that we have nothing concrete to connect him with Mr Ignatieff's death. We still don't. All we have is your suspicion. Certainly nothing showed up on the close-circuit pictures."

"There are pictures?"

For the first time since I'd seen him, the policeman

looked uncomfortable. He coughed, got up and asked if I wanted a coffee. I told him no thanks and asked again about pictures.

"Yes, there's a close-circuit system covering the yard. You didn't know that?"

I said no, but since I wasn't at the yard much except to ride horses, I wasn't overly surprised about that. Yeats, though, clearly didn't like the idea of having given something away.

"So what do the pictures show?" I pressed him.

He coughed again. "We have film of the victim entering the yard, looking around, and heading down that alleyway. In fact we have pictures from the past number of weeks of the same thing. We believe that stable box might have been a rendezvous point."

"For buying drugs?"

"Maybe. I suppose."

I sat back and looked around. Poor Anatoly. What a rotten way to lose your life, I thought. Not that there was any particular good way. But getting killed for whatever bit of dope he could afford seemed so pathetic.

"So Wolf must appear on the tapes as well, right?" I said, straightening up abruptly.

"Wrong."

"How can that be?"

"There's a question, Mr Dee. And it's one we'll have to answer. Maybe Mr Wolf himself will be able to help us."

But Christy had gone to ground. Rumours of sightings were plentiful but days passed and there was no sign of him being picked up. I wasn't too surprised, or worried. He was much too clever a customer to make it easy for the police, and much too cunning to be still around.

8

The drip that Bailey had detected soon turned heavier and, the day after, there came the soggy gush of a definite thaw. Slowly but surely the racing game prepared to pick up speed and our boss appeared to want to set the pace. She was first out every morning, even ahead of Eamon, who was normally the one to open doors, check the horses and start the feeding.

Any mistake with grooming or tack was being met with a booming voice of doom from Bailey. One unfortunate youngster arrived late and ran into her turning a corner. The glare alone left him too tongue-tied to even attempt an excuse. As it was, her renewed energy and exasperation seemed to remind everyone of what they had to do. As always, those at the top set the tone and despite, or maybe because of, what had happened, Bailey was determined to be upbeat. I had a fair idea of the effort that took.

One evening, after making some phone calls, I returned to the house to find her staring up at her grandfather's portrait and talking quietly to it. It was barely a whisper and impossible to make out from the kitchen. But the tone alone was enough to make me turn around and leave immediately. Bailey called me back.

"There's no need to be embarrassed. I'm not losing it," she said. "I find it helpful sometimes. Always have done. He was a wonderful man, my grandfather. Built this place from nothing. Everything we are comes from him. I think my own father found that hard to deal with. He felt that expectation heavy on him. They weren't very much alike, and the old man intimidated him a bit. I've always taken comfort from this picture though. It probably sounds mad but I've always thrashed things out with him. Just having his memory nearby helps me."

At first there was a steady flow of visitors to the murder scene which still had a Garda standing sentry during the day. At night it was left in Banjo's care. But when the stable was finished with, the Guards disappeared, and, almost guiltily, more and more signs of normality started to emerge. Spontaneous laughter at someone getting dropped off a horse lasted longer. Grumbling at Eamon's roster arrangements reclaimed its vigour. All the signs of a stable getting back to normal – inevitable and in a way admirable.

In fact, the rhythm of the stable was coming back without us even realising it. I rode every lot and even managed to get schooling over poles into some of them. Then there was the mucking out. Eamon casually directed me to three horses. It was hard physical work dragging straw bales around the place, lifting buckets of water and sweating through the endless sweeping with the big yard-brush.

"It'll do you good to see what us poor slobs have to do back here while you're off at the races living in the limelight," Eamon grinned. "We don't want you getting too high and mighty."

But I enjoyed it. Maybe, unconsciously, the sight of the police tape had made me want to assert my strength and health, fighting off fears with raucous activity. But I chose to reason it through as rent for my luxurious new bed and board. Whatever the reason, I went into the house in the evenings with a luxuriant ache in my limbs which felt pretty good.

Because of Bailey's abhorrence of cooking, I got drafted in as chef under the new regime. It wasn't a problem. The dietary constraints of keeping at a decent riding weight meant that I had long since learned to rustle up meals on my own. Dinner the first couple of nights consisted of vegetables and chicken, boiled together with gravy powder to thicken the whole thing into a passable attempt at a stew. Thrown onto some rice, it didn't look too bad either. For a woman who professed herself to be uninterested in food, my boss tucked into it with some relish.

"This is nice. I could get used to it," she announced. "Isn't food supposed to be a substitute for sex? I'd watch out if I were you."

I couldn't muster such relish myself. The damn gravy powder was new to my system which in the past had rebelled against such exotics as cheese and ketchup. Would this play havoc with my weight too? As it was, I decided to leave the daily dread of standing on the scales until nearer a race day and tucked in. The hell with it: what kind of life couldn't contain a little gravy?

One evening, Franco and Charlotte, complete with wine, joined us. Apparently it was a tradition they had – tucking into a bottle and chatting the night away.

Charlotte delegated the help to the kitchen to find a corkscrew. I got the distinct impression she wouldn't have minded if I'd toddled off to my quarters afterwards. Her attitude was more amusing than anything else. Whatever it was about Charlotte, the idea of taking umbrage at anything she might say was hard to imagine. The woman seemed too slight in every way to provoke anger. Which made her choice of mate seem peculiar.

Bringing the bottle-opener into the drawing room, I looked at Franco as he sat sullenly watching the TV. Big and brawny, just the way he sat looked aggressive, legs wide apart, dominating the space in front of him. There was a bristling ferocity to the man which didn't need language. He automatically put people on their guard.

"I'll just head off," I said, putting the bottle down on the table. "Leave you guys to it."

Bailey jumped up and grabbed my arm. Pulling me towards the sofa, she practically pushed me down into it. Her eyes implored me to shut up. Charlotte sat down next to me and delivered a smile that could have cut glass.

I could guess why Bailey wanted me to stay. She seemed almost to puncture in the evenings. That energy and passion she brought to the yard left her spent. All she wanted was to sit and watch the TV with a drink. There was also the reality that the once boisterously confident trainer was facing a much more uncertain world than she was used to. Still stricken by the death of a young man who she would always feel died on her watch, she was also coming to terms with an undercurrent of activity in her yard that she had been completely oblivious to.

A hot-bed of gossip anyway, the Curragh was alive with the news of how Christy Wolf was the prime suspect for Anatoly's murder. The papers, no doubt helped by leaky police sources, had quickly picked up on the drugs angle and presented the yard as some dope-ravaged battleground.

The police had pored over the big horse box that Wolf

had driven, taking away any amount of material to be forensically analysed. Once again there was a round of interviews with everyone who had even the slightest connection to the suspect.

Not sure of much any more, Bailey's instinct was to throw herself even more into working with the horses. It was also obvious that she was concerned about me.

"That dreadful Wolf is out there, Liam," she said now, and not for the first time. "And who knows what he might do next. He might try and hurt you. I don't know what I'd do if something happened."

"Relax. I can look after myself," I reassured her.

My guess was that Christy was well gone from the Curragh. I still found myself looking over my shoulder more than usual though.

Charlotte continued to chatter about various things, not even needing a response. An actor in a film, a cushion cover or even the label on the wine bottle were worth five minutes each to her. Then she zeroed in on me.

"Seeing anyone these days, Liam?"

I glanced at Franco but he didn't even flinch. Just kept staring at the TV and sipping his wine. Idly I wondered if he knew that his wife had gone out a couple of times with the help. It was years ago, of course, but it struck me that Franco might be the jealous type. Except there wasn't a flicker.

"No. Nobody special," I replied.

"Really? The brave jockey not getting any?"

There really was a job waiting for her at the United Nations, I thought. Again there was nothing from the other two. I turned and looked at her. She had hardly aged in the ten years since we'd fooled around in the flat I used to share with some other lads in the nearby town. Still blonde, still pretty, and still completely unreadable. A few more lines around the eyes maybe but that was nothing. I'd seen pictures of myself from a decade previously and I might as well have been a different person.

There had been an undeniable if brief thrill for that youth in squiring the boss's daughter to a couple of events and there was no doubt she looked well on anyone's arm. But there was no spark at all; for her too. Maybe she'd done it simply to piss off Mummy. Except I remember Bailey managing to disguise any doubts she might have had about her daughter and her jockey hooking up. Yet again Bailey's tactics were up to par. She probably knew better than anyone what an unlikely pair we made but let us find out in our own time.

"Guess not," I answered Charlotte. She would have to do better than that.

"Maybe soon, eh?"

"Who can tell?"

"Oh, I don't know. I've noticed you casting your eyes towards a certain Ukrainian. Blonde too."

She looked at me with a quizzical smile and a raised eyebrow.

I took another quick look sideways, but if Bailey or Franco were listening they made a good job of not letting on. My interrogator, though, was waiting expectantly.

"You ought to know I'm too old to blush, Charlotte."

That was enough for her to give a little laugh of satisfaction and start off on another subject. She had provoked a reaction, a slight letting of blood. Mission Accomplished. Charlotte moved on to a newsreader's hairstyle and then a friend's scurrilous love life. I wasn't sure which friend, or if it was the one person. It didn't matter anyway. What did was that Charlotte had caught me mooning over Lara like some lovesick schoolboy. The woman had a nose like a bloodhound for such things but, even so, I must have been acting like a teenager. Even worse was the realisation that she was right.

I'd found myself looking out for Lara. Taking the circuitous route to the water tap just so I could walk nearer to where she was. Or manoeuvring myself to stand next to her when lifting bales from the straw shed. Not once had there been even a sign of recognition. Mind you, she could hardly be blamed for that, with this mad stalker zooming in and out of her eye-line like a sniper trying to get a better shot. Contrary to what I'd just told Charlotte, I could feel myself blushing at the embarrassment of it all. Suddenly there was a paper on the table nearby that needed my full attention. I hid behind the latest tales of misery and celebrity, trying to get some semblance of normality back onto my face.

It wasn't like I was some pea-green innocent. There had been relationships of various lengths and intensities over the years. Many had been fun, some not so, and one had been serious enough for me to consider the idea of settling down. It didn't work out and that was a good thing. At twenty-six I knew only racing and ultimately she had wanted more than that. It would have been a disaster. Painful at the time though. Since then, it was mostly casual. Hardly the frenetic wham-bam-thank-you-mam popular image of jockeys on the tear, but okay all the same.

What did I know of Lara anyway? She rode well enough, even though the length of iron she used was more show-jumping than racing. But the horses stayed balanced underneath and there was an efficiency to her that I knew would appeal to Bailey. There was no hauling-at-the-mouth bravado with the reins that could mess up a sensitive mind and a carefully planned programme.

However, what Bailey really liked was the skill Lara brought to treating those horses whose bones creaked. People who treat bad backs and joints, both equine and human, have always been prized. The tradition of the bone-man is as long as the Curragh straight. Most of the old-style operators were tough farmers who couldn't explain what they were doing or how they did it. More of their younger colleagues had paperwork, but ultimately they too relied on the feel of their hands. It was wonderful to watch: fingers gingerly working their way over a sore area until they found the sensitive spot and then the click of bone returning home. The best part, though, was the audible groan of relief from the horse and the way it relaxed from the position it had adopted to compensate for the pain. Some of the most gifted horses I'd ridden over the years never fulfilled their potential because of that pain. All the talent in the world let down by a faulty chassis.

This reverie on the misfortune of my love life was interrupted by a phone call from the office. The voice that started to speak to the answer machine was that of another trainer and Bailey sprang up to take the call. We heard her laugh once and then she returned.

"Good news! That was Alistair Jones. He was driving down the country today and dropped into Thurles on the way back. Talked to the course manager. He says the ground will be ready in a couple of days. It looks like we're back in action, people."

9

The yard seemed to be re-energised, its very purpose restored. All the grinding labour, the organisation, the dreams invested in every new young horse entering the gates had only one aim: to get to the racecourse and win. The long days of inactivity emphasised the point. Now our own little bull's-eye was back on the horizon.

Of course, in the wider context the whole thing seemed more frivolous than ever. One horse passing a finish post in front of another didn't mean much in the big picture. But that didn't make it futile. Too many people's hopes were consumed by this epic irrelevance for that to be the case. Commitment alone gave it meaning.

But such high-falutin' navel-gazing didn't count when faced with no sign of Johnno and time ticking on. Over the years, I'd learned the time needed to get to every racecourse down to the last minute. Thurles was a quick hour-long drive from the Curragh. Johnno's tardiness threatened to make it even quicker. Our hardy amateur was bumming a lift from us and making a meal of it. I knew he was down to ride a horse in the last race, one of the amateur flat contests universally known as bumpers. Johnno eventually bounced his BMW into the yard with brakes squealing and wheels spinning for grip.

"Sorry about that, chief. Got caught in work."

"No sweat, let's go."

"Wait a sec. I've got to get my instructions."

He ran into the house to find out how Bailey wanted him to ride the horse. She wasn't going to the races herself. The prospect of having to deal with reporters asking questions and photographers taking her picture outweighed the idea of seeing the horses run. The previous day's papers had rehashed the murder story, complete with profiles and pictures. I'd even seen my own mug staring out a few times, characterised as being the loyal but taciturn former champion jockey. The sad part, though, was that grainy black-and-white picture of Anatoly staring out from every page. I found myself wondering about it: where it was taken and when, had he been as grave and sad as it suggested or was it one of those posed passport photos? And how desperately sad that it should become the only representation of his life. How Bailey felt, Lord alone knew, but at least she could opt out of directly helping a slow news week.

My foot was tapping with impatience by the time Johnno emerged and jumped into my replacement car that the garage were in no hurry to have back. I looked at the clock and calculated that we should be okay. There was a back way that avoided the town which only regulars knew about.

"Sorry, Liam, but I wanted to see how Bailey was bearing up. Tell her I'd help in any way I could."

"And?"

"She's been badly shaken, hasn't she?"

"Yes. She liked the kid. And she feels guilty."

"It's not her fault."

"I know. But logic doesn't matter in a situation like this."

"I guess not," he said. "I got the impression she'd fall down completely if it wasn't for having you around. But what a bastard this Wolf is! Who could do something like that to such a kid? And why can't they find him?"

"I'm guessing it's not such an easy job. Wolf might be many things, but stupid isn't one of them."

Johnno was uncharacteristically quiet after that as we sped south. I counted down the minutes between the well-known points of geography. It wasn't long before we passed the location of one of my 'heartbreak hills'.

It was a fanciful term I'd never actually mentioned to anyone. But there were times I'd felt close to oblivion on my assorted collection of heartbreakers. These were sharply steep hills I'd discovered over the years on my way to racecourses. Now there was at least one on all the main routes around the country. There I would slog my guts out for twenty minutes or half an hour, trying to lose a critical pound or two before going on to the course. The whole idea was to build up a sweat, so I would put on the heavy sweaters I habitually kept in the boot and run like blazes for as long as I could without passing out. Then it was back into the car and pray that enough had been lost so I could make the weight.

It was primitive and soul-destroying but it worked. Most of the time. There were other times I'd reached the top of a hill and cry, legs aching and chest heaving, but dry. Those were the occasions I learned to what degree I really wanted to be a professional rider, if it was really worth it. But the answer was always yes. And if sweat wouldn't come that way, then there were other ways. Everyone had their own particular torture. One jockey I knew spent much of his life immersed in dung heaps. He would shovel a hole and get his wife to fill it back in with him inside. The man swore by it, said the heat generated was something else and beat any sauna.

However there was only so much mouth-parching heat a person could take. The really desperate always ended up making themselves sick or using diuretics. Everyone resorted to them at least once and some a lot more than that. But I couldn't live with the pee-pills. Running your guts out was bad, but no morale could survive the constant pissing and worry that your insides were turning to rubble.

This time, though, I drove thankfully past the small wood that contained the steep, spongy path I knew so well. The scales that morning hadn't told a good story but it hadn't been catastrophically bad either. About ten and a half stone stripped was the aim. It meant that, with paper-thin boots, I could ride at ten stone eight or nine. Since race weights went from ten stone to twelve, that left me on the right end of the range. Too close to eleven stone and a career became untenable. The battle with weight was my competition with myself. That morning, I had tentatively stepped on to Bailey's bathroom scales and through squinted eyes discovered I was 10.10. Not too bad, considering I'd let things slide a little. A few runs, a few sweats in the sauna and no more gravy powder should see me okay. But then Bailey's scales weren't familiar. There was a chance they were inaccurate. First thing I'd do when we got to the races would be to jump on the official scales. Luckily though, I didn't have to do under eleven stone in any of my five races.

Sure enough, Thurles town centre was choked with race-traffic, but a nip down some of the side-streets brought us to the back of the track. A helpful gateman took in the badges that Johnno flashed and let us drive down the road reserved for ambulances following the horses in each race. Another gateman let us into the car park, where an ambulance was waiting to drive out on the track. I recognised the driver's face from the any number of times I'd returned with him, either sitting in the cab or stretched in the back. He nodded, knowing as well as I did that it was only a matter of time before he would have to pick me up again. There weren't too many jobs where it was a case of when rather than if you got hurt, but in case anyone forgot, the ambulance was always a couple of hundred yards behind to remind him.

After the freeze, the racing circus had come out in force and brought a thick cold rain with it. Exhaust fumes from arriving horse boxes hung in the air and joined the breaths of the hundreds walking through the gates. A country always in thrall to racing was coming back for a much-needed fix. The atmosphere was one of restrained excitement and a conscious pleasure at spending a midweek afternoon somewhere far more intoxicating than work. It was going to be a large crowd.

We queued up at the complimentary gate and, yet again, I marvelled at the range of people this weird and wonderful sport attracted. Clichéd tweedy types stood shoulder to shoulder with spivs that looked as if they were only one bet away from penury. Just past the entry stile stood the almost obligatory national politician who was being harangued into buying a race card by an old man in a flat cap and wellingtons.

Johnno tapped me on the shoulder.

"Bet you're glad to be back in harness."

The jockeys' changing area was at the end of a weigh room that had stayed just about the same for half a century and was as far from the popular image of racing glamour as it was possible to get. Everything was pared down to the essentials. Nothing covered the concrete floor and no pictures broke up the bare cold of the walls. Near the scales, heavily wrapped-up stewards sat freezing on chairs that looked like they'd been borrowed from the local school. One electric heater sat plugged in near the big board that gave the non-runners and jockey changes for the day. Condensation ran down the wall.

Crammed into the small area were haughty trainers and harassed stable lads, along with officials, stewards, reporters and any number of sundry local worthies eager to be seen at the centre of things. I quickly skipped through the throng and followed Johnno into the comparative oasis of calm that was the jockeys' room. Which in essence was a bench.

Here too, at the heart of it all, the bare essential theme continued. Hard benches ran along the four walls and looked in on a small square of other benches that were cornered by four six-foot poles joined together at the top by thick beams. Off these hung an assortment of saddles, riding boots, girths, helmets, colours and goggles. Including amateurs, about forty jockeys were riding today and, after a two-week break, it seemed everyone was keen to be there early.

Rushing about in an organised panic were the valets, those hardy souls who looked after our equipment, brought it to the races, laid it out and generally did the work their title suggested, except in the sort of ribaldly profane manner that no gentleman of leisure would ever tolerate. They were a rare breed, many of them ex-jockeys who couldn't make a go of it from riding, or else had got too heavy, but who knew nothing else but this shifting lifestyle. Helping us to get out on to the track seemed to be the next best thing to going out there themselves. As I stripped down, standing on the bench to spare myself the cold floor until the last moment, my own valet Sam English walked up and handed me a new set of boots.

"Feel the material on them. Like a baby's arse."

They were indeed soft. Sam often did that, buying a new set of pants or a new helmet on spec for one of the dozen of so jockeys he looked after. He believed in sending his boys out looking their best. He was one of the old school whose standards never dropped. If there was a shine to be had, then he got it. I'd got lucky from the very start with Sam. He'd known Eamon from years before and steered himself my way on the very first day I rode. Ever since, it was assumed that we were a pair. Never anything on paper, no formal agreement. Just an understanding that I was the lucky one. And I was too. There had been the inevitable low times when injury, bad luck or a simple lack of winners meant that a little pick-me-up was vital. Somehow Sam always had the right word at the right time.

I got down to my boxers and padded past the white-coat man on duty at the door on my way to the scales. There was over half an hour to when we would have to weigh out for the first race, so there was no problem just stepping on to check. It was a simple metal device, like an upturned tray, except for the black panel with the green digits that whirred in response to my weight. They quickly settled. Dry-mouthed, I waited for the luminous result. 10.10 it was. Trust Bailey to have things exactly right.

Back inside, my colours for the day were hanging on a hook and I checked a race card to see which one was up first. Then came the well-worn routine. The ladies' tights that always gave the uninitiated a giggle but were perfect for some light warmth, next up the breeches and boots, followed by a light vest over which went a back protector. That left only the silks.

I was buttoning these when the hubbub was suddenly interrupted by peals of laughter from the opposite corner. Johnno's voice suddenly soared to a peak as he hit the punch line that sent those around him into paroxysms. Johnno was always a popular guy.

My own reputation, I suspected, was a lot quieter, partly because I was now at the veteran stage. My new rivals had been kids back when I was starting to carve out a career. Now, they were the new and hungry faces. Afraid of nothing and willing to get on anything if it had a chance. I was still confident enough of my own ability to compete, but nevertheless I found myself checking in the mirror for grey hairs. And then there was inclination. Not everyone could be as ebullient and inclusive as old Johnno, no matter how much we might want to be. There had been times when I'd looked at him and envied his social ease. But, eventually, everyone grows into the skin they've got. The trick, I guessed, was realising it. One of the benefits of age. Or was that just an old man making excuses?

Sam tightened the cap onto my helmet, shoved an even amount of lead weight into pockets on both sides of the saddle, and I went to the scales. Two other guys were in the queue and I also noticed a figure hovering at the side.

Reggie McGuire was a large man with a personality to match. As one of the mainstays of the racing media, he also possessed a rather regal presence which meant that he rarely ventured from the press room. In fact, he had been known to summon his victims to him. Few refused the invitation. He now caught my eye and leaned forward.

"Any chance of a word, me old cock?"

Quite why Reggie had adopted the accent of a 1950s' cockney car salesman remained a mystery that never quite dissolved into an answer. Some of his colleagues had let it be known that the genteel suburbs of Epsom were the closest their man had ever come to any kind of Bow Bell. But this was the picture of himself that Reggie McGuire wanted to portray to the world. Others dismissed him as an old loon who knew damn all about the game and was nothing more than a pest who was always asking questions. Bailey, I knew, was one of that camp. The two of them were about the same age and Reggie's readily acknowledged ignorance of all things equine seemed to rub Bailey up like a rasp. Post-race press conferences had been known to turn heated at a query she judged to be silly. Which, of course, was why one of his favourite pastimes was winding her up into a fury and then diligently noting down the floridly colourful results.

He himself argued that not knowing a horse's arse from its nose meant nothing to a racing journalist. Stories were what counted and, whatever about his ignorance of the animal itself, no one could argue that McGuire didn't get stories. For as long as I could remember he had been essential reading. No doubt his editor would put up with Reggie sounding like the Mad Mullah of Mullingar as long as good copy kept coming in.

"Things have been a bit hectic recently, I see, Liam."

"A bit."

"How's Tiny Tears bearing up?"

It was his nickname for Bailey. The incongruous moniker he'd used for years. There were other less brave souls who had shortened it to a plain and simple, 'TT', which, in turn, had resulted in a less benign derivative. But I still liked Reggie. There was a fun to him that was appealing and, for some reason, he'd been mostly kind in his references to me over the years, only one or two rides a season earning a 'moronic' review.

"She'll be okay."

"Good. Listen, while I have you, any news on Patrician and what you're going to do?"

I should have known. Getting the line on what race Patrician would run in at Cheltenham was a big target in the press room. Especially getting it ahead of everyone else. There was a sudden competitive light in Reggie's eyes which almost made me regret having to deny him his story.

"You know I can't tell you anything. Bailey would have my balls. And anyway, as far as I'm aware, no decision has been made."

"But you think he should go for the Gold Cup, don't you?"

"No comment," I laughed. "Definitely no comment."

"Off the record?"

"Still no go. I can't."

"Be off then," he sighed. "You're no use to me."

"Sorry."

"I know," he said, glancing at his race card. "You'll probably win the first, won't you?"

"He's got a chance. If he's fit enough, it'll take a good one to beat him. And if he takes to jumping."

"Worth a bet?"

"You could do worse."

If they were in the mood, some of McGuire's more unscrupulous colleagues could theoretically have drummed up a whole lot of controversy on the back of that little exchange. 'Supplying information' is how it might be seen. In return for a favour from someone of influence. A disgrace, a threat to the integrity of the sport, shady dealings in shady places, champion jockey in tips shocker: the headlines wrote themselves. Never mind the reality, just run with the prejudice – every punter's natural instinct to believe the worst.

Yet it was an exchange that occurred every minute of every day on a race course. Not so much inside information as banal conversation. McGuire wasn't going to head to the ring and bet his mortgage on what I'd just told him. There was nothing in what I'd said that he wouldn't know already from looking at his form card. But no one would want to believe that. Just as no one wanted inside information to exist at all – unless they were the ones getting it.

10

Eamon was waiting in the parade ring, phone stuck to his ear and a smile playing on his face. That was an Eamon I knew much better than the anxious figure who had been rushing around the yard for the last few days. Clearly the return to action was perking him up.

Like Johnno, he was a man who seemed to thrive on company. In the past I'd wondered idly if his cheerfulness covered a more sombre temperament but had come to the conclusion that some people really are just the way they seem. Eamon told me once that he woke in the mornings and smiled at the idea of going into work. Which was no bad boast after thirty-five years.

"That was the owner wondering if he should back this thing."

"What did you tell him?"

"Said if he needed to back at these odds, he shouldn't be gambling at all. But he's a greedy sod."

The greedy sod was a new owner I'd never met. But he clearly fancied his chances. Bailey's instructions the previous night had been the usual: win if you can. Contrary to public perception these were almost always the instructions. The real Wild West days had been years before. For some, though, a race was incomplete without a bet. I glanced up at a TV screen and noted that my horse was odds on. Eamon was right. The owner must be greedy.

His horse was called King Titus, a four-year-old who had won a number of races on the flat and was now having his first start as a jumper. I watched as the stocky bay figure fidgeted his way around the parade ring. King Titus was jig-jogging and throwing his head up and down but they looked like mannerisms to me rather than nervousness. His coat wasn't sweaty and there was no anxiety in his eye. I'd ridden him at home a few times, including one school over hurdles. He had jumped pretty well and, as expected, had plenty of speed between the obstacles. But it was one thing to jump well at home on his own. Surrounded by others at racing pace on very soft ground was a different matter. Today we would find out if King Titus had the courage to go with his speed.

The bell for mounting sounded and we walked towards the horse. He was being led by the young man who had almost hurt himself swallowing a sandwich in Bailey's dining room. What the hell was his name? I really had to start making an effort. Eamon swept the warm blanket off the horse's rump and legged me up.

"Just do another round of the parade ring, Sergei, and then take him out," Eamon said helpfully.

Sergei didn't look up but marched forward resolutely, keeping in step with the lad in front. The crowd around the ring were starting to make their way to the stands to secure a viewing spot and I began the ritual of tying a buckle in the reins and untying the lowest plait in the horse's mane. There was no reaction from Sergei. Usually, there were growls of disapproval when I did this. Bailey liked her horses to be plaited, which meant extra work for the staff. However, since a few quid was usually awarded by the racecourse for the best-turned-out animal, there was rarely any quarrel. And I usually didn't go on an untying rampage until the judging was over and we were leaving the parade ring. But there was always a groan from the lads when one of their intricate designs was loosened and stood up like a particularly rebellious kiss-curl. I could understand their dismay. But I always liked to be able to grab a hold of the mane if I needed to during a race. Mostly it was a mental thing, in the way every jockey liked to take a horse to a fence and give him a look at it before the start. Never once had a poor jumper looked at the obstacle and suddenly gone 'Eureka!'. But we all still continued to trot them up. Neither had anyone ever heard of a clawing hand securing a piece of mane to keep a partnership intact, but some of us still persisted in upsetting the lads. Irrational stuff, but since I was the one travelling at 30 mph, I reserved the right to have a foible or two.

"How is he, Sergei?"

I wasn't sure of his English but asking the lad about the horse was a logical pre-race superstition that I always followed. They were the ones who knew the horse's character best, recognised if the individual was in a bad mood, or was sulking against the rain, or if he had travelled poorly and was now resenting everything to do with the game. Every piece of information helped when dealing with a partner that couldn't tell you if he was in crap form and didn't feel like putting it in today.

Sergei looked up but didn't lose his stride.

"He is very good. A happy horse," he said. "But he very excited. He want to run."

"Thanks. I'll remember that."

"I have fifty euro on him," he added, grinning.

I laughed. To hell with the greedy-sod owner. Getting King Titus home in front would mean a helluva lot more to this kid.

"I'll do my best, Sergei."

For his part, King Titus felt as if he wanted to do his best as well. After weeks confined to gallops on the all-weather, the feel of grass under his feet seemed to galvanise his enthusiasm to run. It wasn't surprising. Already battle-hardened from the flat, he knew that hitting the turf meant he would be required to race very shortly. He was clearly excited at the prospect, but containing all his enthusiasm until the proper time was going to be a challenge.

The track was triangular-shaped, with a tight bend going away from the stands leading to a long back straight. From there it was a long pull up to the highest point of the course and the home straight which was mostly downhill until the last furlong. The undulations made it more of a test of stamina than it looked. On very soft ground, and with the rain getting heavier, it was going to be a real slog. Any unnecessary extravagance would take its toll down the long final straight.

The signals from King Titus told me that one glimpse of daylight and he would be over the horizon. It was like that sometimes with horses that were too fresh and eager. Usually they needed a race to get all that fizzing over-the-top wellness out of them. The trick was to make the first race as easy as possible. Driving and battering an exhausted animal was the best way to sour him for life. King Titus was tough, but this was a new game. Our main aim was for him to go home with good memories and looking forward to his next trip away.

The start was a scene I knew from thousands of times before. We circled round, stopping only to get the girths tightened, with the conversations remaining reassuringly constant. Who is going to make the pace? Who is fancied? What kind of chance does that outsider with the good action have? Did you see the girl with that flute of a trainer? Where'll we go after racing? By the way, where's that hundred you owe me? It was the soundtrack to my life, as earthy and fundamental as the game itself.

But where once I had revelled in the heartiness of it all, now there was only doubt. Maybe it was just boredom. After all, hearing anything often enough gets tiresome. These youngsters' lives might be all birds and booze but, at thirty-four, was that enough? I wasn't talking better than them, just different. The starter climbing his steps shook me out of the reverie. King Titus deserved my full attention. I pushed my way into the pack, jostling for position behind the tape and found myself with only one horse between me and the rail. No going back now. The tape flew away and King Titus sprang forward.

The previous night, Bailey and I agreed to ride him on the outside. It meant going farther but also allowed a raw horse a full view of his jumps. That was no longer an option. His excessive energy meant that there was no chance of getting into a rhythm if the whole of County Tipperary ranged out in front of him like some soggy steppe. We wouldn't even make the finish. So I decided on a change of plan. Bury him in the pack, trust that his jumping held up, and hope against hope that he'd relax.

Riding against instructions was a simple matter. Once you did it, only a win justified the decision. In the past I'd ridden what I felt were excellent races but against instructions and so I returned to sulphuric receptions. Bailey wasn't the worst that way, mainly because she was able to read a race. It was amazing how many trainers couldn't. They just ended up spouting the jargon they'd heard from the jockeys in the grandstand. Still, I knew only a win would prevent raised eyebrows. To hell with it, I thought. Let's see what we can do.

Far from charging for the hills, King Titus started to behave like the little professional he was. Compared to the pace of flat races, we were going at a gentle doddle. But, although the reins were alive in my hand, the strain was one of contained eagerness rather than run-like-hell fervour. Even when a clump of soft earth churned up by the horses in front slapped into his nose, King Titus didn't react. In fact, if anything, he seemed almost bemused by the whole thing. This was going better than I could have dared hope.

The first hurdle must have seemed like a surprise from nowhere. Suddenly, instead of a wall of other horses in front of him, there was this thing. There was no time for any measured stride or encouragement. It was up to him. I let the reins go loose, sat back and trusted in King Titus's judgement. In the end he bunny-hopped over the angled, timber obstacle. All four legs in the air and all four hitting the ground at the same time. But he stayed upright and there was no mistaking the signal of recognition that surged to my hands. So that's what that was! One of those things from home. The boost in confidence seemed almost physical and he immediately started searching for the next hurdle.

All the work was going to pay off. He always enjoyed jumping, felt it was fun. The best ones usually did. Those who hated it made their feelings clear pretty soon. All the practice in the world was useless if there was no pleasure in it for them. But King Titus thought it was all a gas.

Except now I didn't want him to enjoy it too much yet. I slightly tightened my hold on his mouth. The last thing anyone wanted, least of all me, was a tug of war. But one of us had to be in control and it was best for both of us if it was me. Silently, I prayed and cajoled and ordered and threatened and pleaded with him to relax. It was a sort of primeval communication I would be too embarrassed to translate for anyone. But I also knew it to be as real and vital as the instinctive block of muscle and tissue underneath me. The second hurdle was approaching when King Titus accepted that it might be a good idea if I ran the show – for a while at least.

There was more room to see the second flight and both of us saw a stride at the same time. I tucked in low, clicked my tongue and gave him a slight tap of the whip down his shoulder. Once again there was recognition at the signals. He sailed flamboyantly over, giving it way too much air. Next to me, I heard a shout as another horse gave it no air at all and the jockey colourfully vented his verdict. By the next hurdle, the competition around us had thinned out even more and there was space to attack the obstacle. Once again we got a stride and this time he jumped it perfectly, just flicking the top and wasting as little time in the air as possible. I could feel his increasing confidence. We were a good twenty lengths off the leaders but I reckoned most of the ten or so horses in front us would feel the pace later. It was time to start thinking of winning.

Galloping down the straight for the first time, I slowly eased off the rail towards the outside. The ground felt a little better there and King Titus was happy and settled. His jumping was remarkable for a newcomer. The second one in the straight we met all wrong, but he put himself right and lost only a length in the process. I'd have patted him on the neck except changing my hands was not an option. Things were working out better than okay. There was a joy to King Titus that I couldn't have guessed at. The jockey's shouts and the crack of hurdles being pounded into the ground often frightened novices, but this one didn't back off a yard. He was going to be good. Maybe even good enough to win first time out.

Along the top, with half a mile to go, most of the leaders started to weaken. Hardly surprising considering the ground was like glue. Just getting their feet out was proving difficult. I angled even wider as tired horses struggled and retreated, and, turning into the straight, we were practically in the middle of the track. Up ahead were just two horses, one under pressure and the other in the catbird seat, an American term that just about summed up his enviable position. The leader was knackered and it was only a matter of time before he was swallowed up.

I got low into King Titus, almost tasting his mane, urging him forward with my calves and changing my hands on the reins in the unmistakable command to run faster. He responded like a trooper. Our big danger went into the lead after the second last and I could see it was ridden by Jim Gallagher, one of the game's rising stars and a hard guy to beat. He must think he has the race won, I figured, and sure enough he put his whip down and allowed his horse to coast into the last hurdle. It cost him.

King Titus threw another spectacular leap, but this time it was low and fast and suddenly there was only a length between us. Jim started shouting and throwing everything at his horse, but the momentum had switched. Fifty yards from the line, King Titus hit the front and passed the post a length clear.

It was all I could do not to laugh out loud as we slowly

pulled up. He still had enough energy left in him to eventually stop well ahead of the others, ears pricked and loving the attention. I patted his neck repeatedly and told him he was a great fella. I meant it too. He was loving it and, because it had been fun, he would continue to love it. There might even be a new little star at the McFarlane yard. I pulled down my mud-splattered goggles and turned my face up to the elements. Winning felt just as good as ever and the rain washed away any doubts. How could I give all this up?

Sergei looked thrilled. He led the horse back to the winner's enclosure where favourite backers gave King Titus an appreciative round of applause. Eamon was grinning and everything suddenly didn't seem so bad. I weighed in and returned to my bench to change for my next ride. There were a few minutes to spare so I rang Bailey.

"Some plainclothes policemen have just taken Lara away," she said immediately. "They say it's for questioning. What are they questioning her for? What has she got to do with Christy Wolf?"

"Questioning can mean anything," I said, trying to reassure her. "It doesn't have to mean the worst. Don't jump to conclusions. What did they say?"

"That's all they said: questioning. Then they just led her away. What is going on here? Everything is so messed up."

"Don't worry. I'll go straight to the station when I'm finished here. Well done with the winner, by the way."

"Thanks. Well done you," she replied.

Her voice sounded dreadfully dispirited. Reality was back with a vengeance.

11

I stepped warily into the police station and saw Vaz being restrained by two large officers. The big man was on full throttle, shouting at everyone, in what was presumably Russian, and using every ounce of his considerable strength to try and free himself. His hard weather-beaten face was purple with rage and effort. The words he was using might have been unfamiliar but there was no mistaking the tone. As I stood there trying to take it all in, another officer burst through a door.

"Come here, you bastard!"

Those words snapped me awake. As the third policeman threw his arms around Vaz's neck, I went towards the mêlée, wanting to do something but not sure what.

"Keep back!" One of the officers hanging onto an arm shouted the warning.

Whether I distracted him or he simply weakened, his grip suddenly relaxed and Vaz lashed out, moving so quickly that his fist connected before I'd even realised what was happening. It was more of a stun shot than a bone-breaker but, nevertheless, my eye started to hurt like hell. Retreating hurriedly back into a corner, I felt around. He'd struck me underneath my right eye. Already I could feel things swelling. No doubt there would be shiner to advertise my slow reactions. Still, it was nothing to concern any doctor. Only my pride was chipped. Just a pity it hurt so much.

Contact did, however, seem to sate Vaz's immediate thirst for blood. Two officers still clung to his arms, but the third straightened me up and made me give him a look.

"Ah, that's nothing. It'll be gone in a day or two."

There was even a little chuckle and he grinned at another man whom I suddenly noticed, staring out from behind the main reception counter. It was all bonhomie: too much so. Obviously someone clipped inside the station might mean a bit of a stink for them.

"Relax, it's not a problem. I'm actually here to see this guy," I said, pointing to Vaz.

"Why?"

"Apparently we both know someone you've got in here for questioning."

From his reaction, Vaz was clearly even more incredulous than me at the idea of Lara being picked up and brought to Newbridge station.

I'd driven on my own through the dark, wet evening. Johnno had organised a lift back to Bailey's later to pick up his car. It suited me, allowing for a quick getaway after the last of my five rides. There hadn't been another winner, but Bailey's other runner, an honest old stager in the handicap chase, had done well to be third, running on at his usual moderate best. It was a good sign. The freeze-up hadn't taken too much of the edge off them.

Damn, my eye hurts, I thought, as Vaz finally shook off his tormentors and sat down at the other end of the hall.

Not surprisingly, everybody else had cleared out of the way. There had been a couple standing nearby who had the unmistakable waxy skin of those doomed to addiction, but even they'd had the good sense to take off when confronted by a rampaging Vaz. My shoes sounded unnaturally loud on the tiled floor as I walked towards him. He didn't even look up. The cops hung back and waited for something else to kick off, but I was damned if I was going to cause it.

"What's happening? Where's Lara?"

"She is there, somewhere," he said, pointing to a door. His expression was stony. No other word described it. There wasn't a flicker of emotion when just seconds before that was all there had been. But there was no doubting the mass of simmering resentment underneath. If King Titus had been a ball of energy earlier in the day, this man was a spring just waiting to explode. He held his hands together and leaned forward, his elbows resting halfway up his legs. It took an effort of will to sit next to him, but I had to find out what was happening.

"What's going on, Vaz?"

There was no reaction to my using his name, nor to the cops edging closer towards us. I gestured them away.

"Please, Vaz. I can't help if I don't know what's going on."

"Oh, you are going to help?"

"If I can, yes."

"Right. Because you are different?"

At that moment, a familiar voice emerged from behind the counter. I walked up, looked inside and sure enough Yeats was leaning over a computer, muttering to himself about how much he missed paper.

"Have you a second, Inspector Yeats?"

"We're being very formal, aren't we, Mr Dee?"

"In this situation, it might be best."

"Oh dear, that sounds ominous. What's wrong with your eye?"

"I was racing today."

"Oh, right," he said disinterestedly. "Okay, I can guess why you're here. All I can say is that our enquiries are continuing."

"Don't fob me off like that. I thought we had an understanding. You know: me helping you out. How about a little something back?"

"Such as?"

"Such as why have you picked her up?"

Vaz materialised at my shoulder like some vengeful Cossack. Physically he intimidated the hell out of me, but Yeats simply looked at him, clearly trying to figure out where he'd seen him before. Vaz beat him to the punch.

"You are a liar! You said you will find Anatoly's killer and all you do is arrest one of us. This is shit. No one is interested in finding out the truth."

"Hold on, sir," said Yeats, who now clearly remembered Vaz. "No one has been arrested. Miss Kuznetsov is merely helping us with our enquiries."

"That is rubbish. Why is she here? Why are you not looking for who killed Anatoly? Why have you not found that Christy Wolf?"

"We are devoting all our energy and resources to finding whoever's responsible. It's not fair to say we are not interested. We are interested."

"No, sir. Your only interest is saving your own back."

Vaz turned and walked away. I went after him, through the front door, almost trotting to keep up. I didn't know what I was going to do. The idea of another punch didn't exactly appeal and the man was clearly still upset.

Suddenly, though, he stopped and stood still. The cold night air was heavy with misty rain, drifting lazily through the beams of the street lights. Traffic hummed beside us but each deep breath Vaz took was clearly audible. The reaction to all that spent emotion was starting. Suddenly, he didn't seem so formidable, as if someone had let the air out of that huge mass of indignation.

"Look, I'm going to go back there and try to work something out," I said. "But I think it would be best if you came with me."

"I am not going back."

"Then at least stay in my car until I come out. It's parked over there."

There was a second where he was clearly deliberating whether or not I was worth another smack, but thankfully good sense won out. I opened the car and Vaz sat in. He didn't say anything and there wasn't much else I could say. Anyway, I was scrambling to think of something I might be able to do back at the station.

Yeats had left the reception area and for a second I was afraid he might have gone altogether. But the sergeant on duty took a look at my eye and decided it might be best at least to humour me. It didn't hurt either that he obviously knew who I was.

"Any joy today?"

King Titus seemed such a long time ago, hardly the six hours the clock said.

"Yeah. One winner. And a third."

"Was that the McFarlane horse in the first?"

"Yeah. Did you back him?"

"Nah," he said scornfully. "Too short for me. Anything coming up?"

Being asked for tips was the bane of every jockey's life.

Give some punter a winner and it's what's expected of you anyway. Give a loser, and you don't know your arse from your elbow. My standard line was that if I could reliably tip winners, I'd be sitting on a beach in Barbados and not slogging my guts out in the wind and rain. This time, though, I figured it might pay to come up with a name. My mind was suddenly blank. Hundreds of horses a year, but only Patrician came into my head.

"Patrician is going well. Improving all the time."

"Which race will he run in though? Is he going for the Gold Cup?"

Bailey would have gone spare if she'd heard me, and McGuire's laptop would have been just a blur, but I simply smiled and nodded. What did it matter anyway? The Gold Cup was weeks away. Even if this cop knew every tout and bookie in Kildare, it would hardly be the end of the world. I decided to put a cherry on top.

"He's the best I've ever ridden."

There was an almost audible whir as he swiftly calculated odds, risk and the fact that the jockey himself was telling him all this stuff. Never mind the fact that he probably knew jockeys were the worst tipsters in the world. I'd given him what he assumed was a glimpse of the inside.

"I realise it's a pain in the arse, Sergeant, but is there any way you could get Mr Yeats out for me? Just for a minute. I need to speak to him."

"Sit down over there and I'll see what I can do."

Inside a minute I was being escorted through the large door that Vaz had pointed out earlier and down a long corridor. The sergeant came with me and stopped at the end. He knocked and I heard a muffled grunt.

"In you go," he said. "Thanks for the tip."

Yeats looked anything but grateful for the pleasure of my

company. He was sitting behind a bare desk but with his chair tilted far enough back that his head was resting against folders that sat on a series of shelves. It was a tiny room. A small glass cabinet full of books was on the left as I walked in but, apart from the lamp next to a computer on his desk, and another chair for visitors, that was the extent of the furniture. There was no window and no hint of the outside world. I knew I would quickly go mad in such a room and, from the bare essentials on view, I reckoned Yeats spent a minimum amount of time in there too. He looked at me from his contemplative position and then let the seat softly fall forward.

"What did you say to the sergeant?"

His tone was more amused than annoyed, but there was a new tiredness to the voice that fitted that doleful face a lot more. The man must have been under serious pressure. I didn't envy him.

"I gave him a tip."

"That figures. Will it win?"

"Who knows?"

"And who cares, right?"

That wry grin returned and he resumed his former position against the files behind him.

"Sorry about outside, Inspector. I'm not trying to mess anyone around."

"That's nice of you."

"Why Lara?"

In a split second his stare turned a lot less friendly. He didn't move – there wasn't even a flicker – but I could feel myself starting to shift in my chair. Now there was a hardness that explained better than any words why the man was in charge of a murder investigation. If Lara had been on the receiving end of this for a few hours, then she would know all about it. I suddenly thought of Franco and his rabid dismissal of this man. Very wrong, Franco, very wrong indeed.

"I don't have to tell you anything, Mr Dee. You do know that, don't you?"

"I know."

"So, why should I?"

"Right now, I can't think of a single reason," I said. Or at least I couldn't think of one that would mean anything to him. "But, like you said before, I might be able to help you out."

He pondered this with a frown that suggested he already deeply regretted suggesting the deal. And I could see he was also wondering how it was me, and not him, who was trying to cash in on our little arrangement. It didn't make sense and I realised how ridiculous I must look to him: a silly jockey, out of his depth, behaving like some cartoon figure riding to the rescue. It was stupid and Yeats would be just the kind of man to point this out.

Despite every effort, there was no mistaking the noise of me shifting in my seat. Somehow, though, I held his stare. After what seemed a very long time, he appeared to make up his mind.

"This is strictly between us. I mean that. Any bleating to your boss, or to the press, or anyone, and I'll be displeased. Understand?"

I understood. The idea of getting on the wrong side of this man was not attractive.

"She was picked up because her name and address were on a scrap of paper found in the young fella's clothes back in the hostel. More importantly, we also found a small sachet of cocaine there."

"Okay," I said, feeling far from okay about where this might be going.

"The amount was so small, it had to be for personal use. But there's a much bigger picture to all this. There has been a sharp rise in the number of Eastern Europeans coming to Ireland and being caught with significant amounts of drugs. Our intelligence people now say there is no question but that there are supply routes coming into this country from that part of the world. It's also no coincidence that the number of Eastern European nationals at the centre of gun crimes in this country is increasing."

"Are you saying that that's what this is about?"

"I don't know, but it certainly can't be ruled out."

"But what's that got to do with Lara? You can't think she's involved in drugs. This is about Wolf and crooks and –"

"I don't know if she is or not. But what I do know is that the Ukrainian Embassy has sent us details of the arrest of Rudi Kuznetsov, twenty-two, from Odessa, the brother of Lara Kuznetsov. He was picked up in Moscow airport last year for possession of two million euros' worth of cocaine. He's currently doing ten years. So, you see, Mr Dee, if you were in my position I think the least you would do is ask Ms Kuznetsov if she knew anything about cocaine found in the dead lad's digs and what exactly was the nature of her friendship with him. Wouldn't you?"

It wasn't a question he wanted me to answer.

"There is no record of Ms Kuznetsov ever coming to the attention of the authorities, either here or in the Ukraine," he added.

"All of which means what?"

"All of which means that the situation will be kept under review."

"Can she leave here now?"

"I have to ask her another couple of questions. But then, yes, she can leave."

"You don't really believe she has anything to do with this, do you?"

The only response was a small smile. It was all way too slight. Even I could see it was just an exercise in joining up dots that might lead anywhere you wanted them to go. Yeats knew that better than anyone. Why else was he sitting there talking to me? If there was something serious happening, I could have offered that sergeant the ride on Patrician and still be sitting in the lobby. Yeats stood up, stretched and said he would see me at the duty desk.

Less than five minutes later Lara came out, closely followed by Yeats, who gave her forms to sign. He tried some minor chit-chat which was met with stiff silence. She was still wearing jeans, Wellington boots and a heavy anorak from work, while her hair was tied up in a bun under a baseball cap. Yeats gave up on the small talk and pointed to me.

"Mr Dee here can take you home, I'm sure. Thank you for your co-operation."

All he got in return was a glare that made me think it must have been a pretty even match in that interview room after all. She strode proudly out of the station and turned left.

"Sorry, my car is down this way."

"I will walk."

"Vaz is waiting for you there."

Momentarily the tall figure wavered and then turned and walked back with me. Vaz got out of the car and there was a big hug that provoked in me a stab of envy. Lara climbed in the back seat and we gratefully made our escape.

It was a relatively quiet journey to Vaz's hostel. Roadworks meant it took longer than usual to get there and it was only the big man who felt the need to fill the silence.

There was undoubted delight at Lara being let go, but I suspected there was regret at having stuck one on the stable jockey. I copped him having a couple of sneaky looks at my eye which felt as if it was swelling quite nicely thank you. He needn't have worried – I wasn't going to go whinging to Bailey, but it was sore enough for me to enjoy letting him sweat for a while.

In fact, it worked well enough for me to learn that he had a wife and three kids back home who would not be able to survive on their small farm without the money he was making in Ireland. As emotional blackmail went, it was pretty unsubtle, but there was no mistaking the genuine loneliness and longing in his voice. I'd looked at a globe back at Bailey's just to see exactly where the Ukraine was and it seemed very far away indeed – far too far away from three children. When Vaz got out and hesitantly said goodnight, I shook hands and said I'd see him in the morning. Relief flooded over his face. He said goodnight to Lara, clearly asking in their own language if she would be okay with this strange Irishman, and then held the door for her to climb in the front beside me – presumably to give me directions.

We drove off and I told her that I already knew the digs from years before when some friends had stayed there. Mrs O'Sullivan was an old woman even then and she provided room and board, along with a famously acerbic mouth, to those a long way from home. The view generally was that she took people in as much for the company as the money, even though she disguised the fact rather well.

The silence resumed and I settled in for a tense drive to her lodgings.

"Why were you there when I came out?" Lara suddenly asked.

"Bailey asked me to see if you were okay."

There was no response. We stopped and waited for some lights to change. Lara sat almost to attention. We seemed to be waiting a long time for green.

"I'm sure everything will be fine."

"You are sure about that?" she said scornfully.

"I just mean –"

"What I am sure is that I have just spent six hours in a police interrogation centre. And they wanted to know if I had killed my friend because of drugs."

"I don't think they believe that."

"It doesn't matter what they believe! All they want is somebody to blame and there is nobody better than us."

"What do you mean?"

"You don't know what I mean? Don't treat me like a child. What better way to look at this. Oh, just more of those foreigners killing each other. It happens all the time. Just let them get on with it, as long as it doesn't affect any of us. We're all the same to you people – Russians, Ukrainians, Lithuanians, Poles, it doesn't matter. We're only the help, doing what you Irish are not prepared to do. We're your cheap servants, or your cleaners, and if we're not good enough for that, then we are good for being whores or strippers, isn't that right?"

Bitterness and rage and desperate grief poured out. There was no point arguing or trying to mollify her. I simply drove on and waited for the torrent to abate.

"It is the same in the yard. All these remarks. No one cares that a young boy is dead. The only thing the police care about is making sure their records look good. So they have to find someone. Why have they not found this Christy Wolf? They do not seem like they want to search very hard, do they?"

"For what it's worth, I don't believe Inspector Yeats

thinks you had anything to do with the murder. He was just ruling things out. Your brother being in jail meant he had to talk to you."

"My brother? Did he tell you about my brother?"

"Well, yes, he did."

"Stop the car."

"There's no need. We're nearly –"

"Stop the car now!"

One punch was enough for one evening. I pulled over and she climbed out quickly. Mrs O'Sullivan's house was just around the corner and I watched as Lara marched towards it. There was nowhere just there to turn the car, so I slowly drove in the same direction and saw her disappearing through the front door.

12

Standing on Bailey's scales and looking at the result, I actually stepped down and checked that the needle had returned to zero properly before getting on again. But there was no mistake. Hoping against hope, I even got off and on once more. The tiny black marks just kept mocking me. I was ten stone twelve. It was all I could do not to scream out loud, knowing the painful process of getting off the extra weight was waiting to squeeze me dry.

The lack of racing and my new living arrangements were obviously throwing my system into disarray, but gaining a couple of pounds in less than a day was ridiculous. Especially after five rides the previous afternoon. All I'd had to eat yesterday evening was a sandwich Bailey had pushed on me when I'd eventually got back. Could that really be worth two pounds? Part of me was tempted to jump on the bathroom scales again but instead I went back to the bedroom and put on running gear.

The bag was always ready: tracksuit, runners and a couple of sweatshirts. Usually quite a hum emerged from it, but, surprisingly, this time the gear was freshly laundered. Bailey's housekeeper must have washed it. Only then did I notice shirts and underwear piled on the dressing table, all neatly ironed and folded. Something a guy could definitely get used to. My watch said six fifteen. I hadn't been able to sleep much anyway: might as well get on with it.

The yard was still asleep and the new dawn was hardly making a dent in the black sky. I pulled up my hoody and tied it tight around my head. It was a familiar routine: a few stretching exercises, check the watch and try to think of something interesting to ponder about while running. I usually used the time to think of upcoming races and the tactics I, and the opposition, might use. But nearly always it drifted off into something completely different. Like taking up where a movie or a programme had left off and wondering what the characters might do next. What happened to Hawkeye and Trapper John after they left *M*A*S*H*, for instance? Did they meet up for pints? Or where did Rick and Renault get to after leaving Casablanca? Stupid stuff, but at least some sort of help in trying to block out the pain.

Hate didn't even come close to describing my attitude to running. Only one thing was worse and that was sitting for hours in a sauna. So I kept running. Usually an hour every day. Which amounted to forty miles a week. The aim was to wring the body of water. There were times when I would see soft drinks and my throat would contract with a desire that no woman ever came close to provoking. But only sometimes. Mostly, the problem was just the physical pain of running every day.

My Achilles tendons sometimes felt like tightly wound piano wire. The first two miles could sometimes be an exercise in quick hobbling. After that, it was a simple matter of coping with lungs that felt as if they wanted to escape through my mouth. The temptation to slow down was constant, but that wouldn't drive the sweat out, so it became an effort of will. In one way, though, I was lucky. A lot of jockeys wouldn't run because it built up muscle in their legs and muscle weighs more than fat. By some genetic throw of the dice, that at least wasn't a problem I had.

I walked quickly down the road towards the all-weather gallops. It would be another hour before the first horses appeared, so that gave me just enough time. The surface felt wonderfully spongy. Along with having slackened off for the previous week, it meant that things felt a lot less sore than usual. My breathing was laboured and no doubt I sounded like a bellows to the early-rising thrushes and blackbirds that were bouncing busily on the grass. But I also knew that would pass. The pipes just had to open. It all felt quite pleasant really, which meant having to up the pace significantly. I put my head down, got the arms pumping and had daydreams of tall, icy blondes.

The first of the lads were arriving when I returned. Sweat was pouring off me and my leg muscles were demanding mercy but I kept going, through the gate and around the house to the back door. Only then did I stop.

Eamon's voice came from the kitchen.

"You're in England today, aren't you?"

"Yeah," I gasped.

"What do you have to do?"

"Ten stone nine in the handicap hurdle."

"Are you in trouble?" he asked, coming to the door.

"No. I'll do it. But there's no way I can ride out."

"No problem. What's wrong with your eye?"

"Oh, the horse in the last race yesterday threw his head up and caught me. It's nothing."

He nodded and headed for the yard. I took off my

sneakers before going inside and climbing the stairs. There was no sign of Bailey, so I went straight to the bathroom and stripped. My silent persecutor was waiting. The needle shook and hovered at 10.9 which was better than expected. Three pounds gone. Another two and we might be in business if I used the smallest possible saddle.

The bath took five minutes to fill. Nothing but hot water until the very end when I added a touch of cold. Its effect was minimal but getting into scalding hot water was as much a mental as physical test. I grabbed the handles on either side of the bath and hung over the water, legs stretched out like a skinny gymnast. My way was to slowly but surely lower myself into the steaming bath. There were others who preferred to throw themselves in and get it over with. Either way, everything depended on forcing yourself to actually do it. The first minute was the worst. Then the body started to compensate for having to endure this lunacy. It always did if you waited long enough. Often that was the only hope to cling to as you watched your skin redden like a sore tomato.

I stayed in it up to my neck for quarter of an hour. I towelled down and caught my reflection in a full-length mirror in the corner. Paler lobsters had been served up in restaurants. In the past, such baths used to create a thirst that would drive me nearly insane but, as with most things, I'd got used to sometimes peeling my tongue off the roof of my mouth. The whole idea was to lose water, not add any.

The scales said 10.7 when I stood on them again. Relief flooded through me. I might even be able to have a cup of tea now. There was a sauna at Newbury and I would have time for a stint in that if I got there early enough. I got dressed with a lighter heart than had seemed likely earlier. No doubt doctors would throw their hands in the air at the idea of losing so much in that time, but I'd never heard of an alternative. The dangers of bone diseases and organ problems later in life were constantly being stressed by the medical people but owners and trainers didn't want to hear about our well-being. They wanted a jockey to ride at the correct weight. Platitudes might be thrown about when some poor unfortunate got hurt, or even worse, but the reality in racing has always been that excuses are cheap. If one jockey isn't prepared to do the weight, there are plenty of others who are. And it didn't matter if the weights rose to twenty stone. Jockeys have always wasted, even for just the tiniest edge.

Downstairs, Bailey was poring over form books and, from the notebook at her side, it was obvious she was ringing owners to let them know how their pride and joys were getting on.

Her response the previous night to what I'd told her about Lara had been blunt: "It's all rubbish. They're grasping at straws if they think that girl had anything to do with it. And I'm going to make a point of telling her so in the morning."

I'd left out the bit about cocaine and a brother doing a stretch in a gulag: Yeats had asked me to keep schtum. Bailey's initial bemusement on the subject of drugs had turned into hatred. It had never been baldly stated but equally it had always been understood that if I got myself mixed up in anything dodgy, be it gambling, booze or any other kind of substance, the chop wouldn't be long in coming. But by now she knew that I found my highs and lows out on the racecourse without resorting to the artificial variety. Deliberation on the matter of tea, however, was a different matter. I eventually decided to risk half a cup and was making it when Charlotte walked in from the yard.

"So you decided to join us. That's good of you."

"I won't be riding out. I'm in Newbury today."

"Damn. That means re-jigging the schedule."

She made it sound as if I was deliberately trying to make her life harder. A number of responses sprang to mind, but the process of choosing one was interrupted by Bailey's entrance.

"Eamon says you're sweating. Everything alright?"

"Yeah."

She didn't pursue it. Like most trainers, Bailey left all that to the jockey. She knew what weight I could do at a push and with some advance warning, but might ask me to reach it only two or three times a year for an important handicap. Even then, it was delivered as more of a request. But we both knew that when she requested, it was expected to happen. I regarded that as a simple professional requirement, like a painter having paint or a singer a voice.

"What you got today?" she asked me. Bailey was my principal employer but when she didn't have a runner in a race, I was free to look elsewhere. And if there was no racing in Ireland, it was only a short hop across the Irish Sea to make up for it.

"There's Lanark Boy in the Game Spirit and I'm on Valley Forge for Johnston in the Trial."

That grabbed her attention. Newbury had the last of the established trials for the Gold Cup. After this, there was only the runway to Cheltenham. It was the last chance saloon to make a case for inclusion. Bailey knew as well as me that Valley Forge was a 50-1 outsider for the big prize, but he was reliable trial tackle, and he would tell us a lot about Tenterhook, one of the major Gold Cup fancies who was running against him.

"I'll look at that on the telly," she said.

"Mightn't be a bad idea."

Patrician wasn't even mentioned. There was no need. I realised that an awful lot was left unsaid between us. Whatever mental shorthand we used seemed to work. Charlotte of course was a different matter, but the relevance of my trip to England slowly dawned on her and I was seen off with a hearty "Bring home some good news".

The first lot were coming back from exercise as I walked to the car. Eamon was among them and clearly had decided to let the horses have a break in the paddock closest to the gate. Lara was standing near the rail at the driveway, holding her horse on a loose rein, letting him gratefully tear at the short grass. She looked down at the horse's head and idly played with the mane. His tail flicked once in mild irritation, but he left it at that. Only then did I spot that Eamon was holding Patrician in the middle of the string.

So many people's lives were revolving around this big dark animal. Even the lads who looked after other horses and so didn't even come close to riding him out had a lot of hope invested. To be able to say you'd worked in the yard that contained a Gold Cup winner would be a proud boast for years to come. In fact, it wouldn't be a boast at all; it would mean a lot more than that. There were old men in the towns around the Curragh who were defined by the great horses they had worked with fifty years previously. In horse-mad Kildare, such things mattered. I knew I was no different. Now that racing was back in full swing, I couldn't allow myself the luxury of imagining all the time how good Patrician might be. Once every half-hour would have to do.

But the centre of all this attention merely wanted to have another minute eating. I'd seen Eamon look at his watch and tug gently on the reins only to give in and indulge

Patrician's reluctance to budge – proof that colossal investment can show up in the tiniest gesture.

I was getting into the car when I heard Lara call my name which sounded different with a Russian-sounding accent: more rounded with the careful pronunciation. A lot more exotic too. I really needed to get a grip.

I went over to her.

"I just wanted to say thank you and apologise for the way I behaved last night," she said.

I was suddenly very aware that the only sound was coming from the horses eating grass. The conversations and laughs had dried up. Some sly grins were being directed towards us. The reference to last night even had Eamon eying me quizzically. I leaned on the fence and told her softly to forget about it.

"No, you were very kind. Vaz told me what he did, and how you spoke to that man Yeats."

"How are you feeling?"

"I am fine. How is your eye?"

"It's a lot better thanks."

There was silence after that until Eamon shouted for everyone to head back to the yard. Lara tugged at her horse, who reluctantly straightened his head. I started to make for the car but Lara spoke again.

"Take care of yourself today."

"Thanks. You too."

Maybe I was delusional, but it seemed as if she had looked at me for longer than was strictly necessary. What I knew for certain was that even the idea she might have done so put me in better form than had seemed remotely possible when I'd got up that morning.

13

As I walked towards Martin French in the parade ring, it struck me that he was the perfect advertisement for those who believe that money doesn't bring happiness. His jowly face rarely cracked a smile and, if it moved at all, it was usually into a vindictive smirk at someone else's misfortune. His wife stood next to him while their horse, Valley Forge, walked around us.

"It's a bit nippy," I volunteered to the man whose green and yellow colours I had on.

"A bit."

It sounded like he resented making even that effort without getting something in return. Valley Forge's trainer raised his eyes to heaven, but was hardly going to say anything. After all, Valley Forge was his best horse. It takes all sorts, I told myself as I got on and tried to think of a way of beating Tenterhook.

If Patrician was the bright young thing in Ireland then Tenterhook was his English equivalent. He was a year older, but only now starting to achieve his potential. Just two months earlier he had surprised everyone by beating all bar the Gold Cup champion in the King George. Just a little more improvement and he would be a serious contender. Today would provide the answer.

My own expectations were low. Valley Forge was talented but not getting any better. He was one of those frustrating horses that are too good for handicaps and yet fall short of the real top-notchers. As we circled at the start, various scenarios went through my head but not one of them worked out with a win. Tenterhook's jumping was solid, so I would be unlikely to harass him into mistakes and he had won over longer distances than the three miles we'd have to race. Still, one never knew.

Only four runners sometimes means a false pace but Tenterhook's rider was having none of that. He led from the start and set a good tempo as we turned out of the back straight, flew the cross fence and made our way to the straight for the first time. Five fences ranged in front of us, dividing the long view into what looked like paddy fields. Newbury was a galloping track with two long stretches that put a premium on a horse's stamina and jumping ability. Meet the first fence right and the rest usually took care of themselves. Or at least that was the theory. I set my sights on the take-off board at the bottom of the fence ahead and tried to judge it so that Valley Forge could jump it without having to change stride. Like the intelligent and experienced racer he was, my big bay partner had the same idea. He didn't miss a beat and I hardly had to move as we sailed over, just a couple of lengths behind the favourite.

Valley Forge was going easily and felt well. He also seemed to be enjoying the quick pace and the cold, bright winter day. Getting a horse into a rhythm was half the battle and travelling at pace on a good one over these big fences still produced a conscious joy in me. We turned away from the stands and I thought that if French could sample this kind of controlled brio, he might even loosen up once in a while.

We weren't quite right at the first down the back but Valley Forge responded to the pull on the bit, put in a short stride, and fiddled over it. The disruption gave Tenterhook another couple of lengths' advantage and I figured if he was as good as he was supposed to be, then now was the time for him to stretch on. But he didn't. I rousted Valley Forge into the next obstacle and he took off too soon, almost outside the wing of the fence. The reins stretched almost to the buckle as I sat and prayed for him to get to the other side. Not only did he get there, he landed running and put himself right for the other fences. The next four were incident-free and, as we turned to face the cross fence again, I could hear Tenterhook a couple of lengths ahead being urged to go faster. But Valley Forge now cruised up to within a length. Unless I was very wrong, this was no Gold Cup horse in front of us. In fact, we could beat him. And if Valley Forge could beat one of the best around, what might Patrician do to them all?

The last thing I expected was a mistake. We were going so well. I took a slight pull coming to the fence so that Valley Forge would come back on his hocks a little. No need for heroics just yet. One-two-three, tuck in and urge him up with mind and body: it was a routine as familiar to the horse as eating and galloping. But, for some reason, he didn't want to do the routine. Instead, he came up a full stride early. No buckle was going to provide enough grip for this. In mid-air the horse's back twisted as he fought to get over the big black fence. Suddenly, there was nothing in front of me. At thirty miles an hour, we were momentarily going in different directions. The moment was enough.

Hard as I tried, gravity still won out. Valley Forge hit the ground and briefly rolled over on top of me. His instinct to get up took over immediately and, in a scramble of limbs, he was back upright again. That should have been the end of it: a race that might have been won thrown away by carelessness. But then the awful reality struck home. My right foot was still caught in the stirrup and in my all but upside-down position I couldn't shake it free. The horse stood still as I struggled. Then the two other horses in the race jumped the fence and his competitive instincts took over. Valley Forge started to gallop after them.

It was the nightmare situation. I was helpless. As the horse gathered speed, I was being thrown about like a rag-doll. It felt as if my insides were in a liquidiser. Trying to get the foot out of the stirrup was next to impossible. Everyone knew the only way to do that was to get the horse to stop. But Valley Forge didn't want to stop. I tried to arch my back into some sort of position which might change the angle I was caught in but it was useless. My last clear thought was not about death but about paralysis. Dear God, don't put me in a wheelchair. Then my head hammered off the ground and everything blurred.

It could have been only for a split-second. The start of a section of running rail that divided the hurdles and chase tracks was just ahead. A tall pole made out of the same birch they used in the fences was at the nearest end. The black timber shimmered as my vision wobbled but then sprang back into sharp, vivid focus. I didn't want to think about the damage that would be done to me if I hit that pole at speed. I heard myself swear and tried to move my foot one last time. It was useless. Heavy steel-tipped hooves whistled and thundered around my head. My body felt like it was empty of everything except pain. No life flashing past, no sudden illumination, no last-second spiritual acceptance. This was it. What a stupid way to die.

Except I didn't. Suddenly I was no longer moving. I hadn't been aware of keeping my eyes closed but opening them now, I saw white rails and in the distance a flight of hurdles. Wind whistled around my ears and brought with it snatches of the course commentary. I lay on my side and opened my mouth to taste the green grass. It still had some moisture on it from the previous night's frost. After a few seconds of not daring to move, I told my toes to wriggle and they responded. Then I moved a leg. I wasn't paralysed. Some primeval instinct kicked in and I moved a hand to my groin. Everything seemed intact. Only then did I move my head. About fifty yards away Valley Forge was standing quietly, head up, staring at the stands in the distance. I dropped my head back and pushed my face into the grass, opening my mouth wide to taste the world again.

"Are you okay, son?"

One of the ambulance personnel was leaning over and staring into my eyes. It suddenly felt all wrong, having this large, bearded man with a huge garish jacket kneeling next to me. I wanted him to go away. He wasn't alone either. I saw more legs skittering around and heard the clanging sounds of machines and equipment being unfolded. Why couldn't they leave me alone? It felt right just lying there.

"Can you hear what I'm saying, son? Don't move. We'll sort you out."

A stretcher suddenly appeared. It was time to return to the world. Time to get my finger out and sit up. I pushed myself up. Then I unhooked the helmet and took it off. My bearded and earnest saviour ignored my assurances that I was alright. Instead he held up two fingers.

"Are you trying to tell me to eff off?"

That was greeted with a smile, an assurance that he really would tell me to eff off if I kept on being so smart and, by the way, could I move my legs? I made to get up but, instead, was told to remain seated while a thin light was shone into my eyes. This prompted a buzz of discussion.

"You're a lucky man. Bloody lucky. The doctor will have to have a look at you in the first-aid room, but it looks like you've got away with it. Think you can stand up?"

My legs were shaky but, by leaning on one of the crew, I was able to make it into the ambulance. It drove slowly back and the official doctor was waiting when the doors opened. So were quite a number of other people, including a camera crew. Next to them was one of the television reporters whose name I couldn't remember.

"How are you feeling, Liam?" he asked, thrusting a microphone out in front of me.

The doctor was having none of that. "Please make way!" he shouted and cleared a path to the medical room. I gave the reporter a nod and followed the doctor into the small room. There I saw the television coverage of what had happened. Because there had been so few runners, individual cameras had been devoted to all four horses and the one on me had captured every moment. It looked horrific. I had bounced around like a ping-pong ball in a gale. A number of times my head crashed into the ground with a ferocity I hadn't really felt. Thank God for helmets. Flopping to the ground just seemed to happen. There was no sudden jink from the horse, no dramatic last-minute reprieve. One second I was hanging – the next I was on the ground. It was all frighteningly random. The film was repeated while I was checked out but I turned away.

"Somehow, Liam, you look to have got away with it. No

bones broken, no concussion and your leg is okay. Whoever you're praying to, keep doing it." The doctor grinned. "You're riding in Ireland tomorrow, right? You're going to have to pass the medic there, but you should be alright. How, I don't know."

He handed me back the helmet and said he would put down 'shaken' on his official report. There was that word again. I was escorted by a racecourse official through some corridors and we somehow got back to the jockeys' room without seeing anyone else. I sat down and stared at the ground. My colleagues kept their distance at first, unsure about how to deal with me. But one of the senior lads tapped me on the shoulder, sat down and informed the room I'd make a lousy rodeo rider. The laughter that simple remark generated showed their relief. Anyone expecting tears, hugs and expressions of solidarity would be disappointed. But the jokes and slaps on the back spoke volumes. After all, no one knew better than these guys. The possibility was there for all of us every time we threw a leg across a horse. If the gestures appeared old-fashioned, that didn't make the depth behind them any less.

14

On the plane back, the memory wouldn't go away. Mulling over something that frightening couldn't do any good, so the two people sitting next to me were treated to a non-stop flow of inane chatter that had them looking at their watches halfway through the flight. It was useless of course. The more I struggled, the more dominant the images became. That black birch pole just kept racing towards me even quicker. I leaned my head against the window and peered out at the white wing tip shuddering just metres away, thinking about death and pain and oblivion. No doubt my neighbours were happy I was finally quiet.

Making for the car park, I switched on my phone. There were twenty-two messages. Some were from reporters enquiring about the accident which was, apparently, featuring prominently on all the news channels. I deleted as I went. One, though, was from my mother whose voice cracked with worry towards the end. She obviously had been looking at the news. I rang her.

"Ma, I'm fine. Just a little bruised, that's all."

My mother still managed not to show her fear in front of me on the rare occasions she came to the races, but the ever-present danger lying in wait at each of the black fences meant an almost daily effort to blank out what might happen. My dad explained it one night over a drink and made me swear not to let on. My mother's effort was considerable, but the idea of me knowing about it would be terrible.

Knowing what my father had told me, I felt the woman's courage was amazing. All she said was to get something to eat, that I looked too thin. I said I would and we both knew I wouldn't. It was desperately unfair to put her through such anguish. Maybe such selfishness could have been excused by youth, but what excuse was there now? She even managed to sound light-hearted when I rang off and I found out that shame tasted pretty much the same as fear.

The last message was from Bailey, telling me to ring her straight away. I excused myself that task. Better to get some miles out of the way first. I got on the M50, pointed the car south and thought instead about Anatoly. I found myself hoping that the death blow had been quick, and that he hadn't seen it coming.

It wasn't even half past seven when I got back to the stable, which was far too early. I didn't know what I wanted to happen but sitting around in the kitchen and brooding was not a good idea. Better to get out. I was trying to decide where when Bailey came out of the drawing room. She threw her arms around me with a wincing ferocity and delivered a kiss to my cheek.

"Thank God you're alright. You are alright, aren't you?"

"Yeah. Just a bit bruised."

"We thought you were finished. We really did."

Charlotte and Franco were sitting in the drawing room with a depleted bottle of whiskey perched on a table between them. Franco's expression didn't betray too much anguish and I'd given up trying to read his wife years ago. Still, Charlotte stood up and gave me a perfunctory hug while Bailey poured herself a drink and asked if I wanted one. I shook my head and figured she must have made quite an impression on the bottle already. Her capacity for the hard stuff was legendary.

"You're a very lucky boy. I couldn't believe what was happening. It looked such a soft fall, and then there you were," Bailey said.

"Mummy was terribly upset," Charlotte chirped. "I was in the kitchen and heard this terrible cry. The tears were streaming down her face after you got up again."

"Yeah. You'd swear you were her son or something," said Franco, betraying a slight slur in his voice. So, it hadn't been only Bailey making the impression on the bottle.

Charlotte retreated to the kitchen and I joined Bailey on the big sofa. Franco was sitting opposite and it was only then that I realised how drunk he was. Slouched into the seat and leaning at an angle, he sloshed his drink around before demolishing it in one go. He straightened up to replenish the glass and I caught Bailey looking disapprovingly.

They made a strange combination: the big hearty trainer and the big brooding sculptor. One devoted to the living, breathing animal and the other to stone and marble that needed all his skill just to imitate life. Despite the potential for fireworks, I'd never heard about them clashing. Underneath all that bravado, Franco obviously understood that keeping his mother-in-law on side meant an easier life for him. And although I suspected Bailey made allowances for his often boorish behaviour, I also guessed that she was more than a little intimidated by this strange man that her daughter had chosen to marry.

The television news had my 'miraculous escape' as their quirky end-of-bulletin item. The pictures hadn't lost their potency. I tried to look away but Bailey grabbed my arm.

"*There* – that's when I thought you were cooked. My God, your head didn't half bounce." She laughed with obvious relief.

"Yeah. By the way, I was nearly going to win until it happened."

"Really? I thought Tenterhook had a lot left."

"No, there wasn't much there. I was starting to fancy my chances."

I hoped I'd managed to switch Bailey's attention to the dark-bay athlete housed outside. Sure enough, there was a silence interrupted only by Franco making another attack on the bottle and Charlotte's return with plates of sausages, chicken nuggets and chips.

"Tuck in everyone," she announced. "Sorry, Liam."

I grinned but my hungry stomach almost did a back-flip at the smell. It was on the tip of my tongue to ask for a fork, but I suspected Bailey might reserve one of those looks for me if I did. Sweating in the morning and pigging out in the evening would not be what she wanted from her stable jockey. I swallowed my hunger and waited for some response about Patrician.

"Have a think about it, Liam. I know you want to go for the Gold Cup but just have a good think about it. Study the form of the others and see how you might ride him against them. We'll decide next week, alright?"

There was no point pushing it. Bailey would only dig her heels in anyway. She was clearly playing for time. Both of us knew the form and tactics of every Gold Cup contender back to the day they were foaled. More time wouldn't make any difference to that. But at least she'd said something. Now I could escape with my duty done. The idea of listening to Charlotte rambling on about everything and nothing and of looking at her husband getting twisted wasn't how I wanted to end the day. And for once the idea of pondering Patrician's future wasn't doing much for me either.

It was still early. Time to get out. I thought of ringing Johnno. A night on the town with his infectious joie de vivre might be just what I needed. Johnno was always good for a laugh, always knew the cool places to visit and he invariably managed to get talking to the best-looking girls. But I didn't feel like it tonight. Instead, I walked into the kitchen and kept going through to the office.

I found her number easily enough and dialled as I walked back to the kitchen. Just as the phone started to ring, Bailey came in searching for ketchup. She was in mid-root at the back of a cupboard when a voice answered.

"Is Lara there?" I asked and noticed Bailey's head re-emerge with eyebrows raised. What the hell. I really was too old to be blushing.

"Yes. Lara speaking. Who is this?"

"It's Liam Dee. I hope I'm not getting you at a bad time."

There was a pause, which I suspected wasn't good. Either she had forgotten me or was debating whether or not to put the phone down.

"What do you want?"

There was a directness there that I figured wasn't meant to be aggressive, but which still didn't do much for morale. Only for Bailey standing nearby, the temptation to hang up and forget about it might have been overwhelming. But that was ridiculous. This kind of funk was supposed to happen when you're fifteen. I gritted my teeth and ploughed on. Now getting to the end of the call was the only objective I had.

"I wondered if you were doing anything tonight and, if not, would you like to go for a drink?"

"With you?"

"With me."

"I don't know. I am supposed to be in Dublin tonight."

"That's fine. I was just wondering, that's all. There's no sweat."

"But I suppose you could come too. If you wanted."

"Sure. I can drive, if that would suit. Will I see you in about an hour?"

She said that would be fine and hung up. I kept the phone to my ear for a second longer, trying to compose myself. I was aware of a grin on my face that probably looked silly in the extreme and would no doubt have Bailey ripping the piss out of me for a long time to come. But who cared?

I waited for the quip but instead the big woman paused only briefly.

"It's about time you got your finger out."

15

On the drive to Dublin, I learned more about Lara Kuznetsov. She came from Odessa, on the Black Sea, in the south of Ukraine. Home was on the slopes of the hills that surround the city and, during the summer, she said the blue of the nearby sea was enough to hurt your eyes. Her mother was there now with a younger sister. They were all close. There was no mention of her brother and I wasn't going to bring him up again. In fact, it would have suited me to just listen to her talking.

She looked magnificent, wearing jeans, black boots and a white blouse under a black jacket. She had a bulky anorak with her in case of rain. The clothes accentuated her tall, willowy figure that in itself would have been enough to transfix anybody. That she also possessed a mane of thick blonde hair that fell halfway down her back, and eyes that made me want to be a better man than I was, seemed an almost ridiculous accumulation of beauty in one person. It was all I could do to keep my own eyes on the road and the hour-long journey went by far too quickly.

She also seemed very different to the quietly proud person who worked in the yard. Her conversation was surprisingly easy, although her verdict on the dumb driver might have been different. Some shred of a long-forgotten geography class had remained in my head, so that I was hesitantly able to volunteer that the Dnieper flowed into the Black Sea somewhere near Odessa. There was a delighted reaction and plenty of surprise that an Irishman might know that. Just the mention of the river had her smiling and promoting the beauty of a vast country I'd barely even been aware of before. I retrospectively sent my thanks to Mr Lyons and his peculiar interest in the great rivers of Europe.

"My uncle has a farm, on the steppe, and every summer we would visit. It is where I learned to ride. Many ponies were there and our cousins would take us all over the countryside. Sometimes we would be away for days, camping and exploring. I loved it so much, and horses got into my blood. Even years later, when I went to university, they wouldn't go away. I did a physiotherapy degree but there was a veterinarian class in the college too and I attended some of those. My mother told me to stop wasting my time, but I think she was also secretly pleased. After all, she has Cossack blood."

"Now you're going to tell me that Cossacks have forgotten more about horses than we in Ireland will ever know."

"It is true!"

Her laugh was surprisingly light and it easily took me far away from the memory of what had happened that afternoon. There was a joy to this woman I couldn't have even guessed at before. The laughing lasted until I asked why she had picked Ireland.

"An agency in Kiev advertises for horse people to come here. You have to understand: the money we can send back is huge compared to what is available at home. My mother is not rich and she is not young any more. I can ride horses and I can speak English – I always loved the language in school – so I answered the ad. There were interviews and that is where I met Anatoly."

There was a brief silence. I glanced at her as we stopped at traffic lights but I couldn't read her face. She didn't seem upset. There were no tears. If anything, there was only a wistful smile. I was beginning to realise that the strident image she presented to the world was very far from the complete picture.

"He was so nice – this innocent little boy from the country. His village is so remote, it doesn't even have a proper road going through it. Only some dirt track. He had never left before, never been in Kiev. He got there in the back of a lorry transporting cattle. All he could talk about was how the poor animals were squashed in so tight they couldn't even get the air into their lungs to moan properly."

"He must have liked you very much."

"I tried to help him. Silly things like making him follow me in the airport in case he got lost. He trusted people."

"He certainly trusted you."

"Why do you say that?"

"He told you he was gay."

"He did not have to tell me," she smiled. "It was obvious. I think he hated being different. On the plane he was so scared. I tried to keep talking to keep his mind occupied and when I asked if he'd left a sweetheart behind, he just got very red. I told him not to be concerned and held his hand. He just wanted to talk about it, I think. To find out if it was okay. So silly, isn't it? How can it not be okay to love someone?"

We slowly made our way to the city centre and eventually found a car park that stayed open twenty-four hours. As we walked through Temple Bar and side-stepped the first drunken victims of the night's stag parties, she asked me about my own family. So I told her about my parents and my sister, the solicitor. All very middle-class Dublin. Plenty of complaints, but no major worries.

"Not very exciting, I'm afraid," I concluded.

"Family is about warmth, not excitement."

"I suppose so."

"Since you helped me with the police, and you know about it anyway, let me explain about my brother."

"Honestly, there's no need."

"I know there isn't. But I have nothing to be ashamed of. And my brother is a good boy."

We were passing the famous front entrance into Trinity College and, as a shortcut to where we were going, I led her inside it. Notice boards surrounded us. Pinned to the walls were the usual notes from all the societies informing their members about upcoming sporting fixtures, meetings, platforms and piss-ups. Usually it was jammed with students and tourists waiting for tours, but a Saturday evening in Dublin clearly demanded more exhilarating entertainment. So we had the draughty stone corridor to ourselves.

She halted abruptly and turned to face me, looking directly into my eyes.

"Rudi was a student, in Kiev. Very intelligent. A scientist. But being a student so far from home costs a lot money. Far too much for him to earn in some spare-time job. We don't know anybody rich and it looked like he would have to leave and get a job to help support our mother and our sister who is still in school. And then he was made an offer.

"You have to understand that nothing is certain in Ukraine, like it is in Ireland. Not even the government. And so much is corrupt. That doesn't mean the people are any more criminal than anywhere else. It just means everything is still young and new and boundaries are being tested all the time. The only really rich people now are criminals. You can see them in Odessa, Kiev, all the big towns. Driving around in their western cars, treating people with contempt, feeding on everyone's fear and weakness. But you can also see how someone young might look at them and be impressed.

"Rudi is an intelligent boy but, in many ways, he is as naïve as Anatoly. He became friends with people in this world and it all looked so easy. That is what he told me afterwards. It was so easy. These people had so much money. They would light their cigarettes with hundred-dollar bills for a joke. It meant nothing. Rudy is twenty-two. It does not matter how intelligent you are – if you see everyone getting away with breaking the law and making a fortune, then you will at least be tempted. It seemed the answer to everyone's problems. One job and he would get enough money to pay for college and look after everyone.

"Except he was arrested in Moscow. Rudi had his best suit on and he thought he looked like a businessman. But he must have looked like a schoolboy trying too hard. He was sweating so much with fear, he was picked out. Now he is paying the price. But Rudi is no gangster and no Mafia person. What he did, he did for us, not for himself."

There was sadness in her voice but also a fierce loyalty. This was far too bright a woman not to have wondered what might have happened had Rudi got away with that first run. Would the rush, and collecting the money, have prevented him from turning away? Intelligence wasn't some sort of automatic defence against becoming a criminal. I knew that myself, having ridden for more iffy owners over the years than I cared to remember. Most of them would have bought and sold their jockey without him even knowing about it. Betting and the prospect of easy money had always made racing as much a sport of chancers as kings. But that didn't mean they walked about with stupid signs on.

"What are you thinking?" Lara asked.

Those eyes were piercing into me. This could be one very short night. I dithered but knew that trying to waffle my way out of trouble was not going to work. After all that had happened to her, this woman's bullshit-detector was finely tuned.

"I was thinking it might not be the worst thing in the world that he got caught."

A flicker of what I hoped was recognition flashed across her face and the expected torrent of Slavic abuse didn't start ringing around my ears. Instead, she turned and stared at a poster about the Communist Party of Ireland's latest guest speaker. Apparently, the country could be saved only by a complete change of mind-set by the establishment. A wry smile played on her lips, the kind an indulgent grandparent gives. I waited for a response, but no words came. Instead Lara pushed her arm into mine and we walked outside.

Our destination was a pub I hadn't been in for a very long time. It had a famous old marble counter stained with many years of spilt pints and forgotten cigarettes. Mercifully, there had been little or no change, no plastic shiny modernisation that would look dated in a decade. Behind the counter, a large wooden clock beat its slow time alongside yellowing photographs of past sporting heroes. There hadn't been an upstairs when I'd been there last but now we followed the 'reserved' signs to where about sixty people were gathered around a small bar, making plenty of noise.

"We meet here once a month. It is important to stay in touch. When I first came to this country, I was very lonely. But being able to meet others from my country helped a lot. We travel here from all over Ireland. Some come from Cork for the weekend, others from Sligo. Miles away. But it is important. This reminds us of home."

We moved through the throng and closer to the bar where I bought a couple of drinks from a sour-faced youngster behind the counter. He and I seemed to be the only Irish people in the place and, returning to Lara with the glasses, I noticed some resentful stares in my direction. For some, the night was clearly about getting away from the natives and here was one of them right in their midst. Any tension, however, vanished as the familiar figure of Vaz pushed his way to the bar from the other end of the room. I saw him glance in our direction and then deliver an almost comical double-take. He registered my face, and the fact that I was standing next to Lara, and there was a moment before his own face split into a huge smile. I'd seen terrible anger and sombre acceptance before, but among his own Vaz looked a different man.

"Hey," he roared as he happily bullocked his way towards us. "Why didn't you tell me?"

"Tell you what?" I replied.

That got a laugh and I noticed there was even a slight blush on Lara's cheeks when Vaz winked at her. Then there was a lengthy burst of what sounded to me like Russian. Both Ukrainian and Russian were used on a daily basis in Bailey's yard – Lara had told me that Russian was widely spoken in Ukraine. Smiles played on both their faces as they spoke and when they turned their attention back to me there appeared to be agreement.

"Follow me, Liam," Vaz said. "I see you drink vodka.

That is for the weight, yes? Come, I will show you people who really know how to drink vodka!"

I leaned close to Lara in order to make myself heard. She moved too, so that her hair briefly brushed against my face. It felt like a thousand volts surging through me.

"Is everything okay?" I asked.

"Yes, of course. Why shouldn't it be?"

"Because I'm Irish."

"Don't be silly. He also said you had a bad accident today. How are you feeling?"

"Better all the time."

We sat at a table that was already threatening to get top-heavy with empty glasses. Around it were five friends of Vaz and Lara who received the full double-cheek-kissing attention of them all. I got sober handshakes, but there was nothing unfriendly about them. The three men and two women were introduced. Petro and Alexander worked as butchers in Limerick. Maria and her sister Jana were based in Dublin and worked as waitresses in a shopping-centre cafe. The other man, Josef, had been in Ireland the longest and was a computer engineer in Wexford town. He was about forty and, according to Vaz, had set up this informal get-together when he had first came to Ireland a decade earlier. It had grown into a vital link to home for a lot of people.

"It's the same idea as the Irish clubs in London and New York and all around the world," Josef said. "Except we are not exactly a club. After all, we have no place of our own to meet. But that is not important. We hire places like this and we can be ourselves."

"How does that work with someone like me in the place?"

"We simply have to curl our lips, look down our noses and smile nicely!"

Vaz wasn't wrong about the drinking. Everyone tucked in with a relish that quickly had me struggling. There was nothing so stereotypical as a national devotion to vodka either. In fact, I noticed Lara's tipple of choice was a pint of Guinness, albeit with a dash of blackcurrant cordial on top.

"There are people in this country who would have you strung up for that," I told her.

"There are people in my country who would string you up for being so careful with that vodka. Drink up!"

Throughout the evening, there were constant interruptions from people arriving at the table and delivering great bear hugs. Vaz and Lara introduced me to each of them. Invariably I was given a firm handshake, a smile and a welcome. Considering it wasn't long since one of their own had been murdered, the atmosphere was exuberant and, after yet another introduction, I leaned over to Lara.

"Did Anatoly come to these things much?"

"Every one."

"Really?"

"You are wondering why people are not more sad? It doesn't mean we have forgotten Anatoly. We never will. In fact, the night has come early this month because we want to remember him. We want to celebrate his life. This is for him."

I thought of the great tradition of the wake in Ireland. At the time of the greatest sadness, there was always the determined effort to drink and celebrate and scorn death with a great exhibition of life, fun and laughter. How could it be a surprise that the same attitude might exist somewhere else? Especially in a country like Ukraine that had had its heart and soul ripped to pieces just decades earlier. Millions paid the price for being the unwitting pawns in a power game played by maniacs. The family of every person in the room must have been affected in a struggle that put Ireland's painfully small-minded, dirty little conflicts in scornful perspective.

I looked at Vaz, happily getting drunk and loudly urging Lara to play some music. A hard, proud man, but as easily moved to laughter as violence. Josef sat next to him. He had quietly informed me that he'd become quite the racing fan since coming to Ireland. Few things beat a good day at the races, he declared. I'd done him some favours over the years, he added, placing another large vodka in front of me. He even secured a large bottle of slim-line tonic to help me out.

"You are racing tomorrow," he grinned. "I think it is probably best to add some of that."

At one stage, Jana returned from the bar, sat on my knee and loudly proclaimed that if I had anything harder to sit on I should let her know. This was met with peals of laughter and Lara playfully grabbed her hair, pretending to pull her off. Any nervousness at upsetting the ethnic feel of the evening evaporated in a sea of boozy bonhomie of a sort I hadn't enjoyed in a long time. It felt wonderful.

Vaz eventually got his wish and from somewhere a guitar was handed to Lara. She turned around to face the room and quickly tuned the instrument before a hush fell over the place. Expectant faces looked at her as she started to pick the first set of chords. Those same faces became sombre once the words began. No knowledge of the language was needed to understand the tone of the song. Sadness and pain picked their way through to the heart and left only regret. After a verse, there was a hum, made up of a roomful of voices almost whispering in accompaniment. Lara stared into the distance and delivered the song without once looking around. I noticed her fingers played over the strings with a speed and touch that would always remain an intangible mystery to me. Music was a love of mine, but the idea of even attempting to make it was beyond my understanding. Yet this woman was able to play with a feeling that turned the room on her very fingers. I started to feel very, very inadequate. When the song ended, there was a second's silence before thunderous applause broke out. I looked at Lara and she caught my gaze. I couldn't help it. In any language my wish at that moment was far too easy to understand.

Josef stood on a chair and raised his arms to quieten everyone. He started to speak and Lara whispered that he was asking for everyone to pray in memory of Anatoly. The voices rumbled, followed by a full minute of silence broken only by the clink of glasses behind the bar and the whirr of the glass-washer. I noticed more than one person crying and being comforted. Josef spoke again at the end. There would be a bucket at the door when the evening finished. It was for contributions for Anatoly's family in the Ukraine. Give what you can was the tone.

Not surprisingly, there was a lull in the atmosphere after all that, but then I noticed Josef glancing at me.

"Ladies and gentleman," he shouted in English. "It's not every night we have a sports star among us. So let us show him how we enjoy ourselves in Ukraine!"

A loud cheer filled the room with Vaz contributing lustily into my ear. I looked up at Josef who mouthed the word 'sorry' to me. Somehow, and purely in the interests of re-establishing a good atmosphere, I endured the hospitality and unfailing friendliness. There appeared to be no sign of anyone going home and the thought of driving the hundred miles from Dublin to Clonmel in the morning briefly loomed before being dismissed with a mental shrug. A run in the morning would be painful, but somehow it would be endured and the drink's only legacy would be a set of running gear that smelled like a brewery.

"What about the Irish tradition for singing? Would you care to make a contribution?"

Josef was back in his seat, looking quizzically at me, while trying not to notice what was going on to his left where Vaz was making some rather unsubtle attempts to make a move on Jana. The big man briefly caught my eye, winked theatrically and delivered a grin that was almost a caricature of roguish. I laughed and noticed that Jana, while pretending to talk intently to her sister, wasn't exactly straining at the bit to get away. In fact, there was an almost imperceptible slide towards her prospective suitor. Rather like the movement of plates before an earthquake.

"So, will you sing?"

Vaz's vast hairy hand ventured towards Jana whose deeply tanned arm was stretched just too far from her to be comfortable. It was only when their fingers touched that I registered what Josef was proposing.

"Forget it. I don't sing. And if you try to make me, then this Irishman will be heading out the door very fast."

"These things are usually all-Ukrainian anyway," he said, smiling. "But forget the song. I'm happy you came here. You have restored some of my faith."

I was about to ask in what, but he made his way to bar. That was when it struck me that Lara had been away for some time. She had said something about talking to some friends at the other end of the room, but I looked around now and there was no sign of her. More than a tiny panic took over at the idea that she might have cut her losses and gone home. I stood up to get a better look and there she was, standing in a corner looking directly at me. Suddenly it appeared like a decision had been made and she walked towards me.

"It is getting late. I think you'd better take me home."

16

Streaks of sunshine darting through cracks in the curtains woke me. I lay in bed and watched them shimmer in front of me, like lines of music with dust and fluff providing constantly moving notes. When the dust slowly glided out of the light, it was briefly possible to follow it until the changing background of colours swallowed it up. I didn't move for quite some time. Just kept watching my musical light and relishing the ache in my limbs. Looking down, I could see how the blotches of yesterday's fall had turned black and blue and covered my stomach and hips almost entirely.

Lara slept on. She was lying on her front, her face away from me, taking the shallow breaths of a deep and undisturbed sleep. Two of my more adventurous light-streaks made their way like thin guitar strings to the small of her back and beamed into the tawny brown skin that had thrilled and excited me almost beyond endurance just hours before.

The thin sheet barely covered her rump and my eyes

almost started to ache as well as they traced the naked descent to the bottom of her back. It took a conscious effort not to reach over and kiss the valley of her spine and taste the minute blonde hairs that only my light-streaks could find. But that would mean moving and disturbing a moment I wanted to last for as long as possible. So instead of tasting and touching, as I'd helplessly done all night, there was nothing for it but to look and marvel at how lucky one man could get.

There wasn't a blemish on her long brown back that curved now slightly as she lay. My eyes lingered on the escarpment of a slightly raised shoulder blade and then ventured sideways, past some thick blonde hair, and settled on where her arm met her body. The meeting threw up a slight roll of skin that at that moment looked like the most blatantly sensual expression of womanhood I could imagine. My light-streaks would have to come back another time. I leaned over and kissed my provocative piece of heaven.

There was a murmur of unconscious recognition, followed by a low grunt from the back of her throat. Immediately I could feel myself getting aroused. Images and memories collided for attention in my head. I put my hand on her back and started to kiss it. If a malevolent God had told me I could do nothing else for the rest of my life, I'd have thanked him there and then.

We'd first kissed when I opened the front door. My house was only a twenty-minute taxi ride from the city centre and on the way I could feel her hand move across the seat and touch mine. The idea of presenting the driver with a story to tell his mates flashed repeatedly through my brain but, somehow, we managed to just stay holding hands until we got inside and everything became just a blur of touch and sound and taste.

When we had undressed, my bruising was obvious, even in the dark. Lara didn't even blink at this human chessboard in front of her. Instead, she pushed me gently on to the bed, kissing the parts of me that the Newbury earth and Valley Forge's hooves had marked. The sensations were too much. I pulled her on top of me and amazingly my hunger was reciprocated. Tenderness became more urgent and demanding and breathless moans of desire somehow dissolved into spent fulfilment without one of us getting hurt. At the end, she had dug her nails into my back with a ferocity that had me gasping and her delivering that grunt which she was releasing again now.

Lara woke slowly and once again we made each other happy.

Afterwards we lay together, luxuriating in our nakedness with even the final sheet thrown to the floor. Central heating kept the room warm and when Lara got up to visit the bathroom she skipped unabashed from the bed and made for the door.

"Stop showing off," I murmured, and received a bum wriggle and look over the shoulder that could have come from a *Carry On* movie.

It was eight thirty. We must have had only two or three hours' sleep and yet I felt wonderful. The idea of travelling to the races paled significantly compared to spending a whole day with this woman, but duty called. First things first, though. We would have to get back into town and pick up the car. From the bathroom I could hear the hum of the shower. Surprise visits in the steam had never been my thing so Lara was safe for the moment. Instead I padded downstairs to the kitchen, feeling more than a little pleased with life.

If racing had taught me anything, it was that the hardest

falls always come when you're feeling on top of the world. As I tried to prepare Lara a breakfast out of materials from an impoverished fridge, the phone rang. I glanced at it, prepared to ignore its demand for attention, but recognised the number: Yeats. I groaned, but picked up.

"You work unsociable hours, Inspector."

"From what I see in the paper, so do you. Is it true you're riding in Clonmel today?"

"Yes."

"If you can spare me a minute, I'd like to ask you a few questions this time."

"You're going to the races?"

"I was thinking of it, yes. Might as well see what gets you people so worked up. Presumably ordinary people will be let in too? It's not just tinkers and jet-setters, I hope?"

I laughed. That sing-song accent was in good form. Which might mean some sort of progress. There was a definite satisfaction in the way Yeats was curling his tongue around the sardonic jibes.

"Have you found something out?"

"Let's just leave it until I see you at the races. There's nothing seismic or anything. I just want to bounce something off you."

"Okay. I ride in the first and then in the fourth. We can meet up in between. Just come round to the weigh room and ask for me after the first race."

"See you there."

By the time Lara emerged, dressed and looking as if she'd just come off a fashion shoot, I'd managed to rustle up some scrambled eggs and bacon, along with toast and a pot of coffee. There was a wry, almost nervous, smile on her face as she looked at me putting the food on plates. Then we kissed once more and I told her she was the most beautiful woman I had ever seen. It provoked a grin but also a change of subject.

"Didn't you say something last night about having to run and sweat this morning?"

"I'd say we've made that pretty unnecessary."

We took the food into the front room and plonked ourselves down in front of the television. I watched her tuck happily into the breakfast and felt no hunger while munching on my dry toast and black tea. She looked at it once but said nothing and didn't stop enjoying her own. My God, I thought, she gets it. Normally people looked at me eating nothing and felt some need to abstain in sympathy. All that provoked was embarrassment. I hated it.

A taxi company promised a cab would be outside in ten minutes and, since Lara insisted on washing up, I used the time to quickly get dressed and read through the letters that had stacked up inside the door. The night before, they had been just a nuisance to trample over. So I read in the kitchen and Lara washed. There was a silence only broken by the faint drone of the television in the other room. But it wasn't a bad silence. Far from it. A horn sounded outside and we gathered our stuff. I reached for her hand and she grabbed mine tightly. There was so much I wanted to say. It felt like something very special was coming to an end. Once out of the door, the world would be part of us once again. But I couldn't think of anything. It was enough to make me angry. But then she whispered into my ear and everything was alright again.

"I think you're more than amazing," I said back. And we closed the door behind us and climbed into the waiting cab.

Not much needed to be said once we got back into town and were moving under our own steam. She held my hand and put it on her thigh for most of the journey back to

Newbridge. I resented every gear change. The only interruption came from Bailey whose strident early-morning tones blasted through on speakerphone.

"I need to get out of here. The walls are starting to come in. Can you pick me up on the way to Clonmel?"

"Sure. I'll be there in about half an hour."

Outside Mrs O'Sullivan's I was treated to a long, lingering kiss and an order that I had to mind myself today. It felt ridiculously good, as I drove away, to look in the rear-view mirror and see that gorgeous figure wave me off. Even showing up ten minutes later in the stable, I was aware of my face being split by a lovesick grin. It was time to snap out of it.

As it was, there were still some amused looks thrown my way when Bailey appeared and got in next to me. She was dressed to the nines. Having been blessed with a body more voluptuous than svelte, she rarely troubled herself with fashion problems. Jeans at home and dark trouser suits at the track were the usual. There was none of that this time though. A bright red skirt was topped by a cashmere sweater that couldn't have looked casual even if it tried. Long boots hit the knee and the whole effect was topped off by a rather rakishly tilted hat. With that marvellously defiant face at the centre of it all, the effect was rather like some magnificent galleon turning into the guns with full sails up. You didn't have to be Freud to get the message but, even so, I couldn't help but look at her admiringly.

"You can cut that out right now. Anyway, I thought you'd be too played out for that sort of thing."

"What do you mean?"

"Oh please. Either you got laid last night or else you've swallowed a bucket of happy pills."

"I still think you look great, boss."

Despite herself, she was pleased. We drove out in good spirits and had almost made it to the motorway before things changed.

"Damn, I almost forgot. Charlotte wants to come too. Do you mind?"

As driving companions go, I could think of some I would favour over Bailey's daughter but there was no point moaning and groaning. It wasn't like I was going to tell her that her eldest offspring gave me a colossal pain in the rear and that she was the perfect advertisement for keeping kids out of hoity-toity boarding schools. Time to think of something else, I figured. Like streaks of light and white sheets and slim fingers sliding across a guitar.

Typically, Charlotte wasn't ready when we arrived. She came to the door with a hair-dryer practically scalding her scalp and the harassed air of someone who had just got up.

"Give me five minutes. I'm not sure where Franco is. Maybe he's in the back garden. He'd love to see you."

I rather doubted that but, dutifully, Bailey and I traipsed through the house, with its light minimalist furniture, which I had no doubt had cost a tasteful fortune, before emerging into a large square of green grass. Around the borders were some spiky and unweeded shrubs that had Bailey tut-tutting. I half-expected her to get down on her knees and tear at them, but instead she asked if I wanted to see Franco's studio. Pointing to the squat concrete shed at the end of the garden, she started walking.

"Won't he mind being disturbed?" I asked.

"Don't mind Charlotte. The amount he had to drink last night, I'll lay you any amount you like he won't be up before the afternoon."

It was on the tip of my tongue to ask if the resolute pursuit of drunken oblivion was normal for Franco but then I thought I was in no position to pontificate about booze. Not for nothing had I washed my teeth twice earlier, and rooted out a packet of chewing gum after my boss's phone call. I followed Bailey through a door and into a vast open space that didn't seem possible from the front view of the building outside.

"It goes right back for a couple of hundred yards," she said. "Franco couldn't believe it when he saw it first. Perfect for what he does. Charlotte keeps complaining that she can't get him out of here."

The place looked half studio and half building site. Bags of what looked like sand lay torn open all over the place and contributed to a dusty atmosphere that caught at my throat. Tools were scattered on the floor: chisels, trowels, even a shovel, which was wedged in between a tall sculpture and a massive block of what might have been marble. The clutter extended into the distance and I could even see a small forklift parked against a tall warehouse-type door at the far end.

"I don't know how he works in here. Sometimes you come in and you can't even see him for the dust and grime he throws up. He has to wear masks and goggles. Charlotte says she wakes up in the morning with bits of rock and chalk all over the pillows."

I stepped carefully across the floor. There were shelves along the walls with various half-finished heads, fully rounded torsos and limbs placed carefully on top of each other. Everywhere was a sense of uncomplicated physical labour. Any pre-conceived ideas of a foppish artist's garret were clearly ridiculous. This was a man too busy making art to waste time adopting a pose about it. The piece I saw first had its back to me and I picked my way round to look at it properly. Its immediate impact had me balancing on one leg in the midst of the debris.

The large stone block was being transformed into a seven-foot high representation of what was clearly a soldier. From the puttees around his legs, the loose gas mask that hung uselessly from a belt at his side and the pudding-bowl helmet, it looked like a First World War British Tommy. The detail that had been cut into the hard surface was extraordinarily impressive. Slung dismissively over the left shoulder was a Lee Enfield .303 rifle, like the one my grandfather kept under the stairs; he'd been in the FCA, the part-time army, for years and liked nothing better than a cold afternoon on a firing range. Sometimes he'd let me hold the weapon and, as a small boy, the feel of the heavy wood and iron had been intoxicating.

Franco had got everything right: the angle of the bolt, the snub nose of the barrel, the weapon's deadly weight. All the other details of kit and uniform looked accurate too. But that was all they were. Just detail.

The real power was in the angles. Although I suspected Franco was far from finished, a terrible sense of doomed exhaustion already radiated from every inch of the figure. There was a tilt to the soldier's body that told more clearly than any words could about how far he had marched and what horrors he had seen. Franco was leaving the face until later but already the helmet drooped over it as if trying to shield the eyes from any more suffering. Past a swirling great coat that flapped open, it was possible to see legs almost bowed under the effort of keeping going. Whether he was going to the Front or returning from it was unclear. But somehow, Franco's big hands had managed to make it desperately plain in this mass of rock that it was only a matter of time before death would end the effort. It was a stunning piece of work. When I walked back to Bailey, I had to clear my throat before speaking and it wasn't just from the dust.

"That's so good," I said.

"Is that the soldier? Yes, he's been working on it for some time. It's for a new war memorial somewhere in Britain. He got the commission last year and just kept putting it off. Charlotte says he's been like a bear for the past week."

Little wonder, I thought. The imagination and mental discipline needed to produce work like that had to be immense and the reckless attacks on the whiskey bottle the previous night made a lot more sense to me now. Each glass must have been his own sharp two fingers to the spectre of death that clung to this piece of wondrous creation. Part of me envied Franco his talent. Another left me grateful for my own one-dimensional existence with the certainty of the winning post in the distance.

"I think it's sensational," I said.

Bailey looked pleased at my obvious admiration for her son-in-law's work. We slowly moved farther down the room and it was obvious that the unknown soldier was no random brush with beauty. More than once I made utterly spontaneous expressions of delight which had Bailey smiling. When Charlotte eventually showed up, her mother couldn't wait to tell her how much I liked Franco's work.

"Oh, that's good. There isn't much in here at the moment. Most of it is in Dublin. An exhibition is starting next month in the Pavilion Centre. But there's a pair of preview nights for invited guests and the critics next week. So it's all go."

Sure enough, there was no sign of the man himself before we left. Charlotte got into the back seat and we left for the races in good time. I didn't mention I was meeting Yeats in the afternoon. There was no point in spoiling the mood. Bailey was in better form than I'd seen since the morning Anatoly had been found, and Charlotte seemed determined to be on her best behaviour. Catty jibes were at a minimum as we headed towards Carlow and then Kilkenny.

I hadn't told Lara about Yeats either. Not wanting to spoil the mood applied even more to her. Lara was no more a suspect than the man in the moon, but I wasn't the one who'd been in police custody.

Bailey talked about the two horses she was running that day and the way I was supposed to ride them. But mostly she talked about me back in the studio.

"You should have seen his face, Charlotte. I've never seem him so impressed."

The reaction from behind seemed to be one of genuine delight. I guessed that gushing expressions of approval from her mother about Franco were not something Charlotte was used to. She was still quiet, but the atmosphere seemed even more relaxed as we powered our way past Kilkenny and into the last half of our journey, Bailey's good form increasing with every mile.

"One of Franco's friends once told me that hundreds of years from now, people will still be looking at his statues. That, after all the winners I've trained have long been forgotten, Franco will still be remembered. Cheeky bastard."

There was only amusement in her voice however. Franco's pals must have felt his mother-in-law needed taking down a peg or two. But it hadn't even made a dent in her self-assurance.

"It's all bullshit anyway," she continued. "People worrying about their fucking legacy. Childish rubbish about living forever. Do you want to know what eternity is, Liam? I mean real eternity?"

"Oh Mother, not again! He doesn't want to hear this."

"That, Liam, is real eternity. Back there, complaining that I'm embarrassing her. She's the only eternity that matters a damn. The only chance I have, for what it's worth, of any kind of legacy. Just as I was my parents' only chance. It's all that matters. Watching this little, roaring monster that you've created grow up and continue the line. How can some picture or statue or song compare with that?"

"History is full of those who would disagree with you," I said as neutrally as possible.

"To hell with them! I bet most of them never had kids. That's what I'm waiting for. To see Franco and Charlotte with a baby. In the house. To see that eternity. There's nothing else, you know," she said, turning around to look at her daughter. "Mind you, they'd want to get the lead out. You're not getting any younger, darling. If you don't hurry up, I'll have to start looking towards Liam here. Won't I, stud?"

I glanced in the mirror to see Charlotte's reaction, but she was staring out at the countryside and appeared not to have even heard her mother's none too subtle dig. Having got that out of her system, Bailey settled back in her seat and resumed her instructions for the races ahead. Eternity could wait. In racing, the most important race of all is always the next one.

17

Yeats was waiting outside the weigh room with his doleful face on. I'd just been to the first-aid room to be examined by the course doctor, who bended and prodded and pronounced me fit to ride if I was insane enough to want to. I noticed a copy of the *Racing Post* on his desk. There was Valley Forge on the front page with his jockey twisting in mid-air. The only bit in contact with anything was my foot. Over it was a headline: *Miracle Escape*.

On the way in from the car, where the women had remained to perform some last-minute make-up checks, I'd been stopped a few times by concerned well-wishers. No doubt my initial bemusement was dismissed as concussion or Dee being a little punchier than usual. How could they know that a blonde-haired beauty had pushed my mortality to one side?

Yeats had a copy of the same newspaper under his arm. Possibly he was attempting to figure out the reason for this Pied-Piper-like trek by thousands of people to a small track in south Tipperary. Or maybe he was simply trying to fit in.

Neither task looked to be working out for him. More than ever, he appeared a man disenchanted with the world and his place in it. He sounded cheerful enough though.

"You were lucky, I see," he said, gesturing to the paper.

"Very."

"Is it true? Could you have been killed?"

"Possibly."

"Ridiculous way for a grown man to make a living," he sniffed. "As if there isn't enough danger around anyway."

There didn't appear to be much to say to that. We agreed to meet after the first race and I made to walk away. But he called after me.

"Will you win?"

"What does the paper say?"

"They tip you."

"Always believe what you read."

Sam English was waiting inside, looking concerned. I made a point of trying to touch my nose with a finger but kept repeatedly missing. Johnno appeared and got me in a headlock that only added to my collection of bruises. I stripped down and Sam surveyed the damage.

"Not too bad," he said.

"Exactly."

"Right, what saddle do you want to use?"

His boy was in one piece: time to get on with things.

I got ready to ride a horse of Bailey's whose best form gave him the winning of the maiden hurdle. Sure enough he felt good through the race and responded well to a couple of cracks after the last to win by a length. Her horses really were in good nick.

Eamon was waiting to lead us back in and, as we returned to the winner's enclosure, there was a gratifyingly spontaneous round of applause for the proud trainer standing nearby. Bailey's eyes were sparkling at the success. No matter how many winners came along, the thrill of passing the post first never disappeared, though she always said to make the most of it because who knew when the next one might come.

"Good ride, Liam."

"They always are when you win."

An official walked towards the weigh room with me to ask if I could come out for a presentation to the winning connections. There was an unwritten rule in the jockey's room that we facilitated such things. Owners usually wanted it and sponsors liked their photo opportunities. They were a pain in the ass when you were rushing for the next race, but everyone knew that what was good for the game eventually percolated down. So I dutifully smiled for the camera, told the owner his horse had a future and thanked the local supermarket owner for his kind sponsorship. It was hardly a torture.

Yeats was leaning on one of the stout chestnut trees that lined the parade ring as I left. He fell into step beside me and wondered if there was a quiet place where we could talk. Race day was hardly ideal for silence, but we went past the old stand that faced down the home straight and found ourselves leaning on an uphill running rail. Behind us were trees and there was nobody else within thirty yards.

"I backed you – had twenty on at 6-4 – so thanks."

"No problem."

"I went down to the last jump. It's surprising how quickly it all happens. There's just this rumble, and then you're past. Actually the only thing I heard was swearing. Was that you?"

"No," I chuckled. "That was the guy on my inside. He's

always roaring at his horses: trying to scare them into going faster. He can be quite colourful sometimes."

"You don't do that?"

"I've been known to lose it but, as a rule, I try not to. Doesn't achieve much. A bit like yourself."

"I have my moments."

I bet you do, I thought, and waited for him to get to what was really on his mind. There was little point rushing him. Detective Inspectors probably liked to set their own pace. Sure enough, there was a pregnant silence before he spoke again.

"If you had to describe Eamon Dunne in one word, what would it be?"

"Loyal."

"That was quick."

"I didn't realise I was against the clock. Anyway, it wouldn't matter. Loyal is still the word. Why? What about Eamon?"

"There's nothing about him. I just wanted your opinion."

"I've known Eamon Dunne since I was a kid. He has been nothing but kind and generous and helpful to me."

"Look, believe it or not, I am not the enemy here. If you want to lash out, then go flail at one of your nags. I came here because I thought you were a reasonably bright person. One who might be able to detach his brain from his balls long enough to give me a steer. Whether you realise it or not, all investigations are an accumulation of information. There's no Poirot moment in this business – no shining light in the middle of the night. Just a steady build-up of information. I have no reason to believe anything of Eamon Dunne, but it would be nice to get another opinion about him. Or is your loyalty worth more than helping to find a killer?"

Put like that, there was hardly another option. And, if there was, I had no doubt Yeats would have a similarly convincing argument to counter it. Arguing with the man was a one-way ticket to pain, so why bother? But why this concern with Eamon when Wolf was running around free? As the runners for the next race cantered past us on the way to the start, I asked him what he wanted.

"You say Eamon Dunne is loyal. Why?"

"He just is. He's worked for Bailey since she started out, and for her father before that. He's as much a part of the yard as the stones in the walls. I can't imagine him not being there."

"Okay. And your own experience?"

"When I was starting as a jockey, he put himself out for me. Introduced people, took me aside, pointed out where I'd messed up and where I'd done well. In many ways he moulded me. Bailey might have provided the opportunities but it was Eamon who helped me make the most of them. He's a genuinely good man."

"He seems a popular guy alright, especially with women."

"You're off beam. He's just a warm person."

"There are certain people who wouldn't agree with you. At least two people we've interviewed believe he goes beyond the bounds of friendship with the female members of staff."

"That's just badness."

"Do you know someone called Emma Barnes?"

"No."

"She briefly worked in the stable some years ago. I was told Dunne had a relationship with her."

"I very much doubt it."

"But you don't know?"

There wasn't much to say to that. I didn't know. The girl's name meant nothing to me. Every instinct said it was bad-minded bullshit but could I swear to it? No, of course not. And why should I? Playing away from home might not be particularly moral, but peeping under the blankets was not my style. What Eamon did in bed was his affair.

"How well do you know Jonathan Parle?" Yeats asked.

"Well enough. I socialise with him a bit. See him at the races a lot. He's here today."

"What word would you use for him?"

Despite the circumstances, it was impossible to stifle a grin. Johnno's sheer enthusiasm and good humour made sure of that. There was obviously a sharp business brain there too.

"Fun. Johnno's a fun guy. And bright too."

"He's in the yard a lot, isn't he?"

"He goes down about three mornings a week to ride out."

"He doesn't actually work in the yard then? There's no mucking out or anything like that?"

"No. Johnno's an owner first and foremost."

"So he might not be overly familiar with the layout of the yard: where things go or the pokey little corners."

"I suppose not. Why?"

He ignored me. Instead there was a short silence, as if mentally ticking off names from a list. Next up was Charlotte.

"You want a one-word description for her? I'm afraid it needs more than one. A lot more."

"Humour me and try."

"Well, there's no getting away from the fact that some people think she's a bitch. Others would probably dismiss

151

her as some kind of idiot. She's not that. She's just spoilt. There's your word."

"Her mother?"

"You've met Bailey. Make your own mind up."

"Please. Can I have a word?"

"Okay then, how about staunch?"

The race started and we had a clear view of the field running towards us down the straight before turning right. A couple of stragglers were already under pressure. I had some idea how they felt. Even for someone whose job entailed coming up with excuses to disappointed owners a lot of the time, Yeats' questions seemed more than a little fanciful.

"If you don't mind me asking, what are you after?" I said.

"The killing happened in a stable that is usually kept free, right? It's not given specifically to one horse, as is the case with the other boxes. At the time every stable was occupied except for the one where the murder took place."

He looked at me, waiting for a reaction. But my silence was enough for him to keep going.

"Because of the discovery of some narcotics in the victim's personal belongings, and reports of his use of narcotics, we have to pursue the likelihood that there is a criminal drugs element to this affair, We also have Mr Wolf's continuing unavailability."

Again, there was a halt while Yeats waited for my contribution. There was none.

"Then we have Ms Kuznetsov's report that the victim was homosexual. As of now, there has been no back up to that, but, again, I'm inclined not to dismiss it. From what has been said to us, he doesn't appear to have comfortably fitted in with some of the rougher lads in the place. Your friend Mr Parle even used the word 'effeminate'. From what I've seen, some of the customers running around that stable would make a crocodile's back look smooth. But the sex element is something we do have to consider as a possible motive too – even if he wasn't gay."

"Is that why you're throwing names at me? Because you think someone in the yard was having a fling with Anatoly?"

"You find that hard to believe?"

"I guess not. I mean I've never thought of it. I just presumed –"

"Presumed what?"

"Never presume anything, right?" I asked Yeats, who smiled slightly. "But you obviously have some sort of idea that you're thrashing around."

"Why's that?"

"There's no other reason for you to be here talking to me like this."

"Maybe," he said and looked down the track as the race finished.

The sound of cracking whips carried to us from the pair of horses battling at the front. I recognised one set of colours and the jockey carrying them. Roars from the stands couldn't drown out the grunting efforts from the riders and the fervent oath from the losing one as they pulled up in front of us. It acted as a trigger for Yeats.

"This is strictly off the record. I shouldn't tell you anything, but I still live in hope that you might prove useful at some stage."

"So do I."

"A lot hinges on where it happened."

"Why? It's just a box. It's not empty all the time."

"Yes, but someone knew it was empty that night."

"Anatoly would have known."

"Yes, he knew, and I considered why he might have picked such a place to meet someone. For whatever reason. To have sex, to buy drugs. But that's not the important part. What's vital is that the person who killed him knew how to get there without being seen."

"What do you mean, how to get there? You just walk into the yard."

"You can. But how do you know you won't be picked up on CCTV?"

"What's on the pictures?"

"The security man appears, briefly, but nowhere near the murder scene. And there's the victim. He shows up at five minutes past midnight and makes straight for that stable. It's quite clear. He even looks up towards the camera for a second. He glances around quite a lot, but, then again, he isn't really supposed to be there, and he doesn't want the guard to spot him. He then walks towards the alley but we don't see him. The camera is fixed, pointed outwards to cover the stable yard. It doesn't pan wide enough to take in the alley – or all of the yard underneath where it is positioned."

"So there's nothing there that can help."

"Oh but there is. The fact that no one else appears tells us rather a lot. It certainly tells us that the killer knew another way of getting into that stable. Have you been in that alley much?"

"Hardly ever. I wouldn't have any reason to."

"But you know it?"

"Sure. It's a dead end."

Yeats smiled, shook his head and looked pleased with himself. From a pocket he pulled out a series of small black and white photographs that looked like a series of dark

154

splodges. "I took these yesterday. Even in mid-afternoon, the end of the alley, which is a good hundred feet from the edge of the main stable yard, was almost completely dark. It's roofed at the end and that roof angles down to meet the eight-foot back wall. Normally a person wouldn't even get near it. Over the years, the back of the alley had turned into a sort of dump. Barrels and old buckets and all sorts of rubbish thrown in there. But I was standing in the dark trying to think how the killer might have entered when this bird suddenly appeared out of nowhere and nearly gave me a heart attack. It took off past my nose out into the open like it was the most normal thing in the world. So I left the yard and went around the back of the stable block. It was like a jungle there. Just briars and thorns and brambles. But it was wasn't too hard to get through to the part of the wall where the alley is. The eaves of the roof comes right down below the top of it, but all I had to do was look up. There's a good foot-wide gap – more than enough for someone to get through."

A pair of small boys ran uphill towards us, shouting and laughing at the top of their voices. Yeats waited until they had gone past before resuming.

"I scrambled around to see if there was any way of getting up the wall and I found a loose brick that just came away as easy as you like. All I had to do was get my foot in and I could drag myself up. There was no problem with room. All there was on top were a couple of rusty old bits of iron embedded in the wall. I swung over and just dropped down. When I felt around another couple of bricks were loose on that side too. There wouldn't have been any problem climbing back up and out."

It was only when he stopped and looked out at the racecourse that I realised that the boys were walking back with one of them on the verge of tears after apparently falling. They loitered nearby as if looking for some grown-up reassurance and, sure enough, Yeats asked them if their parents were nearby. There were a couple of nods and even an embarrassed little grin. The detective gave the nearest one a tap on the shoulder as they passed by and watched them walk down towards the stands.

"I asked Mrs McFarlane if she knew of the way a person could climb over that wall and she said that it used to be a shortcut out of the yard years before when the lads were rushing back to town. Except someone broke an ankle one day and her father said enough was enough. She had never thought of it since. Barbed wire was put on top of the wall ages ago, she said, and they'd forgotten all about it. She said Eamon Dunne probably organised all that. But there's no barbed wire there now."

"It could have just fallen away."

"I doubt it very much. There's too much shelter from the roof. There's no way barbed wire was suddenly disconnected from its supports by something like the weather. This is how the killer got into the stable. There's no other way he could have. The box itself is inaccessible, apart from the door, and I've explained about the CCTV. And I'm presuming Anatoly didn't know about the shortcut as he took his chances with the camera instead."

"Wolf would know!" I said. "A guy like that knows every shortcut, no matter what kind."

"That is correct. And it is proving most irritating that we can't seem to locate him. Especially on the back of what we found in the stables' horse box."

I waited for Yeats to continue, figuring he was much too canny an operator to drop something like that without being prepared to expand.

156

"Forensics say the murder weapon is a heavy wrench found in a compartment at the side of the vehicle. Heavy traces of blood and hair from the victim are on it."

"Jesus. But no fingerprints, I take it."

"No. The horse box is central to Wolf's business with drugs. We put a squeeze on that stable lad Duignan who was involved too. It didn't take too long for him to bleat. Apparently that box was perfect cover for transporting drugs around the country. Wolf puts in thousands of miles a year to racecourses all over Ireland and he'd built contacts all over the place. It was simple just to meet at the races or pull over somewhere. No one ever suspected a lorry taking horses to the races. It was perfect cover."

"How long was it going for?"

"According to Duignan, at least the last two or three years. When we searched the truck we also found about five grand's worth of stuff hidden in the cab: mostly cocaine, some ecstasy too."

"And Anatoly was buying drugs off him."

"Apparently so. Duignan isn't sure, but he thinks Wolf roughed the kid around a couple of months ago because he owed him a few quid."

"Well, there's your proof!"

"Hardly proof, Mr Dee. Wolf's got a nasty enough reputation when he gets mad: not a man to take liberties with. Still, dealers usually intimidate, not kill."

"Maybe it was more cold-blooded than that? Maybe he had to silence Anatoly?"

"People kill for any amount of reasons," Yeats said evasively. "If indeed it was Wolf."

"You don't think it was him?"

"I'm not saying that."

"But the wrench?"

"Could have been planted. Handy spot. Handy suspect. In any case, there is a fact to take into account. Our estimated time of death with Mr Ignatieff is a little after midnight. You say you saw Wolf over five hours later. And you can't positively identify him either. Both factors are more than a little inconvenient, don't you think?"

18

I told Lara that night. When I arrived at the house, Mrs O'Sullivan opened the door and peered suspiciously through her glasses at the character wanting to speak to her tenant. Years of looking after young and vulnerable boys and girls meant that this old lady could examine any visitor with forensic intensity. I found myself shifting my feet.

"Hello, Mrs O'Sullivan. I haven't seen you in a while. Liam Dee is my name. I used to know a few lads who stayed here."

"The jockey?"

"That's right. It's good to see you again."

"Of course it is," she sniffed. "That's what you're here for, isn't it? To see how I am."

"Em . . . is Lara here?"

"She is," Mrs O'Sullivan replied but made no move to invite me in. Instead, her stare intensified, eyes bearing in like the guns on a pocket battleship. My feet felt as if they were doing the tango.

"Listen to me now. I know what you jockeys are like.

I've seen hundreds of you smelling around the place over the years, all thinking they're the cock o' the walk and looking for a quick rattle. Well, I'm not having that for this girl. She's too good for that: too good for you."

"Mrs O'Sullivan, I assure you my intentions are honourable."

"Huh!" she replied, unconvinced.

"Really. I think she's great. And you're right: she is too good for me. I'm just hoping there's some pity floating around."

"There might be," Lara said.

Standing at the top of the stairs, she was looking pleased with herself.

"How long have you been standing there?" I asked.

"Long enough," she said. "It's okay, Margaret. I think I might be able to handle him. I'll be down in a minute. Just a couple of things I have to do."

Mrs O' still looked doubtful but eventually deigned to let me into the front room where I sat to attention on the chair facing the television. She weighed anchor on the sofa opposite, throwing occasional suspicious looks in my direction. After five long minutes there was still no sign of Lara, nor a thaw from my company. Only then did I see my Cossack quarry peeping through the slightly ajar door and laughing silently at the scene in front of her.

"Hi, Lara. Are you ready?" I smiled determinedly.

"Of course. What's keeping you?"

We got into the car, with Mrs O' looking sternly through the curtains, and I kissed Lara deeply. It felt like taking in oxygen. Maybe it was the nearby glare strengthening the senses, but it seemed as if my hunger was reciprocated. As I pulled away, it was tempting just to drive to Dublin, take this gorgeous woman to bed and say nothing about what

Yeats had said. After all, I'd said nothing to Bailey and Charlotte on the way back from the races. The pair of them had chattered away, Bailey on a high from her second horse winning too, and her daughter maintaining that persistent demand for maternal approval. I'd said little. What was the point of telling them? It wouldn't change anything. Finding Anatoly's killer seemed more difficult than ever. What was the point in letting them know quicker than was necessary?

Lara was different. I drove out of town and pulled into the wide open area to the right of the racecourse.

"Forget it. Cars are not for me," she giggled before picking up on my mood. "What's wrong?"

I told her what Yeats had said. It brought tears to her eyes. I kissed her forehead, held her hands and tried to console her, but it only seemed to make things worse. She got out and turned her face into the bitter east wind blowing across the flat plain: towards home.

"I'm sorry, Lara."

"Don't. What are you sorry for?"

"I'm sorry you're so far from home . . . and yet I'm happy you are too . . . I don't know."

"It's okay."

For six days a week, she worked alongside the same people, sharing grumbles at bad weather, temperamental creatures and mucky conditions. In such circumstances camaraderie had to be strong. The sense of being in it together was vital. Proximity alone usually resulted in a healthy supply in most yards, but Bailey had always been keen to encourage and maintain that esprit de corps. Now, there was no escaping the insidious doubt which had been released.

"It's hard to believe," I said, holding her hand, "that someone we know probably did this."

"Hate can make anyone do anything."

"What do you mean?"

"I mean the hate that people can feel for anyone who is different. It doesn't need much to bring it out."

"Are you talking about racism?"

"That's almost too big a word for it. You say racism to any of the Irish lads in the yard and they think 'black'. They do not use foul words to us because we are white and look like them. But the fear and resentment is always there. Why don't you go back to where you belong? Why should you get a better job than me? You're not even Irish. Ask any of those who were at Anatoly's remembrance party – they will tell you the same thing. You can see people storing up their prejudices behind stiff manners and not being sure how to behave around us. But when that veneer disappears, it can turn into something sinister."

I didn't say anything. She was right – about everything. Race meant nothing to me. It was something that happened to others. Of course, being Irish, I was naturally touchy when it came to prejudices and stereotypes in Britain. I still remembered one of my first visits to an English racecourse when one of the senior English jockeys there called me a "fucking bogman" after a race. I waited, heart thumping with fear, but also anger, until we were back in the jockeys' room, then I threw myself at him. By some miracle some part of me connected with his nose before I was hauled off. Even standing there, shaking with adrenalin, I knew that if someone with any other accent had said it, there wouldn't have been such a problem. But there was a lot of history wound up in that. The idea of such ignorance being thrown at me indiscriminately was another level altogether.

"No, don't misunderstand me," she said. "This is not just the Irish. It's everywhere. If you were in Odessa, you would be different, and you would feel this sense of not really belonging too, of not being allowed to belong. It's mostly in the little things, like people in shops losing patience because one of us cannot speak English very well. But the idea is always there. What if this fear turns to hate?"

I put my arms around her, turned my back to the piercing gale and we stood for some time coming to terms with a world different from the one we had woken up to that morning. Going out wasn't really an option after that.

Back at the house, Mrs O'Sullivan opened the door and shot some dagger-looks in my direction when she saw her lodger's desolate face. But Lara smiled sadly and told her everything was okay. We agreed that we would talk again in the morning. I wanted very much to keep holding her but the old woman put an arm around Lara and brought her inside. There was nothing else for it but to go back to my own temporary home. Bailey was still having dinner at Charlotte and Franco's, so I went straight to bed and had confusing dreams of blonde hair, cameras and eyes watching me from the shadows.

I woke at nearly six, unsure where I was. It was really dark and only a creak from the ancient bed finally broke the uncertainty. There was no racing, so, in theory, it was a day off. I decided to hang around and work in the yard. Bailey might need me later and it would give me the chance to see Lara. I reached for the phone but decided not to call her; she would be over in an hour anyway. I padded downstairs to the kitchen. There was a big torch underneath the sink and I picked it up before heading out into the chilly early-morning air.

At the other end of the yard was a line of boxes with the lights switched on inside. Eamon had already started the day. He was in the large, dusty feed room, scooping nuts into a wheelbarrow and preparing breakfast for his charges. The shrill whistle that always played on his lips while doing this job reached me. For someone whose working day started so early and ended only with a final check on the horses fourteen hours later, Eamon was always remarkably cheerful. Sometimes, on his way back from the pub or the shops, he dropped in just one final time, like a protective father peeping in on a sleeping child. He had three kids of his own. They were lucky, even if they did have to share him with sixty horses.

However, the memory of Yeats and his one-word summaries wouldn't go away. It was impossible to prevent it. Everything told me Wolf was the culprit, but the detective had doubts. It was obvious he had. A logical mind like that would focus on those missing hours and wonder. I wanted to say to hell with logic. It had to be Wolf. Why else would he have run?

Of course, Eamon knew the place like the back of his hand – better than anyone else probably. Over the years almost every brick would at some stage have demanded his attention. He was after all the yard's unofficial handyman. The signs of Eamon's skill at mending, building and welding were everywhere. And watching the familiar figure emerge, pushing the heavy barrow and slamming back bolts on the first stable door, it was impossible to imagine him provoked into the sort of anger needed to kill. Besides, Eamon's sexual proclivities were hardly gay. And I doubted if he'd smoked a cigarette in his entire life. Pints of Guinness were what I'd always assumed his racier side might rise to. Damn Yeats and his theories. And damn him even more because he was probably right. Why else was I now heading for the alley with a torch?

It was longer than I imagined, especially now it was empty after being cleared out by the police investigation team. The morning was still black so it would have been impossible to see anything without the torch. I walked up the alley and deliberately avoided looking into the box which had only its bottom door shut. Silly and superstitious stuff, but it still felt intrusive to stand gawping at a place where someone had been killed so brutally. Instead, I marched as determinedly as possible to the end.

Yeats was shy with his eight feet. From the guts of my six feet, and even with up-stretched arms, I was nowhere near the top of the wall. The torch's beam darted all over the surface, but there was no sign of a loose brick until I moved my hand on the wall and felt something give. Sure enough, holding the torch between my knees I managed to manoeuvre and jiggle one of the bricks free. My right foot fitted easily into the hole and I eased up, grabbing the top. There was enough leverage to allow me to peep over and then pull myself the rest of the way up. There wasn't much to see. Large bushes and withered clumps of nettles swayed in the wind on the other side and it was just about possible to make out something that might resemble a track leading away to the left. But Yeats was right about the gap between the overhanging roof and the wall. There was plenty of room for someone to get up and down.

I scrambled down and shone the torch around my feet. There wasn't even a pinch of dirt left anywhere, never mind the dozens of old oil barrels discarded over the years and forgotten about. There had been no call for anyone to have come this far in for many years past, so it was easy to understand the neglect. Once that shortcut home had been declared 'verboten' there was no need to come down this far at all. Eamon had made doubly sure of that with his barbed wire.

"The cops were all over this place again yesterday while you were at the races."

Eamon was suddenly standing next to me. I hadn't heard a thing. His gumboots muffled any footsteps and I'd been concentrating on what the torch might find on the ground. Now I understood about Yeats and his bird. It was all I could do to not groan out loud with fright.

"You okay?" Eamon asked.

"Yeah. I just didn't hear you. I was just checking out the wall here – I never knew about people climbing over it years back."

"Ah, we'd all forgotten about it."

We moved back towards the yard.

"It all just feels so wrong," I said. "Nothing like this should have happened here. And still, it did."

"I know what you mean. I thought the police being all over the place was over. But then I was driving past on the way into town yesterday and I saw a couple of vans, so I pulled in."

"How long were they at it?"

"A good hour anyway. I tried to ring Bailey but her phone was off. I only got her last night and she sounded as if she was having a few jars."

Back at the yard, Eamon resumed feeding. The cold, quiet morning was no longer silent as Patrician and a copy-cat neighbour both started hammering doors with their feet, demanding that their waiter hurry up.

As I returned the torch, Bailey walked into the kitchen, looking the worse for wear. Knowing her capacity, I assumed that even this mild display of a hangover must have been the result of considerable consumption the night before. There was only a perfunctory nod for me before a root around the medicine cabinet threw up some headache tablets. I brought her a glass of water.

"Thanks," she said.

"No problem."

"I gave it a lash last night. Charlotte made dinner."

"I heard."

"I suppose you also heard about the police being here yesterday?"

"I was looking at the place just now. It really is as clean as a bone."

"Inspector Yeats rang me just after you dropped us off last night."

I could guess then why my boss's intake had been substantially higher than normal. Detective Inspector Yeats could have that effect on people.

"He's coming back here today, with more police. They're going to interview everyone all over again. One after the other, into the office, and sit down and be grilled. Sounds like fun, doesn't it?"

She threw back some tablets and drained the glass. I re-filled it. The happy, exuberant Bailey of the day before had vanished. In her place was this tired, hung-over woman who was starting to look her age. I offered to rustle up some breakfast but she shook her head. Still, I cranked the percolator into life and opened a new bag of coffee.

We sat and waited for the coffee to boil, each thinking our own thoughts and knowing they were probably the same.

The screech of a loose fan-belt outside told us that the vans carrying the lads from town had arrived. I looked out and saw everyone mooching slowly towards the tack room.

Lara was with Vaz and she glanced at the window. I sketched a tiny wave but there was no response. Next to her, Vaz looked as dark and surly as ever.

I finished my coffee and went outside to ride first lot. Bailey would be out for the second – "After I've fixed myself up," she said.

There was no mistaking the atmosphere. There wasn't a raised voice as first lot pulled out and made for the gallops.

I noticed the subtle divisions as people paired off. One of the local lads called Fagan, a loudmouth whose special talent seemed to be testing Eamon's patience, came out of a box, mounted his horse and turned to find himself side by side with Sergei, the quiet, hungry young Ukrainian. Fagan turned right, did a full turn of the group and waited. It was a piece of nothing I would never have noticed before. I turned Patrician and eased him in next to the startled youngster.

"It's about time this horse learned to settle properly," I said to Sergei, who looked embarrassed.

What Lara thought of my useless gesture remained unknown since she was determined to keep her distance in the yard. Only once did we get even slightly close as I later went into the tack room to find a hoof-pick. For a second there was no one around and she smiled.

"Are you okay?" I asked as she brushed against me on the way out.

"Yes. See you tonight."

We rode out for the rest of the morning and at lunchtime I went for a run. Sweat poured out but there was no need for fanciful ideas to try and divert the mind. As the church tower in nearby Kildare peeped through the increasingly heavy rain, the idea persisted that Yeats might be wrong. Stranger things were possible. The man had no god-given right to be right. Who knew why people did what they did. He'd said the same himself. Wolf was a law unto himself at the best of times. The one thing to know about him was that he was best avoided.

19

I unlocked the front door and picked up the few letters inside. Lara's perfume still lingered in the air. It felt good to come home and smell that.

Every so often I was asked about why I continued to live in Dublin. Living around the Curragh would have made more logistic sense and certainly taken a chunk out of the mileage total. Rationally it made no sense to maintain a suburban existence when my working life was so rigorously rural. There was no massive homing instinct behind it, but possibly something else instinctive about needing to be able to step back occasionally from something that could be so all-consuming. I reckoned it was better to be able to drive away sometimes and put distance between myself and whatever was going on, give myself a little perspective.

Since I was thinking about Wolf, seeing him in the front room, sitting on the couch, grinning, there was a second where my perspective felt badly out of whack.

"How're ya, Liam?" he said, standing up and grinning at the shock on my face. "Boo!"

He laughed and started to walk towards me. I backed up, turned and was faced by a large man in a bulging tracksuit. His shaved head and glowering face made me turn back to Wolf.

"Don't worry. Benny is here just to make sure we're not disturbed."

I forced myself to think. Everything was locked up, making any escape all but impossible: back door, windows, the sliding doors out onto the deck at the back. There might be a chance the skylight in the attic was open though. It was a pain to climb up and lock it whenever leaving the house and only a thief with Alpine climbing experience could really expect to get to it. It would mean having to pull down the folding stairs to the attic, and whatever I did wouldn't delay these bastards for long enough to get away with that.

"I told you, relax. I just want to talk," said Christy.

He looked the same old Christy. There didn't seem to be a bother on him, certainly no hint that the police were searching for him on suspicion of murder. He walked through to the kitchen. I realised the kettle was boiling.

"It's a nice place you have," he said. "You should see some of the shite-holes I've had to stay in recently, thanks to you."

He made a cup of tea for Benny and told him to wait outside. He winked at me as the big man left.

"He's a bit simple, but useful all the same," he grinned.

All the friendliness was accompanied by the underlying menace that I always knew was there but seemed dreadfully forbidding now I was on the receiving end. If anything the bonhomie made it worse, making the anticipation drag on longer. I looked around for something that I might use as a weapon but there was nothing close by. He invited me to sit at my kitchen table.

"Seriously, relax. I just want a word."

"Alright," I replied, hardly recognising my own voice.

"I'm told you're tight with this Yeats character."

"Who?"

"Don't act the eejit, Liam. You're tight with him. I know that. What I need him to know, and you need to know, is that I didn't have anything to do with killing that kid."

I said nothing.

"You see, I'm strictly small time, really. Sure, I know the big lads, and I deal with them sometimes because you have to get supplied from somewhere. But I try and keep things as close to home as I can. Nice and easy, know what I mean?"

Again I kept quiet. What was there to say?

"That's why I was there that night. Where better to keep stuff than in the horse box? Nice and secure behind locked gates with me very own security guard. Not that that old bollix Rocky was able to guard much. He was mostly asleep, and half-blind anyway. But still, I could nip in and get whatever I needed whenever I wanted. That CCTV camera is strictly for show. Anyone with any cop-on can see how to stay out of its way. With the horse box always parked out the back of the yard, all I had to do was use the alley, keep close to the walls and walk right underneath the camera. Rocky never knew a thing. Perfect – no one the wiser."

"How long were you doing that?"

"Ages: absolute ages. Never a problem. And now this shit has blown up."

"Why are you telling me all this?"

"Because when you saw me that night, all I was doing was trying to get as far away as possible. The kid was dead when I saw him."

"So why not just tell Yeats this?"

That made him laugh out loud. It was easy to understand why people might come under his influence and want to be liked by Christy. There was an easy charm there that might be surface but none the less attractive for all that.

"Are you for real? I'm perfect for the cops. A guy dealing dope, who'd given the kid a clip a while ago, and who just happens to have been seen doing a runner? I fit like a glove."

"Yeah, but I didn't actually see you. Not your face."

"Yeah. I had the helmet on," he said. "But you clocked me alright, didn't ya? That'd be enough for the cops to nail someone like me. Christ, they'd get the real high hard one out of that, and get all the newspapers off their backs into the bargain."

"So what really happened?"

"All I know is I went up there about five in the morning as normal to do what I had to do. Rocky is usually banjaxed by four anyway and just conks out for the last couple of hours before Dunne comes in. So I get a few bags out of the lorry and I'm nipping back down the alley when something catches me eye over the door of the box. And there he is. Fucked, dead, out of the game. So I get out of there – fast. I've got a grand's worth of coke on me and if I'm caught my whole game is busted wide open. Besides, there's some mad bastard lurking around somewhere on the premises."

"Why should I believe you?"

"Because it's the truth!"

The smiling veneer had vanished now. Instead, the strain of looking over his shoulder all the time began to show in a taut jaw-line and a hard stare that bored into me. I noticed his hands clenched on his knees as he leaned forward. I was out of my depth if he wanted to hurt me.

"But what do you expect me to say to Yeats," I said. "Even if he took any notice, which I doubt, it would be just me repeating stuff second-hand."

"Maybe, but it might make him look somewhere else, for who really did it."

He stood up suddenly enough for me to jerk a little and the sign of weakness made him grin again.

"Tell him the little bollix was queer," Wolf said.

"The police know that."

"Yeah? But do they know what he was getting up to in that box?"

"What do you mean?"

"Look, you'd see people heading into that box sometimes during work. You know – somewhere private. For a quick bit of 'how's your father'. Maybe he was doing the same."

"You never actually saw him?"

"No. But I did get the impression he was at it."

"With who?"

"If I knew that, don't you think I'd have piped up by now?"

He was back at the kettle, waiting for it to boil again and staring out the window at the mountains that rose behind the estate. It was a spectacular view on a clear day and he seemed engrossed in it.

I stood up slowly, not taking my eyes off the back of his head. The front door was no more than twenty feet away. If I got to it, I might be able to surprise Benny. Nobody that massive could move too quickly and I might be able to get past him. It had to be worth a go.

It was only a few seconds but it felt longer as I stared at Wolf, willing him not to turn. Another moment or two. I was at the kitchen door just as he whipped around.

"Benny!" Wolf yelled.

I'd seriously underestimated the big man's agility. He was quickly in front of me, but leaving me a tiny gap to swerve up the stairs. That slight delay was enough for Wolf to grab my leg and fling himself on top of me. He quickly had my arm behind my back, twisting it viciously and pushing my face into the stair-carpet.

"Don't fucking tempt me," he whispered into my ear. "The only person who can even half-put me near the place that night is you. So don't tempt me into doing what I really should do. Got it?"

I got it alright. Fit as I was, there was no competing with Wolf's bulk on top of me. I stopped squirming.

"Now, Liam," he said again, a little louder, and more under control. "You're going to go to the cops and tell them what I told you, right? And you're going to convince them too, right. Because if you don't, well, you know I can find you."

He lifted me up, turned me around and frog-marched me back to the kitchen. Benny came with him, carrying a thick rope I recognised from my own garden shed. The big man expertly started to truss me to a chair as Christy stuck his head under the tap and gulped down some water.

"You jockeys always have more balls than sense, you know that," he said. "All you need for a quiet life is to relax, do this one thing, and then you can get back to getting your feet under the table with the lady of the manor."

I didn't say anything.

"What? You saying you're not in there? You and Bailey aren't getting cosy? Come on. It's obvious. Fair play to you if you can manage it. It's a nice number. Anyway, enough of such foolishness. Whatever about the boss, you play fair by me and you'll be alright."

They took off out the front door and I heard a car revving before driving away. I strained against the rope and tried to find the knot nearest my hands. Benny had tied it well but the rope was big and it was just about possible to get an outstretched finger to the knot. An hour later, sweating and frustrated beyond belief, I finally managed to break free. The first thing I did was ape Christy's drinking from the tap. There was hardly a rush. He'd had more than enough time to get away. And I needed a minute to stop my heart from racing. What could he expect from me with Yeats? A senior police detective was hardly likely to be swayed by some nervy gumshoe jockey. It was ridiculous, almost as crazy as what he was saying about Bailey.

The only reason I wasn't dismissing the whole thing as lunacy was that I was able to stand there and deliberate on the whole thing. My first instinct on seeing him was that I was finished. But he hadn't killed me. He'd threatened it and I didn't doubt for one moment he was capable of following through on that threat. But he hadn't. The reasons sounded mixed-up to me but I was still around and that indicated something. What, I couldn't get my head around. Maybe Yeats could.

Yeats didn't answer his phone but rang back a minute later.

"You're not going to believe this but Christy Wolf was waiting for me when I got home an hour ago," I said.

"Are you OK?"

"Yeah, he tied me up before taking off but yeah, I'm alright. He just wanted me to tell you he had nothing to do with the murder, that he was picking up drugs he keeps stashed in the horse box and, as he was leaving down the alley, he saw Anatoly lying there. He emphasised to me how important it was that I convince you. If anything he seemed almost offended that his business was being disrupted."

It sounded even more incredible second-hand. But all Yeats said was "Hmmn" a few times.

"And you're okay?" he asked.

"Yeah, somehow," I replied.

"I'd say you're a lucky man," Yeats declared.

"You're not wrong. But what am I supposed to do now? You're hardly convinced Christy Wolf is somehow innocent, are you? Just because of this?"

"No. But I wouldn't completely dismiss what he says either," he said.

What other answer had I expected from him?

We talked a little longer and I hung up feeling less than reassured and more than a little tired. It was time I reckoned to grab some shuteye in my own bed for a change. My dreams though were full of ropes and threats and the malevolence that could lie behind a smile.

20

At the last second I heard footsteps. Then my head felt as if it was exploding. There was so little time. Barely enough to register that somebody was behind me. Certainly not enough to do anything about it. There was simply pain and a brief, ludicrous impression that Mrs O'Sullivan really could deliver a helluva blow for someone her size. The old lady's front door started to look bigger and bigger as I slowly fell to my knees.

Life out of the saddle was getting too hard, I reckoned, as the dimpled concrete pavement nestled into my cheek. Another bang to the head, and this one made Vaz's clip in the police station feel like a brush of gossamer wings.

It had been raining and I was lying in a puddle, dirty water working its way into my mouth. Getting rid of it would have taken a single movement, but even that was impossible. Nothing was moving. Paralysis flashed into my head again but how could the entire mass of me suddenly go numb? Some bit would surely respond. I tried with every ounce of determination I could muster to move my head, but still nothing happened.

It was insane. A television was clearly audible from the front room just yards away. The opening bars of music to the six o'clock news carried easily and yet they might as well have come from the moon. My only view consisted of a tired-looking daffodil, the hardy green hedge behind it, and a rusty satellite dish on the side wall of a neighbour's house. There was enough technology around to communicate with space, but I couldn't even make a sound. From the road just ten yards away came a hum of cars passing by, but no one was walking. And even if someone did pass by, would they see me? Mrs O's front hedge rose a fair height over the wall.

I wanted to scream with the pain, but nothing came out. And if the pain was bad, the frustration was worse. I could do nothing except take in more water and then, eventually, and almost gratefully, pass out.

It was good old-fashioned swearing that brought me to. Like a priest whispering the last rites into some poor unfortunate's ear, Mrs O' brought me back with a litany of distraught blasphemy that would have done justice to a docker.

"Jesus Christ Almighty, wake up! Do you hear me? Don't you fucking die on my doorstep!"

It was enough to stir whatever mysterious cogs were required. I opened my eyes to be met with Mrs O' on her knees staring desperately back at me.

"He's awake, love. He's awake."

Only then was I aware of the despairing sobs from behind her. It could only be Lara. I felt fingers in my hair. Definitely time to make a start. My legs moved. Encouraging stuff. Mrs O' reacted by telling me to stay still, but I ignored her. That provoked a call to someone else to call an ambulance, which wasn't good at all.

"No ambulance," I rasped.

Lara was leaning over me, touching me on the face and staring into my eyes. I repeated the "No ambulance" entreaty and, even though my voice sounded as if it had been borrowed from a half-speed Lee Marvin, there was enough there for her.

"Stop, Margaret. Don't do anything yet."

"He needs help, love."

"He's a jockey. He's been out cold before. Let's just give him a minute."

I tried to smile, but it probably came out as some terrible grimace. She really did get it. Both my arms felt like they belonged to someone else, but there was enough strength in them to take my face out of the water. Then they stretched farther. This was good. I'd been knocked out a few times over the years. Nothing needing a hospital bed, but still enough to let me know that this clattering was not going to kill me. Which didn't mean things were exactly jim-dandy just yet either. It took an almighty effort of will to stretch my arms and turn around. But somehow the parts worked and I found myself sitting up. It almost felt like winning the Grand National.

Lara was beside me and after a second's hesitation threw her arms around me. Any protests from my shoulder and neck muscles were ignored. Morale alone made any twinges worthwhile.

"I thought you were dead," she sobbed into my ear. "I really did."

"So did I. But it's okay. You were right. I've been knocked out before."

Her wrist-watch glinted in the street-lights and it took only a little lean of the head to see it wasn't even five past six yet. I'd been out for a couple of minutes max. That wasn't too bad.

"But what happened?" Lara said.

"Didn't see. Somebody hit me."

There were horrified gasps from over our heads. I looked up. Mrs O' was standing above us, alongside an equally elderly lady who she introduced as Mrs Lawlor from next door. Mrs Lawlor looked terrified and I warmed to Mrs O' whose own face was a picture of barely contained panic.

"We really should call an ambulance," said Mrs O', wringing her hands.

"No ambulance, please. It's not necessary. Just help me inside. That would be great."

So the brave jockey was helped into the house by his three visions of mercy, each step provoking winces of pain that had me challenging Mrs O' in the bad-language stakes. It wasn't great for the ego, but I was past caring.

They sat me on a cushioned stool in the front room and Lara gingerly began to examine my head.

Those wonderful green eyes darted anxiously, but just the sight of them made me feel better. And then her fingers moved under my right ear. Pain surged back so fast it almost made me pass out again. An involuntary groan sounded like the death rattle of a bullock being slaughtered and there was a second before I realised it was coming from me. Lara looked horrified and Mrs O' started swearing again.

"I'm sorry, baby, I'm going to have to look at this," Lara whispered, and, put like that, she could have got permission to saw my head off.

I winced as she continued her examination. Mrs O' brought me a welcome cup of steaming hot tea. Whether it was reaction, or the lying down on the wet and cold footpath, I wasn't able to stop my hands from shaking. Even with my mitts wound around the hot cup, like pictures of those unfortunate sailors rescued from torpedoed ships, it was all I could do not to send the tea all over the carpet. Nevertheless, I figured it was time to start explaining.

"I was walking up to the door when I heard footsteps, then there was this awful pain in my head and down I went. The next thing was you were there, thankfully."

"Are you sure about getting help?" asked Mrs O', looking anything but reassured and sneaking a look herself at the back of my head. "There's a massive big bump back here. Your hair is so short, we can see it clearly."

"Is there any blood, or a cut?"

"As far as I can tell, it's only swelling," Lara said. "But we don't know anything medical. You really should go to the hospital."

I put my hand out and she came around to look at me. Her eye make-up had run, sending little black lines over her cheeks.

"If the racing authorities find out I've been concussed, even for just a minute, it means an automatic ban from riding. I can't afford that, especially not with Cheltenham coming up. Anyway, I know myself, I'm fine. It just means a headache for a few days."

"Okay, but we must call the police," she said. "It must have been Christy Wolf."

I'd told her about Wolf's visit a couple of days earlier. Told her about Yeats and his doubts. She'd never liked Wolf. A bully was how she described him, and a parasite, feeding off people's weakness. We'd spent hours going over everything and there was no getting away from the fact that Wolf hadn't eliminated me. However, he'd also left me in no doubt that he could change his mind.

"My mobile is in a pocket. When you find it, Inspector Yeats' number is programmed in. Can you ring him for me?"

Lara beeped the phone into life and found the name. It rang and she handed me the phone. That sing-song accent crackled into my ear with a short but succinct recorded answer. I hung up, uncertain what to say. Then immediately it rang and Yeats' name flashed up.

"Mr Dee, how can I help you?"

"I need to see you right now. It's important. Can you get here?"

"Where's here?"

I told him, recognising the sound as something more like my own voice.

"And by the way, can you bring a doctor?"

"Why?"

"It's nothing serious. Just bring one."

He said he would be with me in fifteen minutes. It took him ten. Somehow, I had visions of sirens and flashing lights suddenly descending on the estate, but when he arrived it was with a single ring of the doorbell and some gracious words for the landlady. However, even Yeats was slightly taken aback when he saw the scene in front of him. Lara was kneeling with her arms around me. I could see the inspector's eyebrows rising, but, to his credit, he said nothing. Instead, he stepped aside for a bespectacled young man who hunched down to examine my head.

"Okay, Mr Dee, what happened?" Yeats asked.

I told him, as matter-of-factly as possible. The footsteps, the pain, the gap between the news' theme music and Lara's watch, and how sore everything felt. Mrs O' crossed herself and even Mrs Lawlor could be heard whispering to the Sacred Heart. Lara's eyes started to fill again and the doctor brusquely informed Yeats that I really should be in hospital.

"I don't need a hospital," I insisted and made to stand up. It was a wobbly journey that required Lara's help. My head swam and every instinct screamed for me to sit back down. But somehow I remained upright.

Then Yeats asked for a minute alone with me. I gratefully sat down again, hanging on to Lara, and with a nod Yeats indicated that she could stay. The two ladies looked peeved at being left out and reluctantly withdrew into the hall. The doctor closed the door behind them all.

Yeats was in at once. "Did you see who?"

"No. It was all over before I even realised what had happened."

"Damn!"

He too left the room and I saw him pacing carefully outside in the garden, staring at the ground, hoping to find something.

I turned around and took Lara's hand.

"Are you okay?"

"Of course," she said. "But you're not. What is happening?"

"I don't know."

I could hear Yeats talking on his mobile and then coming back into the house. In the hall, he asked Mrs O' if she did much gardening. The old woman took this as some sort of horticultural criticism and demanded to be told why the hell he wanted to know. But the detective inspector turned on his best manner and, eventually, she conceded that mowing the lawn was as much as she could do these days. He thanked her and came back to us.

"I've called for the forensics people to come here and check out the garden and surrounding area. We'll do house-to-house enquires too – see if anyone spotted anything."

"So you don't actually need us any more."

"Not immediately, I suppose. It's hospital for you anyway."

"I feel fine. I don't have to go to a hospital. All it needs

is an ice-pack and a bed. But what might be best is if Lara
and I keep a low profile for a few days."

"What do you mean?"

"I mean we should go away. Nobody just happens to be
walking by and then decide to try and cave someone's head
in. It's obviously not safe for me around here. And who's to
know what might happen to anyone close to me, like Lara."

"Possibly. But let's not overreact."

"I don't care about overreacting!" I said, not succeeding
in keeping the temper out of my voice. "Now that they've
followed me to her door, they obviously know I'm seeing
her – even if they didn't before. Or do you want her to act
as a sitting duck?"

Yeats merely raised an eyebrow while Lara squeezed my
hand and I tried to stem my anger. There was nothing to be
gained from going after Yeats. It was just the way his mind
worked after all these years. Maybe it was time to play to
his self-interest.

"Inspector, wouldn't it be better for everyone if my name
didn't come up in your investigation? I know it would suit
me. If the word 'unconscious' appears anywhere in the
media, then I'm faced with time out of the saddle, even if
there's nothing wrong with me. Now is not a good time for
that to happen."

"I can appreciate that."

"And let's face it, you don't exactly need more attention
on your back. It's not being big-headed, but if my name gets
thrown about in connection with this, then there's going to
be more press problems. It will be added hassle for
everyone."

"You're not exactly subtle, Mr Dee. I get the point."

Yeats wandered to the window and stared into the
darkness for a few moments before turning around and

asking the doctor to come back in. By the way he looked at his watch I guessed the medic was late for something far more important than my thick skull. But Yeats took him into a corner from where only fragments of conversation reached us. I'd noticed before how police and doctors were able to mumble coherently among themselves in a way that no civilian could hope to decipher. A few speculative glances were thrown in my direction but the ultimate result was positive.

"Dr Fingal says he is unhappy about not having x-rays, but will reluctantly agree not to insist upon it," said Yeats. "Of course you will have to sign a release form."

A piece of paper appeared from the depths of Fingal's pockets and I gratefully scrawled my name. Then he told me that if I started to experience any dizziness or feel nauseous, I would have to get my sorry ass to the nearest A&E. This was directed at Lara too and she nodded dutifully. Then Dr Fingal disappeared quickly, just as the first squad car showed up.

Yeats escorted us outside.

"Any idea where you'll go?" he asked. "It might be an idea to keep away from places you'd normally frequent."

"We'll be okay," I said, a lot more confidently than I felt. "I'll keep the phone on."

"Sure," he said quietly before looking at Lara. "Ms Kuznetsov, I'm sorry if I upset you before. It wasn't my intention. I'm simply trying to get to the bottom of all this. There was nothing personal in it."

"Thank you, Inspector. But why can't you find Wolf? Please, just find him."

21

Minutes after getting into the car, I fell into a deep sleep and only came to a couple of hours later. There was a tranquil minute after my eyes opened, just resting my head against the gently reverberating plastic door panel and following the headlights flashing past us. Lara drove with a quick purpose, hands light on the wheel. Looking sideways at her was no hardship either. I sat up.

"I let you sleep," she said.

"How long have I been out?"

"A while. I was worried at first, but your breathing was so steady and peaceful I let you sleep."

My neck felt sore after lying at an angle for so long and I rubbed it to try and ease the ache. Only then did I realise that there was only a gentle throb from just above to compete with it. Sitting up straighter didn't alter the sensation either. Tentatively, I even tried shaking my head. Apart from attracting an anxious glance from Lara, there were no urgent physical demands to stop behaving like a damp dog. The throb continued but my vision was okay and, compared to how it had been, there was plenty to be happy about. I was stretching my legs when a roadside sign flashed past announcing that Galway was only sixteen kilometres away.

"We're going to Galway?"

"Are we? I'm not even sure. I've just been driving, staying on the motorway. Is that okay?"

"Jesus, babe, you've been wonderful," I smiled, putting my hand on her thigh. She quickly covered my hand with hers. "I know Galway pretty well. There's a hotel I go to for the festival. They'll take care of us."

"How are you feeling now?"

"A lot better. That sleep has done me good. I'll drive if you want."

"No. Just show me where to go."

As the city lights drew closer, I guided us around the ring road to the western edges of the city until, eventually, we climbed a hill and could see Galway Bay lit up by the seafront lights at Salthill. Farther into the distance, it was just possible to distinguish the long brooding length of north Clare on the other side of the water. Instead of descending to Salthill's shut-up fun parks, we turned right and followed the northern coast of the bay.

The hotel's familiar square mass quickly appeared in front of us and Lara pulled into the car park with a flourish. I gingerly got out, breathing in the cold wind, laced with that unmistakable tang of salt and seaweed from the sea just a couple of miles away. This would do us alright. It wasn't one of the usual festival haunts for the thousands of hard-drinking race fans who poured into Galway in late July, turning the city into a marvellously gluttonous orgy of fun and risk. Other hotels nearer the city centre didn't even bother closing at all for the big week, just simply opening the doors on the Monday, keeping them open, and surveying the damage seven days later. I had enjoyed that lunatic rush to debauch as much as anyone, but had mostly stepped aside for the past few years: age rearing its head again, no doubt.

The most pressing concern was to get a room and the packed car park didn't exactly inspire confidence. The large foyer was empty though and our shoes clacked loudly as we walked to reception. When the young woman behind the counter looked up, I recognised her face. More importantly, she knew mine.

"Mr Dee, isn't it? This isn't your time of year normally. How can I help?"

"We would like a room, please. The best one you have, if it's available."

"That shouldn't be a problem, and for how many nights?"

"I'm not sure. Tonight anyway, and then we'll see."

I handed over my credit card, scrawled on the forms and gratefully led Lara to the elevator. Suddenly, there was nothing more I wanted to do than lie down and rest. From the strain in her eyes, I guessed the same was true for her. The card key proved maddeningly difficult but, finally, we were able to shut the door and lock out the world.

"Are you hungry?" I asked her. "We could get some room service."

"All I want to do is sleep."

"Me too."

If you had said just a couple of days previously that watching this woman take off her clothes would not drive me insane with desire, I would have laughed out loud. Exhaustion was some leveller though. We dropped our clothes to the ground and slid under the sheets. That wonderfully provocative body moved closer and wrapped itself around me. After all the recent assaults on it, my sorry carcass felt like some dead leaf falling slowly into softness. There was an almost physical pain in stretching out and settling into this wonderful comfort. Lara moved closer and the sensation was one of total envelopment. Our hands started to move. Only slight touches, but, despite our fatigue, the response was the same. Slowly, and with the minimum of movement, we turned and put ourselves to sleep, so gently it hardly felt like we had been awake at all.

Although exhaustion quickly claimed the body, my mind was in no mood to relax. Exactly the opposite, in fact. I dreamed I was running down a black corridor with the sound of feet getting closer and closer behind me. Afraid to turn around, there was nothing to look forward at except more darkness. But still I kept running and running until my legs started breaking up and turning into stumps. Only then did I fall and look up and start screaming. There were no faces, nothing human in any way, and nothing to see in the terrible darkness. The only sound was of knives puncturing flesh and tearing into muscle and tissue – my muscle and tissue – and all in silence. Any movement on my part made it worse, ripping me open even further. Staying absolutely still was the sole thing stopping me from being torn open from neck to groin. So only the agony of lying contorted, legs bent and my arms stretched beneath, could stop me from dying. Dear God, I did not want to die.

In the circumstances, waking up feeling pretty okay the following morning was a result. The only physical hint of my overactive subconscious running riot was the position I found myself in. Arms firmly tucked underneath my body and feet planted squarely on the bed as if I was performing the most outrageously supple limbo dance in history. Sure enough, both sets of calf muscles were protesting at the contortion.

Enough light sifted through the curtains from the street-lamps outside for me to see by my watch it was six thirty in the morning. Either because she liked her space, or more probably because she didn't need to be kicked black and blue by her nervy lover, Lara was sleeping soundly at the very edge of the bed. There was a steady rhythm to her breathing; maybe even the suggestion of a snore.

Fumbling in the dark, I eventually found the switch for a small lamp over the big bathroom mirror. When I turned it on, nothing pretty stared back. Haggard was the word that came to mind. I twisted my neck as far as it would go, to see the back of my head, but it wasn't possible. Padding back into the room, I found a tiny make-up mirror near Lara's bag and went back to the bathroom, closing the door behind me again. It felt like trying to get a picture on a pre-historic television set, but a few more twists and turns later I managed to get a glimpse of the damage. Red, angry soreness filled the little mirror. Even feeling it with fingers couldn't warn me about how large and inflamed the bump really was. Because it no longer really hurt, there had been a presumption that things were healing by themselves. But this was enough to have me reaching for a chair.

A few more clumsy touches and I went back out and returned the mirror before sitting on the bed, looking at Lara and coming to terms with how lucky I'd been. A millimetre here or there and it could have been very different.

The fact that someone had deliberately set out to hurt me really sank in only as I sat shivering there in the cold morning air. Suddenly murder and death weren't abstract concepts. Someone wanted me dead, and badly enough to risk an open-air attack in the street. Yet, why hadn't they finished the job, used a knife or gun, caved my head in as they had with Anatoly? Was it a botched murder attempt or a further warning?

It seemed opportunistic rather than planned, but instead of taking any comfort from the idea of such random impetuosity, I felt even more fear. Did I really think such recklessness could be reined in – that, if the intention really was to kill me, after one attempt they would just forget it and go home? If anything, it made the chances of a follow-up even more likely. I climbed back in beside my girl and it wasn't just cold that made me reach for her warm body.

A sleepless hour later, I again slipped out and from the bathroom rang Bailey, blaming flu for our absence from work. Such an admission would normally have had her rumbling with suggestive laughter, but there was nothing light about her mood.

"Charlotte was in tears last night, just totally overwhelmed by all this," she said. "And Eamon is convinced the police believe he has something to do with it. I mean, how ridiculous is that! And it just keeps going, on and on."

Consoling noises about it being over soon and the police having to do their job brought little response. But there was also no mention of my own drama from the night before. Mrs O' and Mrs Lawlor must have been persuaded that it would be in their interests not to repeat such a juicy piece of gossip. No doubt Yeats had been at his most charming and persuasive while, at the same time, leaving no doubt about the extent of his reach if they did spill the beans. It was a combination to respect and enough to probably put even Mrs O's tongue into neutral.

Bailey asked when I would be coming back and the apparent throwaway nature of the remark told me how much she probably needed my support right now. It wasn't exactly model protector behaviour, but there wasn't much else I could do except say that it would be soon. She didn't pursue the matter and told me to mind Lara. It sounded genuine and I hung up feeling less than proud.

We didn't move for most of the day. Lara said she had never slept in such a comfortable bed and the luxurious sheets did have a way of drawing us back to sleep before we woke again to make love, go to the toilet or order food. It didn't mean we ignored the world's harsher realities. Just simply parked them around the corner for when we both might feel more sustained to cope properly. A lot had happened to us, even without falling for each other. Not once did Lara mention the attack and if she didn't want to, I was damned if I would.

"So, Mister Famous Jockey, how long have you been coming here?"

"To the hotel? Only the last couple of years."

"Is that because of the girl we met when we came in?"

"The receptionist? Don't be mad. I don't even know her name."

"But she knows yours," she said, a smile playing on her lips. "And she looked at me very specifically. Like I was a challenge."

"Are you jealous?"

"Hah! Just like a man to think that."

"What else am I supposed to think? Anyway, it feels nice that you're jealous."

"I am not jealous!" she said, biting me gently on the chest. "I just like to know what my competition is."

"Believe me, you have none."

That pleased her, so much so that it was half an hour later before we resurfaced for air. Lying sprawled on the bed, exhausted but content, we said nothing for quite a while until I broke the silence.

"Forget about that. What's *my* competition like?"

"Are we at that point already?"

"Apparently so. If that receptionist is any guide."

"Shut up!"

"Well?"

I learned about two men she had been serious about. The first was in college and he'd been very good-looking and very smart and very worthy: a politics student who thought about the world and its problems. Lara said he used to dazzle her sometimes, so much so that it took her a year and a half to realise he was boring her senseless.

"It felt good for a while to be so serious," she said quietly. "Until I found out he was also being serious to another girl."

Number two, naturally enough, was the opposite. Someone she had known from childhood in Odessa. Once he'd been the disgusting rough boy from the next street who'd insisted on chasing her during lunch break at school. After she returned from college, the chase resumed. Even now, just the mention of Josef's name made her smile. So much fun, she said, so happy. When they broke up, both had laughed and realised that it was inevitable. The last she heard, he had got married to a girl from an adjacent street. Illogically, I felt relieved. Jealousy wasn't normally my style, but there was no getting away from the jumbled emotions just the mention of these guys' names provoked. There had been casual encounters for Lara too. Not many, but enough for her to know they were not what she wanted.

"What about you? What's your story?"

I told her about some of the girls I thought I'd been serious about and the ones who liked the fact that I was a jockey. I said there was a time when our receptionist friend might have provoked an interest. It sounded pretty barren compared to the depth of Lara's feelings for Josef and the politics guy, but the idea of embellishing or editing didn't arise. There was a directness to her gaze as I recounted my sorry romantic history which persuaded me that she would quickly pick up on any false note. Even more importantly, I didn't want to deliver one. Normally, it was easy to shelter behind the easy joke, keep enough distance to protect yourself, even if you weren't aware of doing so. But the last thing I wanted between me and this woman was distance, so I kept talking. Emotional incontinence wasn't really my scene but Lara simply listened, stroked my still black-and-blue stomach and kissed away any embarrassment at the end.

"When I first saw you, I didn't like you very much," she said, grinning.

"Really. Thanks for sharing that. Any particular reason why?"

"You were arrogant. Showing up, riding the horses, and then going away again. And never smiling. I couldn't understand it. All these beautiful horses to ride and you looked like you were working in a dull office."

"And what changed your mind?"

"After Anatoly died, you stayed around more and I could see you were not what I thought. You were shy more than arrogant. And Eamon said you were a good guy."

"Oh, you spoke to Eamon about me, did you?"

"Of course. Eamon is my friend. Your friend too."

Some friend Eamon had, I thought. Just a couple of days before, I almost jumped into the sky with fear when he'd appeared at my shoulder. And now one of the most decent people this friend had ever been fortunate enough to encounter was still technically a suspect in a murder case because I couldn't persuade the senior detective otherwise.

Lara appeared to pick up on my mood and we simply lay there, idly gazing at the mute television beaming in misery from all around the world. Watch enough of this, I thought, and a person really would think twice before going out the door. And there was something grotesque about these suited mouthpieces spouting news-managed fear into the world when there was more than enough of the real thing knocking about.

"I miss Anatoly," Lara said quietly.

"I know."

"I don't want to have to miss you as well," she added and turned her face to mine.

"I promise you won't. Listen to me, and believe this. Everything will be alright, I promise you. The fact that he came after me the reckless way he did means it's only a matter of time before he screws up."

"But what if he harms someone else before that?"

"I think you're starting to realise that Yeats is a pretty shrewd guy. If anyone can figure this out, it's him. And the best thing we can do is help as best we can."

"You really trust him that much?"

"I do."

That faith was put to the test later that same evening.

Eventually we decided the world had to come back in and, while Lara showered, I made some calls. Jack Hobbs might have felt spurned over the comparative lack of recent contact, but the old boy was far too smooth to let on. Instead, it was as if he'd hung up only half an hour before.

"There's nothing in Ireland until Downpatrick on Thursday, but there's a chance the ride on that good novice of Jarvis's might be open over at Wincanton tomorrow. I'm sure I can organise another few rides over there too, young man."

"Sorry, Jack, I can't. Something's come up."

I waited for a response. Jack's natural habitat was the betting ring, which in terms of gossip could make a racing yard look like a Cistercian monastery. He would never come out blatantly and say something. Jack Hobbs was far too stylish for such boorish behaviour. But he wasn't above a leading question. This time there was none. It seemed my head was, thankfully, not particularly newsworthy.

"Can you call the press agency and tell them I'm feeling under the weather at the moment?" I asked. "You know the score. 'I might not be available Thursday' kind of thing. Bailey rarely sends anything up north anyway."

"Sure," Jack replied, unsuspectingly. "There isn't much up there anyway."

"Thanks."

"Mind yourself, young man."

Next up was to check in with my parents. Their answer machine clicked into life courtesy of my dad's cheery invitation to leave a message and go away. I gave the usual I'm-fine-hope-you-are-too-see-you-soon spiel. Anything else would have freaked them out.

Then it was Yeats, who once again rang back the instant I hung up. He screened like an Olympic drug-tester.

"Are you okay?" he asked.

"Yeah, I'm fine."

"Settled in somewhere?"

"Yeah, we're in a hotel in Galway. Any news?"

"I was just about to ring you. We've got some initial forensic results back."

"And?"

"And nothing. We also have the results on all that stuff we took out of the alley."

"Squat again?"

"Right. There's nothing useful on any of it."

Yeats didn't go in for small talk unless it was necessary. But there was no denying the disappointment in his voice. We hung up, promising to get in touch the next day.

As I did, Lara emerged from the steaming bathroom, drying her hair, and wondering if we were going to head out. In the circumstances, there was hardly anything else for it.

"Oh, very definitely. We're heading out. I'm even going to try and show you a good time."

"That sounds great," she grinned.

In the taxi on the way into town, I told her about Yeats and the results, and whatever consolation she might have taken from my earlier speech about impetuosity letting the killer down must have rung pretty hollow.

"Forget it, Liam. We are in a new place and no one knows we are here. Let us enjoy ourselves."

"For tomorrow, who knows?"

"Exactly."

We found a little restaurant with a table overlooking the river. Only a cretin would have looked into this woman's eyes and pondered the calorie content of what we were eating. It was very easy to forget about pounds and ounces and sweat-suits and steaming baths. Such ephemeral crap could take care of itself in the morning. Instead, we ate and drank, laughed and teased, and all in all did a more than passable job of enjoying ourselves.

Afterwards we moved next door to a pub where a guitarist, a fiddler and a bodhrán-player were raising the sort of racket that needed drink to be fully appreciated. So we did just that: Lara with her Guinness and me with my vodka. The atmosphere improved to such an extent that, after a toilet break, I returned to ask the guitarist if he minded letting my girlfriend sing a song. Blushing furiously, she ended up having the instrument thrust into her hands and being almost frog-marched up to join the others. The look I received was rare indeed, but my Cossack girl wasn't done with the surprises yet. No rare Eastern folk-song this time. Even I managed to recognise the opening chords of the local Galway anthem "N-17". The response in the pub was instant bedlam.

She was word perfect, note perfect, and most important of all, perfectly in tune with the sentiment of the song. That peculiarly Irish mix of bounce and regret at living on a foreign soil rang as true from this young woman from Odessa as it would from any drink-addled emigrant in Boston or Birmingham. Lara smiled and moved to the raucous chorus about a narrow, stone-walled road just a few miles from where we were sitting. But it was in the verses of sadness and regret that she could have been talking about anywhere. As she brought the song to a close, there was huge applause and generous grins.

"You do that again and you'll never see this ass shake again!" she said, smiling.

"I don't think I want that."

As heads went in Galway that night, none were lighter or happier than mine.

22

I wasn't even properly awake before I remembered why such nights were so rare. It was a taste of guilt and the bloated regret of a full stomach. A terrible foreboding billowed over me like a black barrage balloon. Keeping my eyes closed was no defence. It was time to face up.

The clock said seven. Lara was sleeping deeply. After returning, we had attacked each other with a fervour that might have had the management knocking at the door. Except we wouldn't have heard them. Lara's wish to lock out the world for a little while more got us through much of the night until exhaustion finally took its toll. But now, the world was firmly knocking and demanding to be let back in.

I went down to the lobby and made for the gym. It was a good one: small, but well-equipped. After walking through the swing doors, a muck sweat came from nowhere at the sight of the little sauna which bitter experience had taught me could do the job only too well. The attendant washing the floor hardly glanced up. I stripped down quickly and padded to the large scales next to the showers.

It said eleven stone. Despair flowed out of me. Call it warped or silly, but given the choice right then of a few more whacks to the head, or doing what needed to be done to get these pounds off, I would happily have offered my skull. Along with despair came a full quotient of anger. How could anyone be so dense? As if the system wouldn't be thrown off course enough by my being battered around like ping-pong ball, I had to make things even worse by gorging. Starved of rich food normally, no wonder my body now wanted to hang on to its unexpected treat. I turned to the attendant.

"Is this thing accurate?"

"Serviced yesterday," he replied sulkily.

There was nothing else for it now. Briefly, I wondered about going into a cubicle and sticking a finger down my throat. But the guy was still mopping the floor and anyway it would, ultimately, do more harm than good to go down that route again. Flipping was a hard habit to get out of.

Back in the room, Lara stirred as I rooted the car keys out of my jacket. She put a brown arm over her eyes and asked sleepily if everything was alright.

"I'm going for a run. Go back to sleep."

"Are you alright?"

"Yeah, yeah."

As always, the running gear was in the boot and I changed into it in the car park. There was even a blast of a horn from some passing car as I was pulling on my track-suit bottoms. Forsaking the normal stretches and warm-up exercises, I turned my face west and started running.

Right from the start it was terrible. Both head and stomach were still suffering from my over-indulgence and, despite the additional protein, I felt as weak as a kitten. Must be the belt to the head, I calculated, and ploughed on. The route was familiar. A large new estate stretched for a good mile and a half before the pavement gave way to a small country road that wound its way inland. I had followed its course for as long as I could a number of times in the past, but never reached a source.

A small stone bridge that covered a glorified drain and looked old enough to be some sort of relief project from the Great Famine was at the end of a relatively straight stretch and clocked up at four miles from the hotel. I'd driven it the year before to make sure. How I wished I could drive it now.

Every step was sore. Anyone driving by and seeing this supposed professional athlete shambling past could have been forgiven for calling an ambulance or the cops. Unshaven, hung-over and grimacing with pain, I must have looked a sight. But however it looked, I felt worse. My leg muscles protested angrily at the sudden return to road work. It came down to concentration. Every turn yielded something new to fix the eyes on and nothing could come between me and making that signpost, or electricity pole, or gate.

Once I reached the bridge and turned around, it got a little easier. Psychologically, heading back was always a help. More important, though, was the sweat that was pouring out through the two T-shirts and into the rugby jersey on top. Halfway back, it was wringing, which made it heavier. In my half-crazed determination, that felt like a good thing: it made the work even harder. By the time the hotel came into view again, my legs felt as if they belonged to someone else.

Stopping at the edge of the car park, I stood hunched

over for a good minute before straightening up. Stars briefly appeared in front of my eyes. There were almost two hundred metres to the front entrance and I had taken only a few steps when a man stepped out of a nearby car and immediately started staring. Suddenly, the air seemed a lot colder. He was a big man, almost fat, but too latently powerful to be dismissed as some unfit blob. There was also an urgency to his movements that had me checking the distance to the hotel's front entrance and wondering if my legs were up to a sprint.

He was about my own age, I reckoned. Neat hair but stubble on his face. A buttoned-up black leather jacket struggled to contain him and, although his trousers were black and business-like, the white runners he was wearing didn't fit in at all. Every instinct screamed dodgy. He continued to stare and then came towards me.

"Hey!" he shouted.

To my left, a taxi drew up to unload what looked like American tourists, but the cab was a good hundred metres away. Behind me was just wall and to the right was where I'd just come from. There was no one else around. I felt desperately vulnerable.

"Hey, you're Liam Dee, aren't you?" he said, holding out his hand. He was obviously puzzled at why this cowering wreck looked as if he was being approached by the Grim Reaper, but he persevered. "My name is John Fahy. I follow the horses a bit and I just wanted to say I think you're a great jockey."

Jesus Christ, a punter! Hesitantly, I extended my own hand, still half-expecting a blade to come flashing towards me.

"I remember you won a race at Galway a couple of years ago. It was one of Bailey McFarlane's. You drove the head off it, won by a neck. I had a pile on you. So I just wanted to say thanks."

"No problem. Thank you," I somehow managed to rattle out.

"I'm just heading into the gym," he said, raising a runner for inspection and patting his belly. "Trying to get this off. Are you alright, Liam?"

"Yeah. I've just been for a bit of a sweat."

"Don't know how you lads do it. Ye're mighty men. Look after yourself."

How mighty could one be when the mind couldn't distinguish between someone simply wanting to say hello and someone wanting to cave your head in? Embarrassment made me circle around for a minute, trying to regain some sort of control. No doubt such a sight would have John Fahy pondering my sanity and it certainly wasn't good to be this jumpy. Nothing could be gained from shying at the whole world.

Lara was dressed and waiting just inside the door. Her arms wound around my neck and the kiss she delivered was soft and warm enough to bolster any sane man's morale. I hardly noticed it, instead untangling her arms from my neck.

"Mind your clothes," I said, making for the bathroom.

I put my mouth under the tap but didn't swallow, instead swishing the water around before spitting it out. Taking some in simply would make me thirstier and there was a lot more I had to do.

"What's wrong, Liam?"

"Nothing. It's just weight."

"Can I do anything?"

"Yeah. Can you manage breakfast yourself? I have to get into the sauna for a while."

"Sure."

"Good."

"Are you sure I can't do anything?"

"No," I snapped, and instantly regretted it. "Sorry, babe, it's just you can't exactly sweat for me. I have to do this myself."

She nodded, kissed me lightly, and left me to change and get into fresh clothes. A minute later and I was climbing out of them again in the changing room. Two large, elderly women were sitting in the sauna, almost bursting out the sides, and looking as if they were settling in for the day. My feet were positively tapping with impatience. After what seemed like an eternity, they finally decided to evacuate the tiny space. Sitting in with a towel around my waist, I reached for the dial and turned the heat right up. My anger rose along with the temperature.

Controlling weight, watching what I ate, following a strict diet: it was all in order to avoid sitting in these bloody things and scalding my lungs until they felt raw. It had taken years to develop a regime that consistently worked. There were times in my youth when the scales had yo-yo'd so much I'd ended up in dark rooms weeping at the anguish of it all. I couldn't go back to that again. This had to be nipped in the bud right now. The dial went even higher.

An hour later, I peeled myself off the seat and stood on the scales. Ten-eleven was the verdict. Another three and we were back in business. But no way could I go back into the box and no way was another run possible. Maybe a bath, but later, definitely not now. Thinking ahead to more of the same was not pleasant. And neither was the morose man who had been laughing, and joking and loving with Lara just hours before.

Sensing that chat wasn't exactly the best course to

follow, she let me trudge around the room in silence. Only when I was dressed did she tentatively propose going for a walk. It made sense. We could get out of the room and also I might be able to ignore the body's demands to take in some liquid. So we went downstairs silently and got into the car, making for the tiny village of Barna a few miles down the road.

Lara actually gasped when we stopped at the little pier that jutted into Galway Bay before taking a right angle to protect the little boats slowly bobbing and creaking in the dark, calm water. Even in summer, a cutting wind usually bullied its way ashore, but not this time. It was cold but also bright, and the breeze carried no venom. Out in the water a trawler slowly chugged past with lobster pots hanging over the sides. A man at the back raised an arm and then I realised it was in response to Lara's animated waving.

"Isn't this beautiful?" she beamed, eyes shining with delight.

I nodded. This was a place to come to in the mornings during race week: somewhere to sit on the stony beach, stare out at the water and just be alone. Normally, the smell of seaweed and salt lifted my heart, but not that day. All I wanted was to get back and resume the torturous pursuit of losing my extra weight.

"Come on, let's walk the pier," Lara urged.

It really was a gorgeous spring day. Even some of the gulls who normally croaked incessantly seemed to be taking a break and were strolling stiff-legged on the stone harbour wall. I felt an arm slip into mine, just like that first night as we left Trinity. The pier was short and didn't take long. So we also stumbled over the stony beach for about a mile before turning back. Lara didn't say much, which suited me. All she did was breathe deeply and murmur about the wonderful view. I wanted to share in it all, but my mind was back in the hotel gym, wondering if a few laps of the swimming pool would shift more weight off. Hardly surprisingly, Lara picked up on the mood.

"Do you want to go back?"

"Yeah."

"Okay then. Will I drive?"

"If you want."

"Maybe I could drop you off and come back here."

"Sure. Whatever you like."

The relief in my voice was obvious: far too obvious. If I could have reached out and grabbed the words, I would have. Her face didn't betray much, but I'd learned already that was when it was time to duck. How I wished something would come spinning through the air now, like a fist or a stone or a look. But, instead, we simply got into the car and returned to the hotel.

"I'm sorry, babe. I really am. It's just I have to get on top of this."

"I understand. I'll see you later."

It would be nice to say that guilt and remorse sent me running for the pier where Lara was and swept her off her feet into a steamy embrace. But wasting doesn't cater for such noble gestures. It's too selfish for that. Everything that doesn't involve you and the scales in this blinkered, morose tango of denial is irrelevant. The world outside is an irritant. Basic social chores become intolerable. All that matters is getting weight off.

It's a ceremony as old as racing and one that demands only one celebrant. Maybe the modern tendency to talk through problems and share the burden could offer some relief, but I doubt it. Quick-fix television answers don't really suit the grim process of wringing a body dry. Jockeys always look for an edge, even if it's largely in the mind. After all, the hardest battle when warring with the scales is in the mind. The authorities could raise the minimum riding weight and throw in some elephant races, but there will always be someone willing to starve themselves in order to get that edge.

So the afternoon was spent in pursuit of pain. Somehow I dragged my ass back out to the road and ran another four miles. Just as far as the bridge. When I turned around, the road looked like a giant grey carpet leading me down somewhere even I knew I didn't want to go, but the walk back was taken at pace. One flat jockey I knew owed a long career to walking. Five hours every day. Weather didn't matter. He was out with his dogs on the Curragh, away for five hours at a time. It seemed a dreadful sentence but he maintained that it beat running. I argued the other way. Running was a bastard, and it created too much muscle in the legs, but at least it got the sweat out quicker. From his close on fifty years, he simply smiled quietly and told me I'd learn. One thing we did agree on though: anything was better than the sweatbox.

Just twenty minutes back in the sauna was all I could take. It was like someone had flicked off the lights. As I staggered out, my towel fell down, but I couldn't even bend to pick it up. Making the bench and sitting down became the only objective. My heart was thumping so hard my chest felt as if it was about to burst open. The back of my head was starting to hurt again too. Staring at the floor didn't help at all and surveying the bruised and battered length of me didn't do much for morale either: all ribs, and bruises and lumpy collar bones.

A memory from childhood of a skinned rabbit that my

mother had brought home one day suddenly returned. She had announced that this desperately thin, meagre beast was a great delicacy and that we were going to have it for dinner. It lay on the kitchen table for some time, head slightly over the edge and peering under the table, while she figured out how to cook it. Even as a kid, it seemed so unfair. Of all the things we could eat, why pick on this miserable little thing? The first tentative thoughts of liberating it from its fate were stirring when my father arrived home, took one look and declared bunny to be off the menu. I reckoned that rabbit would have looked pretty good next to me right now.

A few wary glances were being thrown my way, so it seemed the time had come to stand on the scales again. I padded stiffly to them and watched the needle settle on my fate. Just like at Bailey's, I got off and then on again. It was impossible! How could I still be 10.11? How had nothing changed? Standing there naked, the vulnerability I'd felt that morning in the car park seemed like Churchillian certainty in comparison. Slowly I stepped down and moved to the showers.

A little later, Lara returned and found me sitting on the bed watching some kid's programme on the television. I looked up but said nothing. Instead, she made an announcement.

"I think it's best if I go back to work, Liam. I can't take advantage of Mrs McFarlane like this and it's obvious that I'm doing no good here. There is a train leaving for Dublin in an hour. Can you take me to the station?"

There was a matter-of-factness to the statement that ruled out an argument. She started to gather up clothes that were lying about and folding them into a bag. Even that was done with a certainty that made redundant any idea of convincing her otherwise. She wasn't trying to make a point by any dramatic gestures of annoyance. Lara simply figured taking her chances with some maniac back home was better than staying with me.

I knew what was happening. The best thing that had happened to me in a long time was getting ready to leave. And it had nothing to do with loyalty to Bailey or doing no good. If ever there was a time to throw pride to the wind and get down on one's knees, it was surely now time to drop.

"Why now?"

That's all that came out. Nothing about the possible danger she was leaving herself open to by going back: just a juvenile whine about how this was affecting me – hadn't I enough to be dealing with without her adding to all of it?

This got the scornful look it deserved, but that's what wasting does. It's a sickeningly self-absorbed agony that doesn't even begin to include the idea that anyone else might exist.

For most of my career, it hadn't been a problem because no one else had really existed. At least not enough to make me think about what I was doing. Or maybe doubt it. Part of me recognised all this and understood only too well the significance of it. But not enough of me.

"Can we talk?" I asked.

"Do you want to?"

On the telly a hapless dog was getting beaten up by a vengeful cat armed with an axe. Without sound, the violence was pretty gruesome, just as it always is in cartoons. Good clean family fun. Right then, though, it jarred. And so did this antiseptic hotel room, with its corporate neutrality. Maybe it was simply a case of being pissed off and hungry. Or maybe a symptom of a deeper problem within me – some harmful instinct to lash out. Or perhaps I was simply an ungrateful clown. Whatever the reason, the one thing I knew was that talking felt useless.

"No."

23

One more night in Galway and I was gone too. Suddenly, the party town didn't seem quite so cheerful. During the drive back to Dublin, though, Yeats rang and was not enthusiastic about the idea of me going home. Seeing as he had previously cautioned me against "overreacting" to the attack, this reassessment of the risks wasn't very encouraging.

"Do you want to make it easy for this bastard?"

"All anyone has to do to find me now is pick up a paper. There I am in the runners and riders."

"But don't just sit in your own place waiting. Is there anywhere else? Somewhere that isn't obvious?"

I'd told him after Lara left to keep an eye on her, make sure there was some police presence near where she lived, have a cop practically sitting in her lap if possible. He'd assured me he'd do everything he could.

So now, as a compromise, I found myself inching through heavy evening traffic on the M50 around Dublin before turning off and heading for the northside suburb of

Whitehall. A number of false starts later, including a stop at a shop to check directions, and the right estate finally appeared. After that, there was little problem finding the house. None of the other small but well-maintained semi-detacheds had a brand new BMW parked outside. Jack Hobbs always liked to travel in style.

I'd never been to his place before. There was nothing deliberate in that, no conscious decision to stay away. It wasn't hard to like Jack and the quiet way he pursued the courtesies of life, like actually doing what he said he was going to do. Compared to some of the loud, hard-eyed youngsters operating in the betting ring, Jack, with his sharp suits and wing-commander moustache, conjured up images of a an old-fashioned, rakish playfulness that didn't fool anyone into thinking he hadn't forgotten more than most rivals would ever know.

The call earlier in the day had gone along familiar lines. I could go to Downpatrick after all if he could organise anything at such late notice. Just nothing under eleven stone. Jack in turn wondered about Bailey's Cheltenham plans because an English trainer had been on, wondering if we were free to take a ride in the Triumph Hurdle in a few weeks' time.

"It's not a bad little horse. What's Mrs McFarlane thinking?"

"At the moment, things are in a bit of a heap."

"Of course. Poor woman having to deal with all that. Are you still staying with her?"

"No. Actually, Jack, I was hoping to put the bite on you."

"Really?"

I produced some rubbish about the house being painted and me needing a bed just for one night. There was a brief moment of hesitation from Jack, no doubt asking himself if his client was some sort of weird Johnny no-mates, but typically he regrouped with panache.

"No problem at all. See you later. Look forward to it."

Bailey's name flashing on the phone provoked a wince as I parked outside Jack's house. She wasn't exactly a barrel of laughs at the moment, which was a bit rich coming from someone acting like a bear woken up during winter. Loyalty won out though.

"Hi, boss. Everything alright?"

"Not too bad. At least the police aren't around. How're you?"

"Fine," I lied.

"Anyway, I've been speaking to the owner and we've decided to go for the Gold Cup."

It didn't register for a second. Too much was going on for Patrician and Cheltenham to be contesting a position at the forefront of my thoughts. There was a long blank pause while I raced to catch up.

"The Gold Cup? That's great."

"Yeah. The owner and I took your view on board about how he might miss out completely if we waited another year. Patrician's healthy now. Let's go for it."

"Exactly."

"Just mind him, okay?"

"Understood."

"And tomorrow afternoon, can you come down here? I'm going to tell the press agency the news now and I've got Charlotte ready to ring a few of the journalists. I'm damned if I'm going to be answering the phone non-stop between now and the festival, so we'll get it over with in one day. They can ask all the questions they like and take all the photos. But then that'll be it."

"Not a bad idea."

"I've got permission to do it in the parade ring at the Curragh racecourse. We don't need to give the reptiles any more to write by having them here. Be there at two thirty."

Jack was waiting at the door with a plump, friendly-looking woman whom I presumed was his wife. In front of them was a little boy of about six who shyly pressed backwards into Jack's legs and looked sideways at the stranger walking through the gate.

"Liam, welcome to this part of the world. This is the current Mrs Hobbs, Leah, and this is our grandson, Duncan. Say hello, you little bugger."

Duncan appeared to want to camouflage himself with his granddad's trousers but gave a little smile that had us all grinning. Leah reacted with horror at being called Mrs Hobbs and led the way upstairs to a room whose walls were covered with pictures of movie stars and dogs.

"Our youngest daughter comes home from college at weekends still," Leah explained.

"It's only for one night," I said. "I really appreciate this."

"Don't be silly. It's lovely to have you here. I just hope you stay longer."

"You're very kind."

"Nonsense. Anyone who makes my Jack as happy as you do can do no wrong."

"I don't know about that."

"Well, I do. And Duncan isn't normally shy at all, but he thinks you're some sort of Superman after all his granddad has told him. You should see his room. Walls covered with pictures of horses and you riding most of them. When we heard you were coming to stay, we couldn't get him to go back home. Are you feeling alright? You look very pale."

I said something about a fall and she winced, generously

215

telling me I was too brave for my own good. Dinner came soon after and everyone politely didn't remark on how I pushed the pork chops around the plate, cutting off fat and eating just a few bits of lean meat. It emerged that Duncan was the son of another of Jack and Leah's daughters and lived just a few hundred yards away.

"You're lucky to have your granny and granddad so close," I said and he smiled happily.

"Not that they look like grandparents. You two must have started young."

"Married at nineteen," Jack announced proudly. "When you know, you know."

Afterwards, I walked Duncan home with Jack, each of us holding a hand and lifting the little boy high into the air at imaginary Grand National fences. There was enough uncomplicated joy at this simple game to make even the most miserable streak of piss raise a smile. Duncan would happily have continued ten times around the green and any shyness was lost in his desperate attempts to get us to keep going, but Jack betrayed the first signs of his sixty years by declaring he was knackered. Instead, his daughter treated us to tea, mine a puritan black of course, and showed all the signs of inheriting her parents' graciousness. With the ice broken, Duncan started asking questions about horses and riding and being a jockey when he grew up.

"Is that what you want?"

"Yeah. I go to riding classes and everything."

"Are you good?"

The sofa arm suddenly was attacked by a wooden-spoon-wielding maniac. Time and again the timber rose and fell as the attacker crouched forward into a very passable position and rode like a demon for whatever far-away winning post was in his imagination. Only some maternal screams brought the gallop to a halt and the vivid visit back to my own childhood ended.

"You'll be in for force and frequency!" Jack grinned.

"Tell you what, Duncan," I said. "After Patrician wins the Gold Cup, I'll bring you down to see him if you like?"

The youngster's mouth fell open. Mind you, his granddad's almost did too. He looked over and I nodded. Jack wanted Patrician to go the novice route, said the Gold Cup was a killing ground for young horses who didn't know how to jump properly at speed. My view – that time was more of a killer for any chaser's chance at the big one – hadn't impressed Jack. There's always time, I remembered him saying. How I would have liked to have known about being married at nineteen during that argument. Duncan made me promise about the visit which was hardly a problem and I told him he was a great lad which was even less of a chore.

It was developing into a cold night as we left and Jack proposed a short diversion to a pub nearby. I shrugged and stuck my hands deeper into the fleece pockets, waiting for the inevitable reaction to the Gold Cup decision. But it didn't come.

"Are you in serious trouble with the weight?" he asked, still looking ahead and not breaking stride.

"Is it that obvious?"

"No, not particularly. You always seem to be on the verge of expiring anyway. But this is different, right?"

"A bit. I was eleven stone stripped yesterday."

"Ah."

"Exactly."

"You been sweating?"

"Like a bastard."

"Then stop for a day or two. Simply let things settle down. I got you a couple of rides in the North on Thursday.

217

Don't put yourself through it until after you get there and check the scales. I've seen a lot of guys mess themselves up by sweating too much. After a while, there's nothing left. The important thing is to give yourself a chance to settle. You know that."

Of course I did. But hearing it from someone else somehow made the option more real. There really was nothing to be gained from yo-yoing so much. The next meeting was two days away. Jack was right: leave it until Downpatrick and then see what had to be done.

"Thanks, Jack."

"Don't mention it. I don't want to see you turn yourself into some kind of babbling idiot. After all, the Hobbs house has quite an investment in you."

"Oh yeah?"

"It sure does. Right now the finishing touches are being put to the paperwork on a very new and very cut-price holiday home on the Algarve – along with about fifty acres of mostly dust which just happens to lie adjacent to a golf complex."

"I always wondered what you did with all your money."

"All? Don't kid yourself. I've had to graft all these years. But working for you has made a big difference. I reckon another six months and I'll be able to jack it all in and head for the sun."

"No coming back?"

"Nah. Once you decide, it's best not to look back. You kick on as best you can. I'll miss working with you, though."

"No, you won't."

"I certainly will. I don't like the idea of leaving you in the lurch. I can recommend a few blokes. They'll queue up to take you on. You're a top man, Liam. In every sense – not just as a jockey. It's been a privilege looking after you."

"Jesus, Jack, you'll have me blushing."

"But I still think you're offside with Patrician."

"I'll let the press boys know you think that tomorrow."

Even though it felt like sleeping in a teenage schoolgirl's fantasy, I did at least sleep. Jack could sound wise reading out a shopping list. Giving it a couple of days immediately made things easier. I'd been like a rookie staring far into the future and seeing nothing but work. No one could operate like that. Weight really was a day-by-day thing. Targets had to be short-term. The alternative was mind-bending. Downpatrick gave me something to focus on.

A reminder of how important that was had come only hours earlier while I was driving from Galway. The radio was on and somehow a history programme managed to pierce my self-obsessed fog. It was something about conditions for soldiers in the trenches during World War One. Various academics droned on, interrupted by actors reading out heart-wrenching letters of loneliness, love and fear. Only the most unimaginative person could remain unmoved at the bravery required of young men who barely knew where they were and rarely realised why they were there. History had always been my favourite subject in school, and Franco Hoy's work was still fresh in my mind, so I listened with interest. So much so, that when the programme finished and nothing was left except to remorselessly drone through miles of flat boring countryside, my mind wandered.

I didn't really daydream. Even those occasional lusts for chocolate didn't take over for that long. But this was different. A vision of the future presented itself. Maybe because of what my body had endured before, the mind picked it up and ran feverishly.

It was hardly Hollywood flash. But the more mundane the details, the more attractive it all appeared. Me driving into the university campus near where I lived and parking. Me walking to some lecture hall and taking notes. Me going to the library and poring over books while pretending not to check out the good-looking girl in the corner. Me tucking into sandwiches made with thick bread and full of coleslaw. Me getting a kick out of something new and different. Me drinking pints of beer. Me being normal. It was vivid and seductive and therefore all the more destructive.

Even much later, lying in bed and staring up at the various pooches and posers on the walls, there was no way of ignoring the significance of what had happened. If riding over fences demanded one thing over anything else, it was commitment. Nothing but the idea of winning could matter in a race. It was too dangerous for it to be any other way. If the desire to get over the next obstacle wasn't one hundred per cent, then you were a danger to yourself.

I remembered Sam English once telling me that he knew immediately when he had to stop riding and get into another line of business. Valeting mightn't be exciting, he explained, but at least it let him sleep at night. Doubt had chiselled its way into his brain. Where once he had thrown horses at the fences without a thought, he found himself thinking too much. Instead of asking for big jumps at fences, he started to play the percentages and fiddle his way over the obstacles. For a while he persuaded himself it was just being smart, but one day at the start of a race, he found himself suddenly wanting to be back in the weigh room. If it had been possible, he'd have called for a substitute there and then. Instead, he had to go three miles over fences.

"As soon as you feel any doubt, it's time to go," he advised me years later. "There's no glory in keeping going and ending up crocked. Imagine getting yourself seriously hurt just because you were too scared to stop."

Did daydreaming about something else constitute that kind of jitters? Hardly, I thought. The idea of being so worked up at the start of a race was alien to me. No doubt Sam had been completely honest, but that was him. Everyone's reaction to stress was different. My problem was in getting too far ahead of myself. I turned over and fell asleep, with Jack's voice telling me to leave things until Downpatrick, and the idea of driving home from college to be met by Lara at the door slowly starting to fade.

24

I dropped into the police station on the way to Bailey's press day. The sergeant from the previous week was on the front desk again and actually winked at me while ringing to see if Yeats was available.

"Thanks for that tip-off. I had a little on. And I see he's favourite now after last night's news."

"Have you a good price?" I asked.

"I do now."

The man himself was sitting in his pokey office, surveying a deskful of paperwork, and not looking very happy. By now I'd seen him in all moods from sardonic to having the charm button fully pressed on. There had been the impressively resolute calm with which he had faced down a rampaging Franco and the seemingly genuine regret expressed to Lara. But I had never seen Yeats looking so dispirited. My arrival barely earned a glance and a good minute went by before he threw his pen down and leaned back.

"How's the head?" he asked.

"I'll survive."

"I don't doubt it. Anyone in the horsey world twig what happened?"

"I don't think so."

We were interrupted by the phone and, without enthusiasm, Yeats started scribbling on another scrap of paper. In a corner, I noticed a number of empty sandwich containers peeping out of a waste bin, accompanied by coffee-stained polystyrene cups. Compared to my last visit, there was definitely more of a lived-in feel there. He hung up abruptly and stared at some spot on the wall for some time before speaking.

"I suppose you want to know where we are with the investigation?"

"I guess."

"We have hit something of a wall, Mr Dee, and at the moment, I'm struggling to find any sort of way over it."

"Oh."

"'Oh' is right. The detail of the new interviews has yet to be fully sifted through, but I very much doubt if anything dramatic is going to come out of it. Forensics continue to tell me everything that isn't useful but damn all that is, and most of the crap you see in front of you is the translated report from the Ukrainian police, who conclude that the victim had no links with criminality of any kind and really was the poor innocent little bastard he appeared to be. I've got a suspect poncing around Dublin as if he hasn't a care in the world. Plus, I now have you sitting in front of me looking like death warmed up with a lump on your head. So, that, Mr Dee, is where we are. Any ideas?"

It wasn't exactly encouraging and he must have seen the worry in my face because his hand waved dismissively.

"Don't listen to me. It's just tiredness. There's only so long a person can continue to hop their head off a wall before they start getting cranky."

And it was then, sitting in the cramped little room at the back of a police station, that I started to feel cold anger seep through me for the first time. Up to then, the emotional spread had reached from sadness to dread to plain relief. But the sheer wickedness of it all now hit me and made me hate my attacker. It was a much more personal desire than I could have imagined, especially now the prospect of his getting away with it seemed to be more real every day.

"Do you believe the person who hit me is the person who killed Anatoly?" I asked, careful to keep it impersonal and impartial and avoid mentioning Christy Wolf by name, in deference to Yeats.

"Hmmn," was his only response.

"Well, there must be a chance he'll try and do it again." Unless, of course, it was intended as a warning. "Why else would you think it a good idea for me to hide away in some place unusual?"

"That's simply a precaution."

"Okay. But if this whole thing is at a dead end, why not try and lure this bastard? Why not let him see where I am and hope he does something. Flush him out."

"Oh, the tethered-goat ploy that the police complaints board has been raving so much about recently." Yeats grinned. "Yes, we've been having great results with that, except for one tiny little problem. What was it again? Oh yes, the authorities don't really approve of us tethering the general public quite so obviously."

"Okay. But you don't seem to have anything else in mind."

"For Christ's sake, this isn't some cop show on the telly. I've told you that nothing happens in a hurry. We will get this bastard. It simply takes time," he said. "I still think that damn alley is important. It demands knowledge."

"Can you establish how many people do actually know about the alley?"

"We checked employment records and tracked down as many of those who've worked at the place over the years as possible. Quite a few of the older people remembered the alley as some kind of shortcut. There's no knowing how many people know. But I reckon someone used that knowledge."

"Christy certainly did. He told me."

"Don't worry. I remember."

"Is there anything at all I can do to help?"

"Nothing along the lines of tethering yourself to anything. Just mind yourself. Where are you staying?"

"In Dublin. With a friend."

"People can be followed."

"Jesus, who's in the TV cop show now?"

"Don't slam the door on your way out."

Twenty minutes later and Reggie McGuire fell into step alongside me as I walked from the car park into the main Curragh racecourse complex for the press conference about Patrician. The parade ring at flat racing's spiritual home already contained a good forty people eager to stare at and photograph what might be jumping's future superstar. Reggie was full of the joys. Between gossiping about one of his female colleagues, and offering me a packet if I'd only do a ghosted column for Cheltenham, he positively gurgled at the idea of winding Bailey up.

"I just love it when that proud old head starts to toss. It's like one of those elephants you see on safari, raising its trunk and screeching at everyone to go away. Beautiful really."

"Look, Reggie, why don't you ease up on her a bit? It's dirty pool, trying to get a rise out of her at the moment."

"But it's one of my few pleasures."

"If you do, I'll think about that column thing."

"But you've never done one."

"There's a first time for everything."

"You're taking the piss."

I shrugged and he promised not to get my boss pawing the ground with temper. Just then, I heard a number of horses coming out of the saddling area. Patrician came first, led by Eamon, and playing to the expectant audience with a series of little kicks and bounces that had his minder snatching at the lead rein. It was behaviour that had more in common with some of the highly strung colts that usually populated the racetrack, rather than a three-mile chaser. But there was a positive hum of appreciation at his appearance.

The press pack had descended in full strength despite the late notice. Reggie, I noticed, slipped in among the local hacks, slightly apart from the large contingent of twenty journalists that had managed to get over from Britain. And, in a display of the journalistic pecking-order, neither would have anything to do with the four television camera crews that prowled around self-consciously, looking for the best positions. Standing against the rail to give the horses as much room as possible, I watched Patrician being followed by five other possible runners Bailey was lining up for Cheltenham. The last of them especially caught my eye. King Titus, the little four-year-old that had won at Thurles, plodded professionally past, led by Lara.

There wasn't a flicker of recognition from her. Maybe she was concentrating on not messing up in front of the media crowd, but King Titus was hardly giving any concern on that score. She strode by, wearing jeans and a bright red anorak, her hair tied up and hidden under a baseball cap.

Even in working gear, there was so much elegance to Lara. I wanted very much to run after her, get down on my knees, say sorry and beg for forgiveness. Just my sort of timing to realise that in front of the international media.

Bailey and Charlotte emerged from the saddling area, the younger woman smoothing down imaginary wrinkles on an outfit that could still have had the price-tag swinging off it, and her mother eyeing the prospect of the next hour with an obvious lack of warmth.

Bailey slowed down before colliding with me.

"Thanks for showing up, Liam."

I wasn't sure if she was being sarcastic. After all, it was the first time she'd seen me in four days. But the greeting seemed genuine enough.

"I hate this. Polite, meaningless bullshit," she seethed. "Come on. Let's get it over with."

Only then did I notice she had been wired for sound. The racecourse manager had organised a system which consisted of a small box attached to her trouser belt and a wire microphone. It dawned on Charlotte and me at the same time that maybe Bailey's disdain for the task ahead might have been broadcast to the mob, but there was no halt to the hum of conversation behind us.

"I'm not an idiot, you two. I do know where the on-off switch is."

She marched towards the presentation podium in the middle of the ring and, flicking the mike into life, thanked everyone for showing up. Her voice carried well and she immediately got down to the business of explaining why Patrician was going for the big race and not the novice. There was no hint of temper as she cogently listed the pluses for taking a risk. There was also a name-check for my contribution to the decision and a rumble of laughter from the audience at the suggestion that her jockey was getting braver with age. I smiled wryly, tried to focus on the speaker, and only stared at King Titus's groom for the time she circled behind the podium.

After explaining about Patrician, Bailey went through the rest of her Cheltenham team and gave an upbeat bulletin on King Titus, who looked to have strengthened up quite a lot since I'd seen him last.

"Whatever about the horse, just look at the bird leading him round," Reggie McGuire whispered into my ear.

He glanced sideways, no doubt expecting some sort of conspiratorial snigger, but then took a step back. Clearly, disguising anger was no longer one of my strong suits. McGuire swallowed. I actually heard his Adam's apple bounce, like some pointy ping-pong ball. Nothing was said, but he retreated back into the safety of the pack.

Bailey wound up her remarks and stepped down to be enveloped by a wall of humanity brandishing tape-recorders and notebooks. I quickly moved to where the horses had been brought into the centre to pose for photographs. Eamon looked stern as a photographer with an English accent asked me to stand with Patrician. Eamon handed over the lead rein and I dutifully stepped in next to the centre of attention. The horse stood perfectly, ears pricked and staring at whatever cloud had grabbed his eye. Lara was less than ten yards away but any idea of getting any nearer to her disappeared as some of the British press peeled off towards me.

"I take it you're happy about the Gold Cup, Liam?"

It was the usual stuff. Good-humoured questions lobbed gently in the hope that the person would catch and run with them. All a million miles from the cut-throat intensity of the media coverage of Anatoly's death. Most of the racing-press boys realised they weren't dealing with end-of-the-world crises and usually were okay to deal with. Disputes were rare. It might not have sat right on the Pulitzer board but it's less than prescient to slag off someone whom you might need to talk to again the following day. In our little world the niceties tended to be observed on both sides. So I dutifully spouted the patter about respecting the opposition and believing in my horse, and the lads scribbled away. Then there were a few television and radio interviews which demanded the same answers and, all the time, I tried to stop myself from staring over everyone's heads at the person I really wanted to speak to. However, it was as things started to break up that a question came from one of the young provincial reporters whom I'd seen but never spoken to before.

"Would it be fair to say your career is winding down? After all, you'll be thirty-five in April. Is retirement anywhere on the horizon?"

There didn't appear to be anything loaded in the question. In fact the guy seemed pleased with himself for simply having asked it. If anything, he was nervous, probably at having to mix it with some very senior colleagues. But his bid to assert himself was at my expense. No one had ever actually thrown the retirement question at me before. Now it hung over me like a doom-laden billboard to professional mortality. Maybe it was paranoia, but it felt as if the circle of people had tightened around me, waiting for a response.

"The 'R' word is so far over the horizon it's fallen off." I smiled determinedly. "In fact, you'll be grey by the time it happens."

My young inquisitor blushed furiously and the others dutifully laughed. I added that only a fool would walk away from the sort of ammunition just then walking back to the unsaddling area. That even provoked a number of "hear-hears", so I asked if anyone needed any more and then headed away hoping there would be no awkward retirement headlines the following day.

Charlotte was flirting prettily with one of the television producers but Bailey used me as an escape route from a lingering bunch of reporters which I noticed included a rather subdued McGuire hovering on the edge.

"I've got to talk to my jockey," she boomed, grabbing hold of my arm. "Keep moving, Liam, and don't look back."

"I thought it went pretty well."

"Yeah, they're okay. Most of them. Even that pond-scum McGuire managed to keep his mouth shut. Doesn't Patrician look well?"

I agreed he did and we headed after him. As we turned a corner, it was obvious that the skittish star of the show was making life difficult for Eamon. Kneeling down to tape some protective gear on the horse's legs for the box-ride home, he was delivering some choice oaths at Patrician to calm down. Eamon's repertoire of abuse for the charges under his care was fruity and extensive. There were horses who would redden with embarrassment if they could understand some of the invective he directed at them. It was all talk though. If a hair was disturbed on a McFarlane runner, Eamon would be down on the ruffler like a bad dream. Especially the good runners. And there was none better than Patrician.

Bailey walked quickly up, grabbed the head collar and spoke soothingly into his ear. Eamon tried to make the most of the lull in activity and I kept walking to the saddle box at the end of the line.

Lara was busy herself, trying to unravel the belt-leads in a large red-and-blue horse blanket. King Titus stood, head lowered, staring out as I approached. He was turning into a proper little gentleman; all the unnecessary fizz had disappeared since his race. I put my hand on his nose and patted him gently, waiting for her to turn around.

"Can I help?"

She straightened up, a last pull at the leads making them fall straight, with the buckles clanging off the concrete.

"Hold this while I give him a brush," she said, handing me the blanket.

There were three empty boxes between us and the next horse. Murmuring sounds could be heard from the lad there. It was time for some grovelling. But before I had a chance to say anything, Lara stood back and I threw the blanket on. King Titus stood perfectly still as I manoeuvred it into position, leaving the belts hanging loose down his sides. Crouching down and leaning under the horse's belly to retrieve the two belt-leads, I was very aware of how close she was.

"I'm sorry, Lara. I really am. I was a complete asshole."

"Forget it. That's all in the past," she replied, crouching down as well to retrieve one of the belts.

We didn't move except to cross the two buckles under the horse so the leads overlapped. Fixing them to the blanket meant standing back up. But still we were near enough for our arms to brush against each other as we padded King Titus for the short journey home. The urge to hold her was painful.

"Look, I could explain myself by saying any number of things, but it wouldn't excuse what happened."

"There is no need to explain anything," she replied, and stood back to look at the horse before turning to me. "You are a good man, Liam. You really are. We had a nice time together, but it is obvious that for you there is no room for anything but racing. Being a jockey is not just your job, it is your life. And I'm not willing to be some hobby to pick up on the side when you have time to kill."

"That's not fair, Lara."

"I'm not arguing with you, Liam. I simply don't like wasting my time. Everything else was forgotten when you woke up that morning. The world could have been exploding around us and you would still have tried to torture yourself running."

"I'm really sorry about that."

"So am I, but that is who you are. It must be terrible to be such a slave to weight. It really must. But I cannot allow it to drag me down too."

"It needn't be like that."

"Of course it must. Liam, don't you see? There is nothing else in your life, and you don't want there to be."

25

A row was brewing when Bailey and I arrived back at the yard. Outside, the horse box was being unloaded, with Patrician still looking lordly as he stepped carefully down the ramp before bunny-hopping to the ground. As he pranced happily, Lara's bright jacket was at the other end of the block, leading King Titus to his box. Maybe it was my mind playing tricks but there looked to be an even greater defiance than normal in her stride. I didn't think it was for my benefit. That sort of arrogance had long since disappeared.

I followed Bailey's own martial bounce towards an increasingly raucous kitchen where Charlotte's voice was shrill enough to make one wonder about the windows. Franco's response, it seemed, was to walk in circles around the room, muttering in a base rumble about how he didn't have to put up with this bullshit. Bailey waited outside for a few seconds, but not, it seemed, out of embarrassment or the wish to give them privacy.

"Always best to know what you're going into," she grinned at me mischievously.

The row was about Franco's driving skills. Or the lack of them. Bailey whispered that he couldn't drive. She made it sound like he wasn't toilet-trained. She also appeared to relish the insults being hurled at her son-in-law and gave no sign of wanting to go in. It was only after some mute imploring from me that she eventually relented.

"This is all very interesting, lads," she boomed, "but what's the problem?"

Charlotte was pouting as if she wanted to run to Mummy, bury her head in her skirts and moan that the mean boy was making her cry. No doubt such behaviour would bring out the protective instinct in certain men, but it was bizarre to see such manipulation close up. Franco almost snorted in derision and even favoured me with an exasperated glance that spoke more eloquently than any words we had exchanged before. There was no such bravado in front of Bailey, however. Physically, he towered over the lot of us but there was no doubting who the dominant personality in the room was.

"I have to get to Dublin tonight," Franco explained. "It's the exhibition centre. They need me to go through site positions for the show. It's in two weeks' time. Things have to be sorted out."

"But I'm meeting Emma and Zoe tonight," Charlotte whined. "I don't want to have to drive into the city."

Franco wasn't anyone's idea of a perfect passenger, but what the hell. It was less than an hour, and, anyway, maintaining the civilities might keep my mind busy.

"I'm going back to Dublin soon. I can give you a lift, if you want?"

"Anywhere near the city centre?"

"Sure. No sweat."

Franco's mood lightened considerably. He even said thanks. Bailey winked but Charlotte sullenly said nothing.

If anything, she looked upset that the air had been let out of this particular drama. I felt a sudden stab of sympathy for her husband. No wonder his reaction to her going higher on the sonar scale was to go in the opposite direction. It must have been exhausting to put up with. Even the indignant way she departed left a smell of resentment in the kitchen. Franco said he had to get some stuff out of their jeep and Bailey eyed him walking after his wife, no doubt hoping the dramatics would not be played out in front of the entire yard.

"In the middle of all that's happened, Liam, I've never asked how things are going with you."

"Same as usual."

"Really?"

There was a tone to her voice that left little doubt that this was no idle enquiry. She sat at the table and motioned for me to do the same. There was something a bit too career-guidance teacher about the gesture, but what was I going to do? Flounce off like her daughter?

"I tried to get you last night. Your mobile was turned off and there was no answer at your house. That's not like you."

"I'm staying with a friend while my place is being painted. It's no big deal."

"Good. It's just that I was talking to Lara yesterday."

"Were you?"

"Yes. I asked her if she was over her illness and she looked at me as if I'd gone mad. Then she said that, yes, she had been sick. So I asked if you'd been looking after her. The girl got quite upset and I brought her in here for a cup of tea."

I wasn't sure what a hackle was but I felt mine rising.

"Don't get thick, Liam. Lara didn't want to say anything

and she didn't really. All I got was that you might be having some trouble with your weight."

This was not on. Never once in my fifteen years' riding for her had Bailey ever asked me about weight. It wasn't her business; she knew that. Racing was full of unwritten rules and understandings and this was one of them. It was the jockey who worried about weight. Once the trainer got involved, it didn't do either party any good.

"All I'll say is that you might consider letting your normal riding weight increase a little. You're not getting younger and it's a reality that people get heavier as they older. Look at me."

I did, and the way I did made her sit up straighter, like she didn't want to be caught unprepared. Obviously Reggie McGuire wasn't the only one able to read my face. But whatever about letting rip at a sarcastic journo, there was no percentage in having a pop at Bailey. Of course, knowing that and acting on it are two different beasts.

"Back off, Bailey. That's my business."

"Hey, you ride for me, which makes it very much my business!"

"And have I ever once messed up in that department? Has there ever been a time when you've been affected? What's changed now?"

"Nothing's changed. It's just that you're obviously not yourself right now. I mean look at you. It's like talking to a ghost. Any more wired and we could use you as a socket."

"My problem, and I'll solve it."

"Like you 'solved' Lara? Nice one, smart boy. You 'solved' that real well. Let me tell you something. I don't have too much faith in the human condition, but I do know that girl is one of the rare good ones. And, for some reason, she's got it bad for you. Why, I don't know, because you wouldn't recognise how good she is, since you're too far up your own arse to see anything."

We were on dangerous ground now. Any more clenched and Bailey's jaw could have belonged to Kirk Douglas. At the same time, though, there was an uncertainty in her eyes that let me know she didn't want to go down that road any more than I did. Ready, but not willing, her face said.

There was a tense pause before I spoke again. Mind you, any notion of it being a climb-down was diluted by what she'd said already. Lara had it bad for me. That's what Bailey believed. There was enough there to cling to, surely?

"It's simply a temporary thing, alright? I took my eye off the ball for a while and it caught up with me. I'll know more after tomorrow."

"I'm sorry. What's happened has messed everything up. I really do think the world of you, Liam. Not just because you're my jockey or any of that rubbish. You've been great during all this. A real friend. Come here."

I was still in her bear hug when Franco returned. There was no idling at the door for him. In he tramped with his big black climbing boots, loudly wondering when we were off because he was under a little bit of time pressure. Bailey released me, threw her son-in-law a dirty look and told us to scarper.

"There's no panic, Liam. Just ring me tomorrow after racing and let me know what happened. We'll sort something out then. And, listen, I'm thinking of giving Patrician a school, just to get his eye in. Saturday morning, at the schooling grounds. Okay?"

Sure it was. She really was a great woman. Concerned and helpful and even able to throw in some hope. I regretted very much offering Franco his bloody lift. A little time to mull over what to do next was what I needed, not pandering to some hot-head who made no effort to disguise his contempt for me. But there was no point talking now. Franco followed me out and it was all he could do not to sit into the back seat.

Maybe Charlotte could relax around her husband, but there was something incessantly aggressive about him that suggested even she might be kept on her toes. He was bristling with impatience as we set off. I was a quick driver anyway – most people in racing are – but when the needle started to climb steeply, I figured I was too old for intimidation.

We'd only gone a few miles when Franco announced that he had to take a leak. It was said in a tone that suggested he didn't much care if it happened in the car. But he helpfully proposed leaving the motorway at the next exit.

"That tatty café where the lorries stop is just up there," he said.

"The Omega? That's been closed for a couple of years."

"It doesn't matter. I can nip around the back."

The look of pain that accompanied this plea was almost enough to make me sorry when the exit lanes were backed up so badly with traffic that using it would clearly have us sitting in snarled immobility for far too long. But only almost. That primal male instinct to clash and defy had come a long way from the cave but only its clothing had changed. Pathetic really, I thought. Which didn't stop me guiltily enjoying the sound of Franco shifting uneasily for the next few miles. Eventually, though, I figured the civilities needed to be restored.

"Is there a lot of work involved in these exhibitions?" I asked as neutrally as possible.

"You could say that," he answered.

Clearly, the idea of conversation wasn't turning him on too much, but he must have figured some singing for his supper was required. There was a deep intake of breath and I was favoured with more.

"In many ways, making the stuff is the easy part. Getting it out there is the most difficult thing in the world."

As far as I could figure out, this was said in all seriousness. There was no self-deprecating grin to dilute the statement; no nod to the real world outside his studio. Clearly Franco was never going to be troubled by a sense of humour. Maybe that was why Bailey would always be the dominant personality in any room they shared. She could be as overbearing and testy as him. There had been times over the years when naughty behaviour breached the line into boorishness, but even Reggie McGuire couldn't deny the humanity that was there too. A lightness that Franco seemed incapable of. Bailey could turn around, shake her head, proclaim to the world she was an eejit, and laugh at herself. Franco's reaction, I suspected, would be to challenge the world, but maybe all of his humanity was directed inward. No way could some un-thinking, insensitive clod create something like that soldier. Empathy poured out of that lifeless block of stone. Enough to make one choke at the despair and waste the human condition seems so good at creating. It was just hard to believe something so beautiful could be made by the hands and mind of the man next to me.

"I really like that piece you're doing on the unknown soldier."

"It's a piece of shit, but it will have to do."

"What do you mean?"

"The fuckers want it now. There's no more time. So they'll get it as it is."

Contempt rolled off his tongue. All that care and attention to detail was in the past; done with.

"It doesn't matter then?" I asked.

"What do you mean it doesn't matter? Of course it matters. Jesus, if art doesn't matter, then those lunatic politicians might as well press the button and be done with it all. Fucking hell: art is the one thing that distinguishes us from the animals. Without it, we're down in the trough too."

"That's a bit bleak, isn't it?"

"Really? What else do we do different? We eat, shit, sleep, fuck, fight, steal and die. Except we also throw in some beauties of our own like cheating, murdering, raping and whatever you're having yourself. The only redeeming feature we have is our creative imagination. Somehow, we have enough in us to create beauty out of nothing, to make something greater than we will ever be ourselves. You can shove your priests, policemen and politicians; they're in the shit along with us all. But art is the only that makes us look up. If that doesn't matter, then there's nothing."

Franco had said more to me in that one minute than in the five years I'd known him. He didn't strike me as one for doubt anyway, but there was a certainty to what he was asserting that defied anyone to argue. Clearly, while chipping for interminable hours at cold rock, he had thought intensely about why he was doing it. Whatever I felt about his conclusions, I could only envy his certitude.

"It was just that you sounded like you didn't care about that particular piece," I said lamely.

"I did. But once it's gone, it's gone."

"When it's finished, it's finished?"

"Oh, it's never finished. There's always some bit you want to change. Some thing that looks wrong. I try never to look at things once they're out of my hands. It drives me nuts. But no one can operate like that. At some stage, you have to cut the line. Say enough is enough. Otherwise, you'd go mad."

There wasn't much I could say to that and Franco appeared to be concentrating on his toilet problems as we silently snaked our way through the city. A couple of hundred metres from the exhibition centre, he asked me to pull over.

"Thanks. I can walk from here and it'll be easier for you to get going."

"Okay. Good luck with it."

"Yeah."

There was an awkward moment where Franco appeared to feel as if he should say something more in return, but he shrugged and shut the door. I watched him as he strode away, walking straight and forcing people to walk around him. A couple of them even looked backwards and grimaced at the huge figure disappearing round the corner. Never had gestures seemed more futile.

26

Johnno Parle's encounters with doubt weren't plentiful either, so when he rang just after I'd arrived back at Jack's, a certain momentum gathered around his invitation to get my sorry arse into town for a few jars. But it didn't need much persuasion. All the logical arguments against a fat jockey tucking into booze for another night ran across my mind like the moving tickers at the bottom of the television news channels. And all of them were ignored in the face of some home-grown logic. After all, Jack had said to let things lie for a couple of days. The deadline was the next day. If there was a time to let rip, it was surely now. For someone desperate to believe, the argument made perfect sense.

Jack offered to drop me into town, but a taxi made more sense. When he asked what was happening, he got the straight, unabridged version. Johnno wanted to go on the piss and I wanted to help him. I was prepared for resistance, but wise old Jack was way ahead of the game. "Good idea," he said. "Let off some steam." So, like a child given permission to break bottles into a bin, I practically skipped outside when the cab arrived.

The mood survived as far as Doyle's Corner where a truck had broken down practically in the lap of some roadworks, causing a tail-back of rush-hour proportions. My driver's reaction was to take off his belt, sigh at the back of the bus ahead, and prepare to sit it out.

"Sorry, chief, but I'm walking," I said, clambering out, paying him, and setting my sights on the city centre.

It wasn't a part of town I knew well but, striding on, I quickly passed the massive cold grey walls of the Mater Hospital and followed my nose towards North Frederick Street and the top of Parnell Square. It was a longish hike, but there was plenty to see along the way. This little part of the north-inner city was turning into a multi-national village. The clash of colours and cultures was obvious just from the shop fronts, making the pallid city of my youth a rapidly fading memory.

Despite that, too many thoughts were swirling around for me to concentrate on the changing face of Ireland. At least Bailey had given some hope that I might turn things around with Lara. Seeing her earlier had only emphasised how much I desired her. Not simply in any obvious physical sense: I wanted her respect just as much. I wanted this woman to like me. Anything else could only come after I'd shown her I wasn't a completely inadequate shit. If there was a master class in how to screw things up, then she'd got a front-row seat in Galway, yet there was still time for me to try and retrieve the situation. If only everything else could be got in order.

It was easy to feel a pang of sympathy for Yeats, stuck in that cramped little office, no doubt with superiors breathing down his neck and nothing to go on. Thank God that was his responsibility. In comparison, being in charge of only myself didn't seem so difficult. So why was I making such a production of it?

It was pretty obvious time was running out on my riding career and it wasn't just age. Sure, the wasting and running and constant aching felt harder, but, if I wanted to, I could still manage to get over all that. The basic question was: did I want to? That stupid daydream on the drive from Galway, and the way I sank into it, seemed to answer that. But how could anyone back away from a horse like Patrician? There was five years at the top with him if he stayed sound. The best really was to come. Maybe enough to turn him into a legend. Was I ready to entrust that to someone else? Not bloody likely.

Except Patrician was only one ride. The glory horse. If it was just him, a jockey could sit at home and get the silks on maybe no more than six times a year. But there were five hundred other bread-and-butter rides waiting to be negotiated too. And about five of those were guaranteed bone-breakers. That was why the occasional big race dessert tasted so sweet. It had been earned the hard way.

Walking past Trinity College, trying not to remember the last time I'd been there, Sam English's story came back to me. Old Sam loved the game so much, he couldn't get away from it. But still he knew immediately when he had to face reality. In one way, he was almost lucky. Once fear got that much of a hold on you, there was no choice but to stay out of the saddle. Mind you, the memory of Sam's last ride was so etched in his brain it must have been truly frightening. I hadn't lost my bottle yet, but maybe it was only a matter of time.

I knew what Sam would say if I were to ask him. That granite-hard face would become even more stony and he would declare, in his low-key manner, that the brave thing to do would be to stop right away. Only fear of the new and the unknown was preventing me, he would say. Then he would deliver a slap to the shoulder, tell me to grow a pair of balls and not be a child about it. No doubt Jack Hobbs would be from the same no-nonsense school. My family would probably break down with relief at me packing it all in, and who knew? Maybe even Lara might think there was something more to me than just being a jockey.

Except a little part of me, hiding at the back of the brain, maybe where I'd been hit outside Mrs O'Sullivan's, said that all of that was only what I wanted to believe. It didn't need courage to stop. Courage was what was needed to point half a ton of racehorse at Becher's Brook and jump over it at speed. Any other definition was self-serving bullshit; just an excuse for bottling out of the job. What was there to be scared of in eating three meals a day and drinking beer and going to school? Nothing, apart from a big belly and a fat arse.

Johnno was in the pub busily tucking into a range of exotically named beers. Typically, he was not alone. Three younger men, all in business suits, and with a loud confidence that seemed like another layer of uniform, sat at the same table. My amateur jockey pal was clearly in full flow and had his school of acolytes laughing hysterically.

"Here he is, lads!" he boomed on spotting me. "The great Liam Dee. Let's hear it for the man who once beat me in a barefoot sprint down the main street of Killarney at four in the morning!"

"That was a long time ago. Before these lads can even remember," I said, smiling.

"Bollocks," said Johnno. "You sound like a maiden aunt and you look like a boiled shite. We're going to have to do something about that."

Which they did. I wanted to dislike Johnno's pals, but couldn't. They worked for him and clearly regarded him as some sort of role model. But although they were still young enough to indulge in hero worship, there was no mistaking the sharpness behind their big grins and loud voices. And no doubting their capacity for booze either.

"What's with this vodka?" one of them called Raymond asked me. "This is a beer place. You've got to have some."

In seconds, a foaming pint of some Czech lager that Johnno assured me was top-notch sat in front of me. Jack's deadline flashed up. To hell with the weight, I thought, and drank deeply. Johnno lifted his own glass in salute.

Clearly, Johnno's career as a jockey was of some fascination to his colleagues.

"What I don't get is how you do the starvation thing," no-nonsense Raymond asked after a couple of hours. "Parle is a butty little bastard, but you're taller than I am. You don't look like a jockey. You look normal."

"He does it by not eating anything. Simple as that," Johnno declared. "Other guys stuff their faces and then flip the lot up in the toilets. You always know them. The yellow teeth gives them away."

"And what do you do?" Raymond asked him.

Johnno picked up a new pint before answering and drank deeply. Half of it disappeared down his throat and he carefully placed the glass back on the table.

"Moderation, boys, in all matters. That's the secret. It's easy enough. You only have to remember one thing. The time to leave the table is when you're enjoying the meal. What you don't do is stay and make a pig of yourself. That screws everything up. Now, who's up for a trip to that pasta place across the road?"

I drew the line at guzzling the square metres of pizza which were presented to us just minutes later, but a decent glass of red wine took the edge off my hunger. Learning about my friend's other life didn't hurt either. Johnno could come across on the racecourse as a rather amiable buffoon – all jokes and bravado. Able enough on a horse, but not someone to take entirely seriously. In the real world, though, it was a different matter.

Even to a financial dumbbell like me, the stories of share issues and currency exchange being thrown around started to become vivid. Johnno lobbed in figures every now and again to put some perspective on the not-so-tall tales his protégés were spinning but the interchange would have been fascinating anyway. These boyish characters were dealing in millions every day, making decisions with percentage fractions that made or broke lives. And just because a few of them still retained a pimple here or there, I'd been ready to write them off. At work, Johnno clearly let them have more rein than he would have been prepared to give any of his horses, but somehow the stories kept coming back to him. The jockey-room joker ultimately was the one calling the shots: the man whose signature went at the bottom of the page. His judgement of money had to be at least matched by his judgement of people. My already high estimation of him rose even higher.

It was midnight before Johnno looked at his watch and announced the time. The reaction among the younger members at the table was so what? Why don't we head for a club? But their boss was not to be persuaded.

"I can't keep up with you youngsters," he grinned, looking as fresh as a daisy.

He pointed to me and gratefully I stood up, shaking hands with the others. They were a good bunch but the idea of clubbing was not on. Unlike Johnno, I knew I must have looked a little hairy: not drunk but not sober either.

He led the way to an ATM near the gates of Dublin Castle and I stood, hands stuffed into pockets, while he got out some cash. Nearby, a newsagent's was selling delicious-smelling coffee and we got some before starting to look for taxis.

"What happened to the back of your head?" Johnno asked.

"Just a fall."

"Yeah? Where'd it happen?"

"Can't remember," I lied. "Those are good blokes you've got working for you."

"They're okay. Subtle, they ain't. But bright lads. Whatever club they go to had better watch out."

"Why aren't you going?"

"Me? I'm too bloody old to be chasing young ones round a dance floor, screeching into their ears about shite."

"You're breaking my heart."

"Piss off. Anyway, what are you having a go at me for? Is it by some chance because you're secure in the gorgeous Lara?"

"Who told you?"

"Bailey mentioned something. I admire your taste, you lucky bastard. Don't know what she sees in you."

"She doesn't either."

"Ah, it's that way."

"What else did Bailey say?"

"Don't miss much, do you? Just that you might be having a few problems. She's concerned, that's all."

"And what's your opinion?" I said, the booze making me stroppy.

"Whoa there. Take a pull. She said you might rear up."

With anyone else, I probably would have, but Johnno was a good guy who was obviously trying to be helpful.

"Sorry. Listen, it was a real good night. I enjoyed it."

"If I can help at all, just ring."

He gave me a tap on the shoulder and jumped into a cab that had just stopped in front of us. A big grin was the last I saw as the car drove away.

It had been some time since I'd last swayed through the city centre at night. Dame Street was still bustling with people, just as it had been years before when a weekend didn't go by without some excuse for hitting town. I found myself fervently hoping I had been a bit more fun then. Rain started to fall and everyone's pace quickened. The nearest taxi rank was a couple of hundred yards ahead in front of Trinity and already a long line had formed. Some things never change, whatever the mood. So, instead, I turned right hoping to flag down a stray cab on its way back.

Out of habit I walked a couple of hundred yards before stopping. One of the city's most famous gay bars was then behind me and a ridiculous childish fear that someone might think I was coming out of there had always made me walk faster past it. There had even been times when the brave jockey had crossed the road, to my shame. Nevertheless, curiosity made me glance back down the street while waving uselessly at taxi-drivers who suddenly seemed to have lost the ability to look to their left.

Two men emerged from under the canopy at the front of the bar and stood in the rain, arms around each other, kissing deeply. Passers-by hardly seemed to notice. If anyone cared in any way about this very public display, they disguised it well. Stupid childish concerns about appearances were evidently the preserve of morons and hungry jockeys. Good on them, I thought, looking back one more time.

The larger of the two had his back to me but there was

something about the way he was leaning over his partner, and the angle of his back, that looked familiar. Unsure, I ignored a passing taxi, stepped closer to the shop-front behind me, and concentrated on the scene. The other guy looked very young, a teenager almost. He was slightly built and seemed almost fragile compared to the man kissing him.

They broke off and spoke briefly. Still the big man had his back to me: massive shoulders practically bursting out of his black jacket. Where did I know him from? Must have been the races. Except how many obviously gay men did I know from the racetrack? It was ridiculous to believe every single person in the racing game was straight, no matter in what context you used the word. No matter how hale and hearty the whole thing might be, it wasn't that divorced from the realities of the world. But no one came to mind. Sure, there were a number of characters whose names provoked the usual sniggering innuendos, but there wasn't one person I could think of who was uncomplicatedly and straight-forwardly gay. The worlds just didn't seem to overlap.

The rain got heavier and provoked some late-night stragglers into running for shelter. It even seemed to break the spell in front of me. The young guy started laughing and grabbed his partner's hand. They made to cross the road but the line of traffic idling at the lights suddenly got a green and started to move. None was prepared to allow anyone across and the big man reacted with a flurry of arms and some obvious abuse. Even then, I didn't fully recognise him. The cars continued to pass until the lights eventually turned red and the two of them squeezed between bumpers and ran to the other footpath. Once there, the younger man turned left but his companion swung around to deliver one final volley at the stream of traffic.

That familiar face was contorted into a mixture of anger and exhilaration, raging at the world that got in his way and yet thrilled at what it might give. His whole being seemed alive with lust, discarded anxiety and whatever he'd used to wash it all down. His normally curly hair was drenched into a flat black cap that sent rain streaming down his cheeks. In the reflected street lights, and the beams from oncoming cars, the effect was of some mythical figure railing at everything and relishing the conflict. Rarely had I ever seen anyone so alive. But then I'd always felt a little inadequate next to Franco Hoy.

27

I started running. Not to escape, or hide, but because too much was happening to stay still. Another primal urge – this time to move and indulge in the physical – took over. Only then could I hope to rein in my mind enough to make sense of it all. No doubt the pissed-up revellers in O'Connell Street and Dorset Street were amused at the figure hurtling past them, splashing his way between road and pavement, but none of it registered. For once, all I wanted was to run and sweat and think. Before long, I'd reached the Cat & Cage pub in Drumcondra and the start of the long climb towards Glasnevin.

It fitted. Franco could have met Anatoly at any time. He was always around the yard, waiting for Charlotte, arriving for dinner, turning up his nose. No one ever really registered him because he wasn't working. But the fact he knew nothing about horses, and cared even less, didn't mean his eyes and ears were closed. Who knew how much information someone could pick up just from hanging around? How hard would it be for him to identify and seduce some lonely youngster thousands of miles from home and desperate for some warmth and affection?

It must have been so easy. This brooding artist, looking as he did, and being so close to the boss, must have seemed almost godlike to the young Ukrainian. I'd heard that Franco could charm but it wasn't a side I'd seen myself. Apparently, it was reserved for the good-looking, the rich and the well-connected. But that was Bailey's bias. Either way, Anatoly could hardly have been much of a challenge. A kid aware of his sexuality but at the same time unsure of it: how attractive Franco's confidence must have been. And then there would have been the secrecy. How intoxicating to know something so significant about someone so strong. The conspiracy could only have brought them closer. Against the world. Enough maybe to make a young man believe that he had found something very special indeed.

Of course I could prove nothing, but coincidences like this simply didn't happen. I searched for my phone and only then remembered why its tinny ring hadn't interfered with the whole evening. It was back at Jack's. I'd left it there charging. A couple walking by were treated to some sudden heartfelt swearing. The one time the thing was out of my grasp was the one time I really needed it. Yeats' number was programmed in. I turned around, looking for a taxi and practically jumped in front of the first one going by. The driver took a look at the sweating, breathless figure and thankfully figured the risk was worthwhile.

There really are no surprises when it comes to what gets people off, I figured on the drive back to Jack's; no presumptions either. Sex might stare at us from every-where, but the urge to disguise and lie about it was still as strong as ever. Maybe it was an essential part of the thrill.

The idea of a married man having sex with another man didn't matter a damn. There was far darker stuff going on in the world than two consensual adults having sex with each other. But what was the impact of this revelation going to be on those closest to Franco when it got out? A young man was dead, killed because of rage or jealousy or fear, it didn't matter. What mattered was justice. But the aftershock of pursuing that justice would resonate so much wider than simply punishing Franco, if he were guilty. His wife would be destroyed, her life exposed as a sham. Charlotte might be silly, but no kind of stupidity deserved that. And how would Bailey react? The murder had shaken her to the core. Would even a woman as resilient as her be able to take such a hit?

As the taxi turned into Jack's estate, a part of me suddenly wanted very badly not to reach my phone. Maybe it was the last lingering effects of the booze, but the idea of sparing innocent people so much grief seemed pretty worthwhile. Franco doing time wouldn't bring Anatoly back and more families would be destroyed if he did end up behind bars. Why put everyone through it? But the thought died quietly. How much more of a betrayal would that be? Who was I to make the judgement? Thankfully, that buck could be passed.

The television was still on but I made straight for my room, fervently praying Yeats was still up too, or at least wasn't a heavy sleeper. Eventually a voice murmured hello. The man sounded like he was still dragging himself into a sitting position in bed.

"Mr Dee, you'd better not be drunk."

"That doesn't matter," I said and told him what I'd seen.

Even from forty miles away, it felt as if I could hear Yeats' brain whirring with the effort of forming an opinion of this new information being thrown at him. Eventually he ventured one.

"It means nothing."

"No, it proves nothing," I replied. "It means a lot."

"Do you know where he is now?"

"No. He could be anywhere. But I have a mobile number for him. It's on my phone."

"Mr Dee, I knew I picked you for a reason. Do you know where Store Street Garda Station is? Meet me there in an hour and a half. Then we'll see if you can be useful again."

I hung up, sat on the bed and wondered how to fill the time until Yeats could get to Dublin. There was no point ringing anyone. They'd all be asleep and what was I going to say? By the way, guess what I saw tonight? Downstairs the television was still humming. Jack might be still up, but talking about rides at Downpatrick was not really a contender for my concentration.

Against the odds, an uneasy doze took over, full of dreams of wrenches and blood and banishing monsters to places so far away they could never reach me. Even unconscious, the idea of having spent an hour sitting and chatting to Franco was enough to make me sweat. What had been the odds of a traffic jam on the drive up from the Curragh? Normally, nothing resembling that tail-back would have been there. Certainly nothing to prevent us making that turn-off and stopping at a derelict building that no one ever went near. What had that been all about? Would I have met the same fate as Anatoly? He and Franco would have been a horrible mismatch in terms of aggression and power. Would I have been able to fight Franco off? The 'what if' questions kept piling in remorselessly until, by a supreme effort, I managed to control my rampaging thoughts.

It was a relief to eventually stand up again and leave.

Yeats was waiting at the front desk and barely nodded before turning and leading me down a warren of corridors to what looked like an interview room. A large desk was laden with recording equipment and there were seats tucked in underneath. Apart from that, the place was empty.

"We shouldn't be bothered in here," he said. "How do you have Mr Hoy's number?"

"Charlotte gave it to me at some stage. She was using his phone at the races one day."

"Okay, let's get on with it. Tell him you need to see him. Urgently."

"For what?"

"I don't know. Just arrange a time and a place and we'll meet him there."

"Jesus!"

Yeats looked at me carefully.

"This is purely in order for us to talk to Mr Hoy. If we can manage to make contact with him in as low-key a manner as possible, that will be best for everyone. There's no question of running him down with lights flashing and sirens blaring. We're just going to ask him to help us with our enquiries."

Yeats knew better than anyone what that apparently neutral phrase really meant, but he was also right about wanting to avoid dramatics. I pressed the button and heard the phone ring in. No reply – just an answer machine.

"Try again," Yeats said.

Again there was no answer. It rang off. I looked up.

"Maybe we should find out if it's changed," I said.

"Just give it another go."

Not until I was expecting to hear the message greeting again did the line rustle into life. Despite the sleep still clearing from it, Franco's voice was unmistakable.

"Hello?"

Even half-asleep, the words were full of attitude.

"Hello, Franco – it's Liam Dee. Sorry for disturbing you."

There was a long pause while he registered my name. In the background I thought I heard a rustling sound and someone being shushed. I waited for the explosion.

"What do you want?"

"I'm sorry, Franco. I know it's the middle of the night."

"What time is it?"

"It's late. Are you still in Dublin?"

"What are you doing ringing me? Yes, I'm still in Dublin. What do you want?"

"I need to speak to you. It's important."

"What about?"

"I'd rather not say. I need to speak to you, man to man. It's a little delicate."

I sensed it was on the tip of his tongue to inform me that he had far more important things to do than meeting up with his mother-in-law's bloody jockey. His exasperation fairly crackled into my ear. Nothing was said for what seemed like a very long time. But then he sighed heavily and came up with a time and a place.

"I'm staying in the south side of the city. There's a pub near here: the Yellow House. You know it?"

"Yeah, I know it."

"It's easier to meet outside that than worry about all the traffic in town. But in the morning!"

"Okay."

We agreed a time and he hung up, all patience exhausted. I looked at my watch. In a few hours the fan was going to be hit big-time. And if I was going to be of any use to anyone, it wasn't here.

"Inspector, I think I'll head down to the Curragh. See if I can be of any help."

"It might be best for everyone concerned if you didn't mention anything about what you saw tonight. It's irrelevant to the case in any concrete sense and I wouldn't like it to cloud the matters we have to pursue. It might also be advisable for your own sake to say nothing."

"But can't I say something to prepare Bailey and Charlotte for the shock?"

"Say nothing. Not even if I phone to inform them. I won't mention you."

He shrugged and then almost tentatively reached over the table to shake hands.

"I realise you must have mixed emotions, being so close to Mrs McFarlane and her daughter, but you've been a big help. Thank you. Basically, this will be an exercise in eliminating another name from the list of suspects. There's no presumption in any of this."

"Yeah?" I smiled ruefully. "Then why are we here?"

On the drive out of town and on to the motorway I tried to imagine what was about to explode. But it was impossible. No one's imagination could encompass the range of emotions that would course through so many people. Just before five o'clock, I pulled in to the side of the road and switched the engine off. The flat green plain of the Curragh was hidden in the darkness, not like that night when I'd crashed and all this horror began. During summers when I first came to the Curragh, I used to love spending afternoons lying in the middle of the bare expanse, reading and listening to the animals grazing. The sound of them tearing at the earth was so peaceful. And the more used they got to the weirdo human amongst them, the closer they ventured. Sometimes they nibbled their way to within feet and, if I stayed completely still, they lay down close enough for me to hear them chewing the cud, moving grass from stomach to stomach and eating all over again. Better times than this.

28

There was barely a sound in the house. Even the old heating pipes which normally gurgled and rattled were resolutely keeping their peace. Outside, second lot were still on the gallops and Vaz and the others were mucking out at the top of the yard. Only the occasional laugh and the loud scrape of a shovel made it down to the house.

Charlotte sat at the kitchen table, waiting for Bailey, staring into whatever private painful vision had been conjured up by this new information thrown at her. She hadn't moved since I'd arrived. The face that normally pouted and prattled was unreadable, frozen into a blank canvas. I didn't know what to say so we sat and waited for her mother.

Bailey's arrival filled the silent vacuum. Presented with a solvable problem, the big woman always seemed to get even bigger with her determination to fix things. There was little doubt from her purposeful march into the kitchen that she believed this too was something that needed only some well-applied common sense.

"Come on, girl," she commanded, practically lifting Charlotte out of her chair. "No moping. This will be sorted out in no time. Don't worry."

Easy for you to say, I thought, and felt more than a touch of sympathy for her daughter. Bailey's attitude to Franco was ambivalent at the best of times. Maybe a part of her was almost happy to see that suspicion and unease confirmed. Now she could set to work protecting her daughter. It could hardly have been more different for Charlotte. Franco was her pick, the ultimate test of her judgement, the one she was supposed to know best of all. And now she was going to a police station in Newbridge to cope with the fallout of something she could hardly have even guessed at.

"It's preposterous," Bailey proclaimed again. "My solicitor is on his way there and we'll fix everything up."

"Really?" Charlotte asked.

"Of course. This is just another police cock-up. Except, this time, someone's going to get a rocket up their arse. Will you mind the fort, Liam?"

"Sure."

On the way to the car, Bailey put an arm around Charlotte and reached across to brush some hair off her face in an achingly maternal gesture that had me cursing Franco all over again.

I wandered outside and felt an almost physical pull taking me towards the alley. The pristine bareness left behind by the forensics people was never going to remain, but it still felt wrong to see a shovel and a yard brush leaning against a wall. Some dead leaves had been blown into the alley by the strong wind and were now rustling around the discarded tools in never-ending circles. I picked up the brush and shovel and thought about placing them somewhere else. But it would have been a silly, meaningless gesture. Whoever had put them there hadn't done so with any disrespect. It was simply a sign of normality returning.

I opened the stable door and stood where Anatoly had died. I looked at the bare concrete of the floor, smoothed to a bright sheen by time and sleeping horses. It was bigger than a normal box, roomier, and there was an unexpected cosiness. The ceiling was quite low and the window gave it a homely feel. Despite the wind outside, there was a calm stillness as I looked around at what might have been a perfect place for two people to secretly love one another.

The yard came alive again as the horses returned, all clattering hooves and clanging tack, with Eamon shouting orders above the racket. I stepped outside. At the front, Lara slid off King Titus, who showed off his happiness with a little fly kick. His reward was a pat on the nose and a smile that reminded me once more what a jackass I had been.

Eamon was gliding from horse to horse listening to their breathing. Even from a distance I could see there were no tell-tale signs of hard blowing, but it was a ritual he liked to go through, like a parent wiping a child's face after the kid has come back from school.

I approached Eamon. "They look good," I said, nodding at the horses.

"Yeah. No problems. What are you doing here? Aren't you in Downpatrick today?"

"There's time. Bailey had to go somewhere."

"She told me. Any idea why?"

"No," I lied.

"The thing is, I was hoping to head off myself for an hour. I don't suppose . . ."

"Sure. I'll ride out next lot. It's not a problem."

"Good man. Owe you one."

I looked at my watch. It took just over two flat-out hours from the Curragh to get to my date with the scales. As long as nothing ran away with me up the gallops, I figured I would have enough time. Eamon pointed me to the veteran old handicapper he had looked after for years and I returned to the car for my gear.

Johnno wasn't around. Clearly the night before had taken more out of him than it appeared when I left him. I walked my horse out, got a leg up and waited for someone to pair off with.

It would be nice and neat to say the only one left was Lara, except it wouldn't be true. Maybe she had someone she liked to ride alongside. Most people did. But I saw that red jacket and clicked my horse up alongside her. She glanced to her left but said nothing. Neither did I. It just felt good to be close to her again. Nothing more and nothing less.

On the walk towards the gallops, there was the usual chat around us but I kept looking ahead and focusing on the horse. He had made the journey so many times before I could have been blindfolded and it would have made no difference. Yet I treated him like Patrician at the start of the Gold Cup, all concentration and attention to detail. Sure enough, the horse and I went through the motions on the gallop, moving easily alongside Lara and her horse. We pulled up and started the walk back, still together, and me afraid to say or do anything in case she told me to go away. It felt silly, in a holding-hands-going-to-school kind of way.

Whoever was leading decided to give the string a pick of grass and we dismounted in the large paddock next to the yard. As the horses reached down for the wet grass, Lara and I both stood, letting the reins hang loose and looking everywhere but where we wanted. No doubt there was much amusement from the others at the little drama being played out in front of them, but I didn't care. This was the closest I'd been to Lara in days and it was agonising.

"I'm sorry," I said quietly.

"I know."

"How have you been?"

"Okay. You?"

"I've been alright."

"You lie. You don't look alright."

There wasn't much to say to that, but the fact she was talking to me at all was progress. I wanted very much to reach out and touch her, tell her I loved her, because I had no doubt I did. The sight of her was enough to make me happy, anxious, scared and every other emotion the damn books and films said I was supposed to feel. If it wasn't so desperately real, the whole thing could be corn on a cob.

"I don't deserve another chance, but if you gave me one, I would make you so happy."

The only sound around us was that of the horses tearing at the grass and the faint murmur of a jet thousands of feet above us.

When I'd been six, my dad patiently made me look up while he explained that the plane was the little bit at the front of the smoke: no one was sitting in the white stuff billowing puffily behind it. There's nowhere to sit, he'd said. No one can hang in mid-air. For quite a long time afterwards I'd dreamed of hanging in thick smoke and then falling thousands of feet. It felt like that now.

Lara didn't move for some time. She looked at her horse, who took a break from eating to stretch a long neck towards her face and breathe heavily down his nostrils. That got a smile.

"Promise?" she asked, turning towards me.

"Oh, I promise."

We held hands. It might not sound much, but the feeling right then beat any sexual gymnastics. This ridiculously beautiful woman was willing to give me another chance. From somewhere behind us, a voice told everyone to take the horses back into the yard. It was all I could do to let go, gather the reins and lift my reluctant partner's head from the ground.

"It'll be lunchtime soon," I said as we brought up the rear of the string.

"Don't you have to go to the races?"

The phone was in my jacket pocket. Jack's number was tattooed on my brain and he picked up almost immediately.

"Was that you tearing out the door in the wee hours?" he asked.

"Yeah. Sorry about that. I didn't mean to wake you."

"Are you alright? Had you a good night?"

It seemed like a week ago already, but I assured him I had. Even speaking, I was aware of the happiness in my voice. He picked up on it too.

"Certainly sounds like it," he said.

"Look, Jack. Can you get on to those trainers and tell them I can't make it to Downpatrick?"

"I suppose so. Is everything alright?"

"Everything's fine. Better than fine. But there's no point pretending I don't need to sort out this weight. It wouldn't be any good today."

"So what shall I tell them?"

"Tell them the truth: my weight isn't right."

"Are you sure?"

"Yes, I'm sure. Thanks, Jack."

I hung up and quickly got my oar in before Lara could speak.

"I know I didn't have to do that, and, no, it was not some stupid gesture for your benefit," I said. "If anything, it was for my benefit."

We walked back to the yard and I gave her hand one more squeeze. When I turned away, she pulled me back and kissed me lightly on the lips. Not surprisingly, that provoked mickey-taking from some of the lads but it didn't matter a damn. If anything, Lara walked her horse back to the box with something of a swagger. Just the sight was enough for me to forget my earlier feelings of more courtly love.

"Hey, Liam!"

I looked over and Vaz was grinning broadly and delivering me a thumbs-up. There was nothing else for it but to shrug, smile and wave back.

I led the horse back into his box, closed the door and leaned my head on his back.

29

Later that evening, I told her about Franco. We were in Mrs O'Sullivan's front room, lying on the couch, watching television but hearing only ourselves. The old lady was away for a few days visiting relatives. We had come back after work and taken advantage. It felt wonderful and right and I told Lara what I'd never said to anyone before. Amazingly, she even said it back. After everything that had happened, it was all ridiculously simple.

In the circumstances there was no other option but to tell her what was still happening just a couple of miles away in the police station. We sat up, me in boxer shorts, her in a T-shirt, and went through everything. She shivered at the idea of the young man the night before looking like Anatoly but there were no tears and no signs of anger at the possibility it had been Franco. I told her I was sorry but she simply put her face close to mine and whispered that she hoped it would all be over soon.

"I dreamed of Anatoly last night," she said later. "On the plane he kept saying how unfair it was that we had to leave home. He kept saying it over and over. Such a childish thing to believe – fair and unfair. He should have got the time to find that out for himself. Everyone deserves that."

We held each other in silence for some time until Lara disentangled herself and went to make coffee. As the sounds came from the kitchen, I wondered about what Bailey and Charlotte were going through. Any guilt I'd felt earlier was gone. Franco was putting them through a terrible emotional wringer, but time would help heal the wounds. The time Anatoly would never get. That he deserved. I pulled myself up for presuming that Franco was guilty.

Bailey had appeared in the yard while we were working at evening stables. Her Mercedes had pulled up, but she went straight into the house and didn't come back out. I was walking towards the car a little later when she re-emerged and threw me a sketchy salute before climbing back in and driving away. The look on her face was enough to tell me that all her morning bounce had disappeared.

"You should ring Mrs McFarlane and find out if she is okay," said Lara, returning with the coffee. "The poor woman must be upset. Mrs Hoy as well."

Of course she was right. Bailey needed support now more than ever, but I didn't want to ring in the middle of something and add to her stress, so I texted to see if it was alright to get in touch.

It was much later before a text reply came. The phone flashed Bailey's name and the message was short and sweet: "C u skool."

She was some woman. Franco might be dragging the family through the mire, but no way was Bailey McFarlane going to allow that to change her tack. I told Lara, who merely nodded as if expecting nothing else.

We had turned off the TV and made for the stairs when

my mobile rang again. It wasn't a number I recognised but something made me answer. Yeats' sing-song accent was at the other end and wasted little time on pleasantries.

"I figured I'd better keep you informed. Are you back in Dublin?"

"No. I'm in Mrs O'Sullivan's."

"Are you now? Things rosier in the garden again?"

"A bit. What's happening?"

"Alright. A visit to your gay bar confirmed that Mr Hoy has been seen there on several occasions with Anatoly – and in compromising positions, shall we say. It's still a stretch but, on the basis that he concealed the relationship, Mr Hoy will continue to assist us with our enquiries. We can hold him for forty-eight hours before deciding if we're going to charge him or not."

"And you're going to use that time to build up a forensics case against him."

"Very impressive, Mr Dee. You have been paying attention."

Yeats was positively chipper. His accent happily dipped and rose. Clearly, the pressure to come up with a result had been significant. Released stress gushed down the phone.

"It's going to be tight. Even with every string pulled, it'll still be a squeeze to get reports back in time," he said.

Lara looked down from the top of the stairs. I mouthed the word 'Yeats' and she nodded seriously. The policeman might have been feeling the joys of spring, but an arrest was the end for him. To many other people it was simply the end of a chapter.

"How's Franco reacting?" I asked.

"Very calmly. When we picked him up, he didn't provide any resistance. He just got into the car and came with us. There wasn't a word out of him until we all sat down and he asked to ring his wife and organise a solicitor. It was all very restrained. Not once has he raised his voice. I thought fireworks were guaranteed, that he'd simply get up and leave. But he's not stupid. He'd twigged even before his lawyer came that refusing to co-operate would look bad for him. So he simply sat there, waited for his solicitor and then played everything we threw at him with a straight bat."

"In what way?"

"He maintains that he might have met Mr Ignatieff at some stage but honestly can't remember. The whole horse game is a mystery to him, he says, and the only contact he has with it is through his wife and mother-in-law. We asked him about his knowledge of the stables and he said he had no interest and kept out of it. When I asked about the wall, he said he knew nothing about it."

"And what about the sex thing?"

"There wasn't even a flinch. I asked him if he was gay or bisexual and all I got back was a shake of the head. No jumping up and down, no 'I'm a married man' sort of stuff. No shock and no surprise. Which from a legal point of view is the perfect response. But he was too cool for it not to be true. Even his lawyer was snorting and shaking his head. Not a word from the man himself though."

"But you're going to arrest him."

"I sure hope so. The forensics boys are at his house now, going over everything. We threw the attack on you at him too, though I'm inclined to think that was one of Wolf's henchmen, and he didn't even blink. He's a cool customer."

"Did you see Bailey and Charlotte?"

"Just briefly. I don't think either one of them wanted to talk to me, but they were around the station all day, I'm told."

"I'll head down and see if I can help them."

"One bit of advice. I know you're very close to them, but

270

it's funny how families stick together at times like this. Even good friends can feel as if they're intruding."

"Right. Thanks."

"And mind how you go when you do get here. There'll probably be some press people around."

"Already?"

"It's a fact of life. All it takes is a phone call. In fact, a snap of you heading into the station would be a pretty good night's work for them. Maybe you should stay away for a bit."

"Okay. Thanks for letting me know everything."

"It's no problem. Glad to see you and Ms Kuznetsov are back together. You look well, the pair of you."

I took a minute to digest what he'd told me and then tried to ring Bailey. Again, there was no answer. She was usually a stickler for the phone, hating the constant interruptions, but always promptly returning calls. Yeats seemed to be on the ball. Hardly surprising really. In the circumstances, how vulnerable would anyone feel, never mind a person whose face is widely known? The natural instinct would be to fall back on one's closest relatives. Charlotte might infuriate her mother but now they had to be strong for each other. I decided to try a final time later and sat down to wait for the television news.

Lara came back into the room just as the headlines were being announced. Sure enough, word had got out. Man arrested on suspicion of murder of Ukrainian stable lad, the announcer boomed. She joined me on the sofa and, while we waited, I told her that Yeats had established that Franco and Anatoly were lovers. I could see pain and pity in her eyes.

It wasn't long before the coverage switched to the police station less than a mile away from us. The reporter was standing almost at an angle to a rising wind that we could hear getting stronger outside. As he struggled to keep his microphone under control, I recognised another reporter passing behind him. It was one of those who had got as far as the front door before being politely told by me to get lost. I found myself hoping Bailey and Charlotte were out of there. My heading down wouldn't have been of much use to anyone.

What was said in the news report was pretty basic. No names and no hints at who it might be. Simply a thirty-nine-year-old man arrested on suspicion of murder. After that was a rehash. Anatoly Ignatieff, nineteen, Ukrainian, stable boy, murdered. A life parsed down to its minimum. I gave Lara's hand a squeeze as she stared grimly at the screen.

"I want to hate him," she said. "I do hate him. But I want to hate him more. I feel like I should be down there, standing outside, demanding justice. Letting the world know how this terrible monster killed my friend. But I only feel cold. Like someone watching all this from above."

"Don't worry about that. Yeats will make sure things are tied up," I said, squeezing her hand tighter. If they can be tied up, said a sceptical voice in my head.

"Thank God I was wrong about him. He is a good man, isn't he?"

"A lot better than most."

Yeats was allowing us to get on with our lives. No more hiding and no more looking over our shoulders. Even sitting there, watching other lives being trampled over, I found it impossible not to look into the future and feel the thrill of anticipation. All of it revolved around Lara. If there was one thing I was sure of, it was that nothing would come before her welfare.

"Has there been any word from Mrs Hoy?" Lara asked.

"I can't get her. She must have gone to ground, trying to cope with everything else that's happening."

"It is terrible for so many people."

"Yes, but nothing can be done about it tonight. Let's see what happens tomorrow."

30

I left Lara asleep and padded downstairs to get dressed. The central heating had only just come on so it was still cold as I put on jeans, boots and a bulky anorak. I needed them. The previous night's wind had turned into a full-blown gale. Outside, a couple of other early risers leaned forwards as they set off to work. Out on the Curragh, it would feel like a serious storm. Schooling on a morning like this didn't seem like a runner, but there hadn't been a peep from Bailey and it wouldn't do me any harm to see her.

In the nearby newsagent's, a brief survey of the papers revealed no screaming headlines about Franco and his famous mother-in-law. I bought a few tabloids which Yeats had told me went to press later than the others, but even they contained only a couple of paragraphs repeating what the television news had said. It was the same on the radio report I listened to on the short drive: no names and no details.

Minutes later, the line of schooling fences appeared in the distance. I drove past the racecourse stands at the Curragh, turned left and slowed down to bump the car onto the cropped grass. To the right was the railway line and a commuter train flashing past on its way to Dublin. No doubt it was packed with people and, for once, I envied them. They might be squeezed in like sardines but at least they were warm sardines. Outside, the gale had been joined for company by rain. There was no way we could risk the Gold Cup favourite in such conditions. But still I waited.

The Curragh looked very bleak, angry dark clouds seemingly pressing down on it. The racecourse stands were no more than a mile away, rearing up out of the ancient plain like some alien Pythonesque cartoon. Only for them, the scattered displays of white plastic railings and the gorse, the wind was tearing across the plain uninterrupted, as it had done for thousands of years.

Gorse grew all over the place here, the only plant hardy enough to thrive in the merciless open space. In some areas it got so tall and thick as to be impenetrable. Hundreds of square metres of thick green obstacles with billions of tiny sharp thorns ready to tear at anything, or anyone, silly enough to get too close. In summer, tiny yellow flowers did nothing to dilute the thorns' prickly threat. But even they weren't around now. Mythical stories of riders thrown from runaway horses into gorse banks taller than themselves were part of Curragh folklore.

Just in front of me, a good acre of gorse looked to be thriving. Parts had grown to at least a couple of metres tall and were thick enough to resist any hurricane. It was something to shelter behind and I suddenly needed a pee. I got out and ran around the green bank, scuttling out of the gale.

Normally, the real early-bird workers would be pounding their way around the nearby sand gallops, but there wasn't a horse or a person to be seen. Hardly surprising in the weather. There was a chill to the wind that I hadn't expected. Combined with the rain, it made the morning thoroughly miserable. I checked for the phone, but realised I'd forgotten it again. A quick look in the general direction of Bailey's revealed nothing. There was no sign of the distinctive maroon horse box motoring over the bridge that crossed the railway line. I could think of better ways of spending a morning. Tucked up next to Lara for one.

I gazed around and felt the vastness of the place. It was unusual for it to be so silent. Normally, there were shouts and yells from work riders competing with the racket of jeeps and machinery. But the army base a few miles away could have ignited its ammunition dump and not be heard over the din of wind and rain. I started to dash back to the car. Only then did I spot the large 4x4 purring towards me.

Tinted windows blanked out whoever was driving. Usually, people rattled around the Curragh in jalopies that had a lot more mileage. The pristine bottle-green jeep slowly approaching didn't look to have had too many wet saddles and bags of horse-nuts thrown into the back of it. No more than ten metres away, the car stopped but the motor was still running. Soaked anyway, I figured there wasn't much chance of getting any wetter. I started towards the jeep to see if someone was lost.

It came straight at me. The engine whined into life and the back wheels skidded momentarily which gave me a vital split second to move. Over such a short distance, there was no chance of it reaching top speed, but enough was generated to send me diving to the left.

Even in mid-air, there was time to register disbelief at what was happening. The guy's foot must have slipped, an idiotic accident caused by some rich kid with too much money and not enough sense. There were enough of them around. It was stretching credulity to think anything else. One attempt at killing me was enough for a week – for a lifetime. All of which took a split second to process, by which time the steel bull-bar in front of the jeep had caught my leg as I jumped out of the way.

Automatically, on hitting the ground, I tucked my body and rolled into a ball. Momentarily face down in the waterlogged grass, a memory flash from the front of Mrs O'Sullivan's house just days before overcame my senses. It provoked the first real sense of fear. But that was quickly replaced by agony. I tried to stand up but couldn't. A searing pain shot up my left leg. The automatic instinct was to lie back down in the wet grass, but no ambulance crew was coming this time. No gentle hands and no soothing voices reassuring me that everything would be back to normal soon.

I hauled myself into a half-sitting, half-lying position, and examined my leg. It didn't look broken. No grotesquely angled bone was sticking out, but reaching down to touch the ankle was enough to send another spasm shooting through me. It was all I could do not to shout out with the pain. Only by staying completely still did it stop. Maybe because I was concentrating so hard on that, or because of the wind banishing every other sound, it was only then that I turned and saw the driver approaching on foot. Relief poured over me like the rain.

"Charlotte! What the hell are you doing with that damn tank?"

She stood and stared at me, her eyes taking in the injured leg. Not a flicker of emotion betrayed itself on her face. The normal blue-eyed effervescent approach to the world might have belonged to someone else. She looked a different person.

That blonde hair was pulled back and hidden under a black cap. Her normally fashionable clothes had been replaced by Wellington boots, old jeans and a faded oilskin jacket. But they were incidentals. Despite the pain and the shock and the cold, I could only stare mutely at her. There was a taut coldness to her that had nothing to do with a lack of make-up or the stress of the last twenty-four hours. Every movement, from leaning down quickly to look at my leg, to turning around to see if anyone was passing nearby, had an inevitability that chilled me more than any wind. She looked like someone with a distasteful job to do and determined to get it out of the way as quickly as possible. Like a vet about to put something out of its misery.

"What's going on?" I asked shakily.

Charlotte didn't even look. Instead, she turned around and walked back to the jeep. No other cars were in the vicinity. Not that it mattered. We were so far in from the road that it would take a minor miracle for someone to see us. I tried to turn, swearing at the pain, but still there was no one on the gallops. Far away, another train belted past, this time on its way south. It might as well have been on the moon.

"Charlotte, what are you doing?" I shouted.

She said nothing as she sat in and started the engine. The white reverse lights pierced through the gloom.

Those lights, and the sight of that big machine spinning and skidding towards me, provoked a terror that no horse or fence had ever come close to. All I knew at that moment was that I didn't want to die, and I wasn't going to just lie there and wait for it to happen.

The gorse was no more than five metres away. With the engine's whine closing rapidly, I scrambled frantically towards that vast bank of green thorns. The pain in my leg was terrible, but nothing compared to the fear. An old rusty Coke can lying on the ground under one of the thick bushes provided a little chink of colour. I kept my eye on it and ignored my protesting leg. Not once did I look back. The sound of the squealing engine was enough. I plunged, groaning with fear and pain, into the middle of the gorse, closing my eyes.

The jeep missed by inches. It went past my feet at a speed I wouldn't have thought possible in reverse gear. The pain from my leg and from the gorse needles was irrelevant. The only thing that mattered was getting out of the way. I tucked myself into my thorny prison and tried to think what to do next.

Charlotte skidded backwards on the mud but quickly got the big vehicle back under control. Again the engine whined, and again I turned and pushed into my green cage. Every stem and branch got thicker until there was no point pretending to crawl anywhere. The only way to make progress was to try and tear through with my hands and shove with my head and shoulders. Suddenly I could feel the hot blast of the jeep's engine. Turning around and throwing myself backwards in a last attempt at making a few precious inches, I watched the massive machine plough through the gorse until its front wheels couldn't advance any more and they started to rise on to the heavy vegetation. Looking up, I could see the wheels spinning just inches from my face. If gravity won out, it would flatten the life out of me. Once more, I closed my eyes and waited for the impact.

But it didn't come. The heat and the stench were terrible, but death stayed a few precious inches away. I braced myself for the end. The noise of the revving and the fumes spewing out of the exhaust were enough to create my very own hell. There wasn't time for regrets or visions of my life flashing before my eyes. There was no time for anything.

However, when it dawned that all the revving in the world wasn't going to work, I turned and ploughed on, tearing and breaking my way through the thick stems and branches. It was a desperate struggle. Despite keeping my face down as much as possible, blood started to pour into my eyes. My clothing was quickly ripped and my hands turned into raw pulp. But I kept going, and anger helped me for the first time.

I embraced the anger, wrapping it around me like a shield. That bitch was not going to kill me! She hadn't managed it before and I would not allow it now. Charlotte of all people was the one who'd hit me outside Mrs O'Sullivan's, I realised, wiping blood out of my eyes. Franco's power would have finished me there and then, but his wife would have had to reach up to make contact. That would have diluted the blow enough to allow me get away with it. I would get away with it now too, I promised myself, reaching up my blood-covered hands to attack another bank of thorny branches.

31

Charlotte stared into the gorse, hands stuffed into her pockets, looking like someone impatiently waiting for a wayward dog to emerge from chasing a rabbit. Maybe it was a pose for anyone watching, but I doubted it. There wasn't an iota of stress in the matter-of-fact way she walked round to the back of the jeep and then laughed. She returned carrying a large can.

"What a stroke of luck. I'm minding my friend's car while she's on holidays and she's such a ditz her husband insists on her having a can of petrol in the car in case she runs out. What do you think, Liam? Will I be able to start a fire in this rain? Keep us warm?"

I didn't doubt it for a second, but said nothing. Exhausted, I lay twisted inside my sanctuary, looking out at her. It felt as if I'd been struggling for miles. In fact I'd made only about five metres, but it was enough. When she had given up on ramming the jeep into the gorse, there was a farcical moment when she had peered into the twisted jungle and our eyes locked. We'd stared at each other. Again, her face betrayed nothing but a mild bemusement that her job wasn't finished. If she could see anything in mine, past all the blood, she didn't react. It was stalemate, until she remembered the petrol.

"You don't really think I'm going to sit back and watch everything that's mine just vanish, do you, Liam? I know you're a jockey, but you can't be that thick."

She was hauling out sheets and blankets from the jeep while casually informing me of her plans, the way someone might talk about their upcoming holidays. If it wasn't so deadly, the whole thing would be ridiculous. Where the hell was everybody? It felt as if I was sitting at the edge of the world. Sure, the weather was bad, but had the Curragh turned into a finishing school all of a sudden? I thought of shouting for help, but quickly dismissed the idea. Even if someone was passing by, it would take a miracle to make out my cries in the wind. Yet, more importantly, shouting would be an acknowledgement of my fear. And, more than anything, I needed to be in some sort of control. For morale's sake, any thoughts of someone riding to the rescue had to be dismissed. I was going to have to get myself out of this.

Now that I wasn't moving, my leg was protesting more than ever at the rough treatment it was receiving. My ankle was seriously damaged, almost definitely broken. I didn't like the idea of looking at the rest of me. My trousers and jacket were cut to ribbons but, at least, still provided some sort of cover. It was my head and hands that were taking the brunt, and blood flooded down my wrists when I raised a hand to wipe my face. Bits of thorn were embedded in my skin, angrily digging deeper every time I moved.

"It's been a nice try, Liam. Just not very subtle. My idiot husband agrees to meet you and the police are waiting? And they just happen to ask him if he's queer? Wow, what a hard one to work out! How did you find out? Did you see him? In some alley? The big tough man getting his rocks off with another pretty boy?"

I said nothing. Charlotte was separating the lighter sheets from the heavy blankets and tearing them into pieces. She may as well have been laying a table. The easy explanation would have been to dismiss this normally annoying but harmless woman as unhinged, but not for one second did I believe that. If anything, she behaved with a calm competence that I wouldn't have believed possible from her.

"Not talking? I can understand that. It must be galling to come so close to getting your hands on everything – my mother, her money, the stables. Burrowing into her life like that, to rob me of everything that should be mine, and now having it all snatched away. I can understand that only too well."

She began stuffing lengths of thin fabric into the bushes, wedging them in so there was no danger that they would fall down.

"It's my own stupidity too, of course. I should have picked a better man to marry. Maybe even you, Liam. We got on okay for a little while, didn't we? It would have been perfect, especially for Mummy. Except you would have got tiresome about the whole sex thing. Typical man, led through life by your dick. Just look at the hoops that silly tart Lara is putting you through. Personally, it's not something I care for. Never have. Which is why Franco looked to be perfect."

Up to then, she had ignored the heavy blankets, but now they were being dragged to the gorse and piled into a heap against it. Only when they were all in place did she turn to the heavy can of petrol.

Charlotte tipped the can over them and the acrid smell of

petrol carried immediately to my nose as it gulped quickly out of the can.

"He's a fine man to look at – Franco. When I brought him home to Mummy, she practically swooned. And all he was interested in was his art. Or so I thought. We tried it once, you know. Not very pleasant, but Franco said it didn't matter. We were good enough together without that. I cried when he told me, Liam. I really did. It was the perfect answer.

"Did you know, Liam, that my brother hasn't been home in ten years? In that time, he has barely spoken to Mummy. He didn't have any interest in the yard, you see – said he wanted nothing to do with horses. He's a banker now, lives in Singapore. I see him every so often if he travels to Europe, but Mummy hardly even mentions his name. And, in that time, all I've ever heard about is the yard, and what it means to be a McFarlane, and how family is the only thing that matters. You've heard her, Liam: the only immortality is through children. How do you think my mother would have reacted to her son-in-law screwing the male help?"

Jesus Christ, I thought, as Charlotte reached into her pocket and pulled out a lighter. One final strip of rag was soaked in petrol and then she set fire to it.

"The little shit was black-mailing us, Liam. Saying he loved Franco, for God's sake. My wonderful husband would stick it into anything. He can't help it. He's got the morals and the self-control of an alley cat. And then your little pal started putting the bite on us for money. You know the score. Eventually the money wouldn't be good enough and he'd start to talk. I had no choice. Just like now."

The pile went up in flames with a whoosh that seemed to pull the air out of my lungs. Anger returned with a vengeance. I refused to be killed. This malevolent bitch could find some other victim. Desperately, I turned around, feeling every new tear and stab, but trying to focus on getting out of there. The flames grabbed hold of the gorse and, despite the rain, started to spread quickly. Already the sound of the blaze was turning my stomach. Twisting and turning, I tried to batter my way out, but my strength was weakening. I couldn't move through much more of it. Going back was impossible. The flames were spreading faster than I could have imagined. Dear God, I prayed, don't let me burn!

Charlotte climbed into her jeep and sped off in a flurry of mud and screeching gears. It was all I could do not to scream with terror. The idea of being alone somehow made it even worse. It didn't matter how illogical that was. Logic is irrelevant in the face of raw instinct. I did not want to die alone. Except some little bit of me refused to dissolve completely. Suddenly the gorse started to thin out a little. There was even some daylight making it through from the other side. It wasn't much, but it was something to cling to. I put every remaining ounce of strength into a final assault. My shoulders strained and my bloody hands tore at the tough branches and somehow enough of a gap appeared to squeeze my head through. It was enough. Some more desperate lunges got my shoulders out and I crawled into open space.

It was a mechanic's nightmare, a place where generations of old machines sat rusting conveniently out of sight. Discarded machinery was strewn everywhere. I'd forgotten about it because the whole reason it had become something of a dump for the Curragh in the first place was precisely because it was hidden away. A large roller sat in front of me and, just a few metres away, was an old-fashioned combine that must have been at least fifty years old. Large clumps of hardy grass grew around these masses of rust. I lay on the hard wet ground and wondered if I'd ever been happier to see anything. This little half-acre courtyard of decay was surrounded by gorse, except for a gap to the left that was big enough to accommodate any periodic new arrivals to this engine graveyard.

Behind me the fire roared despite the even heavier rain. Nothing could stop the bushes being engulfed in flames. Thick black smoke didn't get the chance to rise and instead was taken immediately by the wind in the direction of the huge stands which still managed to peep over the top of the green horizon. Someone would see the smoke and the fire and come to investigate. All I needed to do was sit tight and try to stay as warm as possible. At the same time as that little glimpse of hope appeared, Charlotte drove through the entrance.

Maybe all the terror had been squeezed out by the fire and the desperate crawling escape, but a strange resignation was all I felt as the huge machine teased its way towards me. There was no chance of getting away. The leg had got tired of feeling pain and switched to a numb ache. Even if I could drag myself again, there was nowhere for me to go. She was in no rush to finish the job. Instead, she watched the bloody, broken mess in front of her and waited.

"Come on, you bitch!" I screamed. "Finish it!"

My voice sounded like someone else's. There were no noble last thoughts, no last moment of peace and acceptance. The only taste in my mouth was of bitterness and regret.

"Come on!" I shouted once more.

She reacted to that. The powerful engine gunned into life and I braced myself. Let it be quick, I prayed. The engine roared once more and jumped forward. Except not at me.

It turned in an arc, spraying mud and stones everywhere. One sharp pebble smacked off my eye. In the second it took to shake the sting away, Charlotte had turned the jeep around and was making for the entrance. There were no white lights this time.

Only when it had disappeared did I register the sound of another engine, lighter and less powerful. A car slowly drove past the opening, sliding slightly in the mud. For a second, I thought it had gone too, but then it returned and accelerated onto the hard stony ground. The doors opened and Yeats was running towards me. Then I heard Lara.

"Oh God, no! Liam!"

I tried to pull myself up but it was useless. Instead, Yeats put his hand on my shoulder and told me to remain still. Happy to oblige, I lay back and stared up at my beautiful girl. I think I winked at her, before losing consciousness.

32

Charlotte was found dead less than an hour later. The end was instant. In his statement to police, the distraught lorry driver said that the jeep had veered out in front of him at the last second. There wasn't time to do anything. The lady was underneath before he could react. It was almost like she wanted to die.

The idea was discreetly dismissed. That stretch of road was notorious for accidents. It was just one of those things. Nobody wanted to add to the mess by openly suggesting everyone's private doubts. As a result, Charlotte left life in much the same way she had lived it, presenting a bland face to the world, with much darker instincts lurking just below the surface.

It was early the following morning before I found out. Waking up, and anxiously figuring out my new surroundings, I watched Lara asleep in a chair at the bottom of the bed. Round her shoulders was a red shawl I recognised as being my mother's. What a way for them to meet! There was no sign of my parents. They had carried out these dawn patrols too many times in the past. As I struggled to move up the bed a little, I promised myself they would never again have to go through this hospital ceremony. A nurse pulled back one of the plastic curtains and peered in.

"Are you back with us?" she asked.

I nodded and watched as the nurse gently shook Lara's shoulder. There was a wonderful moment when she opened her eyes and didn't immediately recognise that I too was awake. Just a small smile, and then the shift to full awareness. Her lips tasted wonderful.

"Is there any chance you might become a little bit more boring in future?" she whispered.

"I'm going to bore you for a long, long time."

She kissed lightly around my face which was a beautiful gesture considering that I looked as if I should have been hanging in a butcher's window. We didn't move for quite some time. Only the nurse coming back broke us up. As she checked my blood pressure, Lara held my hand and filled me in on what had happened.

"It is thanks to Inspector Yeats. He arrived at the house and wanted to know where you were. He was so anxious it scared me. You had to be found immediately, he said. So I told him you had gone early to ride Patrician at the schooling grounds. He drove so fast I was sure we would crash. It was terrible. All he said was to keep a look-out for you and Mrs Hoy. Only when I was almost screaming at him to explain, did he tell me she was the one who had killed Anatoly. And then Mr Yeats saw the fire."

We sat holding hands for a long time until I couldn't help but drop off. The last thing I saw was Lara's hand gripping mine. What a lovely way to fall asleep.

I slept for much of the day. A sedative kept everything

comfortably fuzzy and numb as various doctors sombrely examined my ankle and said how lucky I was. It was true too, even though the heavy bandages on my hands and various stitches tattooed across my head might have made it look otherwise. There was also a stench of disinfectant that made any new visitor flinch and take a step back. No chances were being taken with cuts getting dirty. In the afternoon, a young doctor with grey hair and a harassed expression returned to say that the ankle had a fracture and I'd have to use crutches for a few weeks.

"The rest of the stuff is mostly superficial. Cuts and bruises. You were lucky."

"I know."

My parents returned and I filled them in on everything that had happened with Franco and Charlotte.

"Sounds like they deserved each other," my dad said. "You're a fortunate little bugger."

I agreed and told them why I was really lucky. By the time Lara arrived from work, Mum was ready to hug her and immediately invite us home. She recovered quickly enough to have them both eating out of her hand and I lay there watching them with a stupid happy grin on my face. After the parents left, we held hands again and talked before the curtains split to reveal Eamon's smiling face, and behind him Vaz.

"Are we interrupting?" Eamon asked.

"Come in, you two," I said.

"There's a couple more actually," he replied and suddenly in trooped Johnno, followed more hesitantly by Jack. After the scramble for chairs, there was a short awkwardness before Johnno broke the atmosphere.

"You'll do fucking anything for attention!"

It was unexpectedly touching to have the lads piled in

around me. Vaz addressed me seriously and again apologised for having struck out in the station, a story the others urged him to recount, which he did to general amusement. The big man wasn't sure how to react until Lara whispered in Russian and he shook his head.

"The Irish are a very strange people," he said.

Eamon said all the media people were back at the yard in even greater strength, camped outside and asking everyone questions about what kind of person Charlotte was, and how her mother was reacting.

"What a stupid thing to ask," he said. "How would anyone react?"

"All the rest of us can do is pull together and make sure the ship sails on," Johnno added. "We'll keep going until she's ready to think about it again."

There was a quiet determination among them that left me in no doubt the yard was in good hands. How Bailey came through was more important. I'd learned she was a lot more vulnerable than she would like to admit. She had said just after Anatoly's death that no parent should have to bury a child. How on earth could one begin to cope with the emotional turmoil of burying your own child, and one who had murdered? The idea of staying in bed and resting suddenly seemed a grotesque indulgence and it was a good thing the dope started kicking in.

"Easy there, chief," Johnno said. "Everything will still be there when you're ready to get up. There's no point doing yourself more damage."

Everyone started to troop out. Jack gave my arm a squeeze and said I'd missed nothing at Downpatrick anyway. Lara kissed me and said she would be back later; evening stables had to be done first. If it was possible to think more of her, I did just then. Besides, there wasn't much company in me. Sleep was taking over. Gratefully, I shifted myself down the bed and drifted off.

Waking up to Yeats a couple of hours later wasn't quite the same thing as seeing my girl, but pleasing just the same. I stirred at the same time he looked like nodding off. That lugubrious face seemed more weary than ever. Lines that hadn't been there before ran down his cheeks and there was even more grey hair.

"Good to see you looking so well," he smiled.

"I could say the same."

"Yeah, it's been tough."

We didn't say anything for quite some time after that. One of my neighbours had switched on the television at the end of the room. Even though Yeats had his back to it, and the curtain was barring my view, we both listened to the familiar theme music of a popular soap and allowed the story to wash over us. It wasn't an uncomfortable silence and some minutes went by before I broke it.

"Thanks for saving my neck."

"You've actually got Franco to thank."

"What do you mean?"

"There's no way on God's green earth I would have guessed anything if it hadn't been for him. I would have sat, waiting for the lab reports, and looking for them to nail Franco. I was convinced we'd got our guy. Which only shows that you can never presume anything. You'd have been finished except Franco decided he wanted to squawk."

"Why did he do that?"

"He's a calculating bastard, that's why. I could see him all the time we were talking – trying to figure out what we really knew. And, of course, the more we kept insisting he was the one meant he was a step ahead of us all the time. I reckon he was happy to wait until we had the test results and then back himself to beat anything they threw up. He would have been right too. Nothing conclusive came back, but then his solicitor demanded a few minutes for the family to meet. After that, Franco seemed a lot less assured, more uncertain."

"Charlotte said Franco had told her how I'd rung and asked to meet him. She'd copped on straight away what was happening."

"Of course she did, and Franco realised what she was going to do. That's why he started to do some serious thinking. There was a good chance they could get away with Anatoly. Any forensics we could get connecting Charlotte to it could be argued. She was around him all the time, worked in the same place. But you'd be different. That would be much more risky. So he totted up the risk and figured it was worth shopping his wife."

"Thank Christ he did."

"I was at home having a shower when he decided he wanted to talk. Then we had to get his damn solicitor out of bed. The guy didn't miss a beat. He's supposed to be this mad artist hothead and instead he sits there, cool as a breeze, like a politician negotiating a pay rise. The lawyer might as well have still been in the scratcher."

"What did he say?"

"Apparently behind all the bluster, Charlotte was the real boss. Mind you, she was also the main financial source. Franco had been seeing Anatoly for a few months, nothing serious, just some fun, he said. They used to meet quite often at night in that stable box. Anatoly could cycle out and it was close to Franco's house. He'd bring a blanket and it was completely private. Franco would like to do some coke too and often gave Anatoly money to buy some. It was all very nice for a while but then the youngster started getting 'clingy' as Franco put it. He wanted more than just fun. It was serious for him. And he started to get a little too fond of drugs for Franco's taste. So he stopped seeing him."

"And that's when Anatoly started putting the bite on," I said.

"Yes. According to Franco the young man was devastated, threatened to kill himself. Then he threatened to tell Charlotte about them. Apparently she met him and gave him money. But that wasn't enough. Anatoly apparently owed more, probably to your friend Wolf. Then he came after them again, threatening to tell Mrs McFarlane."

"Charlotte couldn't have that."

"Franco says that on the night of the murder his wife told him she was going to meet the young man again and plead with him. But obviously she had decided to 'eliminate the problem', as she would see it. It was only the following morning that she told him what she'd done. Even explained how she'd set up Wolf to take the fall by planting the murder weapon in the horse box."

"And he said nothing."

"Correct. The way he put it was that he couldn't squeal on his wife. All honourable. But he'd eventually realised how wrong he was, which was why he told us eventually. That is one devious, opportunistic individual."

"Is he going to get away with it?"

"No, he's going to do time. But there's no question it will sit well in court that he talked in time to save your hide. If he does three or four years, that'll be it."

"Hardly seems enough."

"No, it does not. Mind you, it's more than Wolf will get."

"You got him?"

"No, we didn't get him. As soon as the news about Mrs Hoy came out, he suddenly appeared at the station. Bold as brass. Just waltzes in, hands out in front of him, telling us he was coming quietly."

"That sounds about right," I said.

"Actually he told me to tell you something."

"What?"

"I'm supposed to tell you 'Boo!' Does that mean something to you?"

"Yeah, it does," I said. "Tell me he's going to be put away."

"Yes. But a guy like that knows the law better than most lawyers. He's reckoned a year or a year and a half is all he'll have to do and then he'll come out and start fresh. Driving that lorry was for peanuts compared to what he was generating from drugs."

The background volume from the soap opera rose as what sounded like a fight broke out. It was enough for Yeats to turn around and throw a brief, sceptical eye on what was happening. Whatever it was didn't seem worthy of mention. Instead, he stretched, yawned comfortably, and made to stand up.

"What about that horse of yours?" he said. "The good one you told our desk sergeant to back. When's it supposed to race?"

"Less than two weeks."

Yeats glanced at my foot peeping out from underneath the sheets, took in the heavy bandaging, and correctly calculated my chances of making it back in time to ride Patrician at Cheltenham. Funnily enough, it was the first time I'd given the matter any thought. He didn't say anything for some time and I realised the hard-minded policeman was looking for a gentle way to say something.

"It doesn't really matter that much, you know," he said eventually.

"No. It doesn't really matter at all."

33

Reggie McGuire promised to ring back. Said he wanted to make sure it was me. So I sat on the edge of the bed, staring at my bandaged foot, and the crutches that would be close friends for the next fortnight, waiting for second thoughts to emerge. There were none. There was nothing but relief. Making the decision had been the hard bit. All that remained was to formalise it.

"I had to ring back," Reggie boomed. "You've never offered me a story in your life. Thought you were someone taking the piss."

"Your professionalism is to be admired," I said, grinning. "That's why you get first crack at my retirement."

"Are you serious? You're jacking it in?"

"Yeah. It's as good a time as any. And I'd rather get out now when it's my choice rather than hang around and be broken up."

"What about Patrician?"

"With any luck, he'll dance up in the Gold Cup."

"Listen, Liam. I hate asking, but people will speculate. Is

your decision anything to do with what's been going on recently? All this stuff about TT's lunatic daughter, her husband and that poor foreign kid?"

There had been little else in the papers and on the television for days. Some of Yeats' colleagues were clearly leaking like sieves and the papers were full of lurid detail and the professionally profound verdicts of so-called experts. It had made me almost relieved to be in hospital and away from the circus in the outside world.

"Absolutely not, Reggie. This is my call."

"How did Bailey take it?"

"I haven't been able to get in touch with her."

There was an awkward silence at that. Before ringing Reggie, I'd contacted other trainers I rode for, and some owners, to let them know. It was purely a courtesy. No one hollered anything back about being let down. Insisting on jockeys riding was not on. Instead, there were only good wishes. But Bailey's phones remained resolutely off. Hardly surprising really.

"Between us, is that really the case?" McGuire asked.

"Off the record, Reggie, that woman you love to rip the piss out of has been superb to me. If there's any regret, it's that I haven't done more for her. She doesn't deserve any of this."

"Enough said then. Tell us about the highlights of your career – the best horses and all that."

That made for an enjoyably nostalgic half hour as I waited for Lara to come and drive us home. The Cheltenham wins, that Grand National that had opened up so much and now seemed as if it had taken place in a long-gone era. Being champion jockey: all the stuff that might be dragged out years in the future when nobody believed the fat old geezer when he said he'd once been a jockey. Reggie eventually said he had enough material.

"For what it's worth, Liam, I think you were the best. A great jockey and a good guy. Even if you never did give me a line."

"Jesus, Reg, I'm going all red."

"Piss off, ingrate. I've got to get busy and make you look competent."

I hung up smiling and noticed Lara standing behind me, with a look of concern on her face.

"What's the matter?" I asked.

"Is it true you are stopping riding?"

"Yeah. I've been thinking about it for some time and it's not been doing me or anyone else any good. Once you don't want to do it one hundred per cent, you're only asking to get hurt. And I can think of punishing this sorry carcass in far nicer ways than on a horse."

She neatly side-stepped away and warned me to behave myself. Instead, we packed up the bits and pieces that had gathered during my hospital stay and made for the car. Over the years I'd got used to leaving hospitals on crutches, but never with such optimism. Now the line of no return was crossed, a future lay open that excited me more than I could have imagined. It would be new and different and from scratch. That college course had suddenly got much closer. Maybe it could wait. Instead, there might be a plane just a few miles away, going God knows where and there was nothing stopping me getting on. Every kind of food and drink was waiting to be tasted, and without guilt. But most of all Lara would be there too. It had struck home rather forcibly that every idealised dream I'd had included her.

We were quickly back in Dublin after having stopped briefly for some groceries. My requests to dump them in the boot and head into town for a huge meal at the fanciest restaurant had been shouted down. What I needed was home cooking, apparently. It was no hassle to give in. We got back to my house and I was immediately ordered to stay out of the way. Again, hardly a hardship. But as I sat in front of the TV, and listened to Lara busily at work in the kitchen, it dawned on me how bare the place was. The evidence of a morning uncomfortably spent in a furniture shop picking out the easiest option lay all around me. If the whole place went up in smoke, there wasn't one thing I would miss.

Despite almost falling over the crutches, I managed to get to the kitchen and watched as Lara tore lettuce, chopped tomatoes and kept an eye on two large steaks that sizzled and spat in a frying pan. The smell of onions and mushrooms was delicious.

"Don't just stand there," she said. "You can lay the table. If there is anything around to put on it."

It was slow progress, but the table got set up. We sat down, pretended the surroundings were okay, and poured German beer that Lara swore was the best in the world. It tasted wonderful. So did the food. I had to remind myself that it was okay to eat as much as I liked. That felt good too.

When we went to bed, we held each other until nothing else was possible but to slowly and inevitably love each other to sleep.

It took something special to rouse me from this warm happiness but the maddening itch from my face and scalp managed it. Before leaving the hospital, I had had strict orders not to scratch. Dire warnings about permanent scars accompanied foul-smelling disinfectant, but relief at getting out overrode all of it. Lying bloated and uncomfortable in bed, with hands clenched by my sides, was a different matter though. Rubbing my head up and down the pillow didn't work. No amount of twisting and turning helped. A few minor scratches provoked nothing only guilt. I looked at the clock: it was five in the morning. There was nothing else for it but to get up.

Outside, little moved under the street lights. Normally the only one leaving at this time of the morning was me, driving to some distant gallop or early morning flight. Those crazy hours and the constant rush to be somewhere else were in the past now. So were the shivering visits to the nearby park to run enough sweat off for the day ahead. All I felt, staring out at the same brave new world, was relief.

The twenty-four-hour rolling news channel droned quietly in the background as I organised a cup of tea and kept an ear cocked for news of Charlotte and Franco. There was none. The evening before, on the car radio, there had been a brief line about Franco being arrested on charges of conspiracy. From what Yeats had said, Franco had no doubt calculated his odds on that too. Three or four years, the inspector had guessed. It definitely didn't seem enough.

I'd just sat down when the sports news started and my own face suddenly appeared on screen. Apparently, the station had quickly picked up on McGuire's story. The determinedly fresh and eager young presenter duly credited the paper with breaking the news that the ride on the Gold Cup favourite Patrician was available after Liam Dee's retirement. Cut to some pictures of Patrician and me winning our last race, and then back to a piece of banter with the co-host about the jockeys waking up to a golden opportunity.

Forgotten and irrelevant already, I decided. Just as it should be. The next race is always the most important. The past is only a form book. I raised my cup of tea and toasted the past.

Stretching the leg out and placing the hot mug on wherever the itch felt particularly bad made things feel a little better. Outside, the clatter of a bin falling over, followed by some heartfelt swearing from next door signalled the start of a new day. The familiar hum from the motorway started to increase and a couple of cars coughed into life down the street. I was concentrating so much that Lara appeared at the door without my knowing it.

"Are you okay?" she asked.

"Yeah. Just got a little itchy and didn't want to wake you."

"Okay. I'm going to take a shower and then go to work."

"Sure. I'll make some breakfast."

It called for a little bit more than my usual black tea and an apple but, despite my spending most of the time leaning against the sink, a small tray of toast and scrambled eggs was waiting when she came out. There was even time to get some clothes on as Lara ate. She was finishing up, putting on a coat while eating the last bit of toast, when I walked into the kitchen.

"I'm off," she said.

"Wait for me."

34

Eamon and I walked slowly to the kitchen door. As we stepped inside, he asked if the paper was right about my retirement. I nodded.

"Good. Maybe you'll get some fat on your bones now," he said, patting me on the arm.

We looked around at what was normally the chaotic headquarters of our little world. Nothing was out of place. An empty sink shone and every cup and plate was where it should be. No smell of rapidly fried and digested food filled the air. A table that normally groaned under the weight of papers, bits of tack and feet thrown on top of it, was bare for the first time I could remember. The atmosphere was enough to make me look at Eamon.

"I tidied up a bit, but she isn't eating and she isn't really talking," he said. "I come in here in the morning and the evening and tell her what's going on and what bits of work we're doing. All she does is nod and go back into the garden. She doesn't go anywhere else. Her ex-husband and all her relatives have tried to talk to her but nothing works."

We slowly made our way into the big drawing room and felt a cool breeze coming through the partially opened windows. At the side of the garden, next to where some daffodils were starting to bloom into life, Bailey sat on a stone bench, her back to the house. She was wearing a dressing-gown and slippers despite the cold wind.

"I'm worried, Liam," Eamon said. "I don't think she has slept since it all happened. It doesn't help that the police still have Charlotte's body. She can't go through that whole grieving process properly."

There was an imploring look in his eyes that ruled out any suggestion from me that I might come back some other time.

I nodded again and he called out gently, "Bailey, there's someone to see you."

She didn't turn around. In fact, she gave no indication she'd even heard him, but then her voice emerged surprisingly clearly.

"I don't want to see anyone, Eamon."

He all but pushed me out and the squeak from the rubber tips at the bottom of my crutches suddenly seemed very loud. The step up onto the grass required some concentration and only after negotiating it did I recognise how her back had stiffened with tension at the alien sounds. She still didn't turn around as I tentatively approached, trying desperately to think of something to say.

I was close enough to reach out and touch her, give a reassuring hug to let this woman know I wanted to comfort her. But it didn't feel right just yet. I hopped around the bench and sat down next to her.

Nothing was said. I glanced to my left. Bailey was looking away into the shrubs and plants that busily competed for space in the fertile earth to the side. The change in her appearance was shocking. That strong brown face looked as if the air had been let out of it. Sunken cheeks lay lifelessly under eyes that had obviously cried themselves to exhaustion. Her hair straggled over her face and there was a terrible weariness to that usually proud body. Bailey was not young, but now she was starting to look old.

We simply sat there for quite some time. No doubt Eamon would have been cursing me for a useless clown if he'd remained watching. But when I turned around there was no one there.

Bailey had to be cold. The wind blew a thin nightgown around her pale feet. Only light slippers protected them and the dressing gown had slipped from her legs, but she didn't seem to notice. I stood up.

"I'll make us some tea."

Everything in the kitchen was where I remembered but a welcome surprise was an unopened Madeira cake at the back of one of the cupboards. A trainer I used to ride for always swore the best pick-me-up after a fall was a shot of brandy and port along with some cake. The booze could wait but getting some food into Bailey wouldn't do any harm.

Getting it out to her though, along with two cups of tea, was a feat of balance and agility to match anything ever seen in a race. But somehow I managed to return to the seat without smashing any other bones. She looked at me long enough to take a cup and a piece of cake. A minute later, I looked again and saw tears pouring silently down her face.

"I'm sorry," she whispered a number of times as her tears continued.

I slipped my arm through hers and pressed against her, determinedly looking straight ahead in case of uselessly adding to the tears myself. We sat like that for some time, the food uneaten, and nothing said, trying to make the world seem a little less bleak. Eventually, she broke the silence. Her tears had dried up, or maybe there were none left.

"How are you feeling?" she asked eventually, looking at my foot.

"I'm okay. Just worried about you."

"No need for that. I'm too old to die."

She put the cup down on the grass. The cake followed and an alert robin emerged to eye it hungrily. We watched as it gathered the courage to hop closer and closer until Bailey leaned down, broke a bit off and threw it towards him. He arranged a piece into his beak and flew off to eat it on top of the nearby wall.

"Bailey, if there's anything I can do . . ."

The uselessness of such a statement was patently obvious to both of us. There was also something in the way that tired body straightened slightly that suggested she was going to ask if I hadn't done enough already. But not for the first time I misjudged the woman.

"I hope you have children, Liam. I really do. Until it happens, you cannot know what love is. It's the most unconditional thing, and it doesn't matter how old they are. You simply feel total love. Not the crap in religion or in books. But the sort that makes you wake up in the night at just the idea of something happening to them. It's what I've always feared most, you know, ever since they were born: something happening to them."

I didn't reply. There was no point. She was right. I didn't know. The only thing I could do was listen.

"My child is dead. I know she killed someone else's child, but she's still my child," Bailey said quietly. "I've made such a mess of everything. Talking about family, and tearing my own apart."

"You can't blame yourself."

"Can't I?" she sniffed. "Do you know the last thing my little girl said to me? She said everything would be okay in the morning. Everything would be fine. She would make sure of it. My child actually believed that killing you would make things okay. I created someone who believed that! And, when it didn't work, my little girl saw nothing else in the world worth living for."

"You don't know that."

"Oh, but I do. Jesus, Liam, she almost killed you too. And all because of this place. A heap of bricks and concrete."

The robin fluttered back in front of us for seconds. Crumbs of cake were strewn under Bailey's feet and our friend hopped impatiently when nothing was thrown out to him. He flew back and forth a number of times, as if storing up courage for a lightning raid, but he repeatedly came up short. Torn between fear and desire, there was nothing for it but sit on a nearby branch and chirp defiance at us. Bailey didn't appear to see or hear him and the little bird suddenly seemed to understand this too. A brown blur shot to the ground and was gone again before either of us could move.

Out of sight, over the high wall to our right, came the sound of the string pulling out for first lot. It was strangely reassuring. Through everything, they had been the one constant, something to cling on to. No matter what else was happening, the horses had to be fed and watered. I took Bailey's hand and held it tightly. She looked at me straight.

"What am I going to do?"

Her voice tailed off plaintively, as if she was directing the question to the wind and not expecting a reply. Yet she clearly needed to hear something, and not just some trite cant about individual responsibility or Charlotte being old enough to make her own decisions. Everything she held dear was either gone or useless. But how could I come up with something to try and stabilise that? It didn't matter, I told myself. I was the one sitting next to her at this critical moment. Now was the time to come up with something.

"You're going to let us help you, that's what," I said almost in a whisper. "Me and Eamon and Lara and Johnno and everyone else. And we'll do it because we think you're great."

The tears came back and she returned my grip. At that moment the robin chose to fly down again and land on my bandaged foot, staring belligerently up at us, demanding our disappearance so he could feed properly. Even in the midst of so much awfulness, there was something so wonderfully defiant about the little creature that Bailey couldn't help blurting out a sobbing chuckle.

"I'm not going to tell you what to do," I continued. "But I know what you will do. You're going to bury your daughter. Nothing else matters now. It'll be terrible, but we'll be here to help as best we can. You'll grieve for your child and slowly come to terms with never feeling the same again. That will take as long as it takes. But, one day, you will wake up and the pain won't be quite as bad. That won't mean you don't love Charlotte any less, or miss her just as much. It will mean you'll have learned to cope a little better. That's all."

Bailey released my hand and leaned down to break off another bit of cake. Our friend bounced off his synthetic perch and practically reached up to take his hard-earned feast. There was no frantic escape this time. Instead, there was a more leisurely examination of his meal. We continued to watch him until the sound of the string returning started to echo towards us.

"They'll be waiting when the day comes," I continued, nodding towards the sound of the horses clattering past. "That doesn't seem important now, but it will be when you're ready. And even though it seems impossible to imagine now, you will be ready again."

We sat and listened to the sounds of the yard, as timeless to this part of the world as the fully fed robin chirping his challenge to any would-be invader. From outside, guffaws and oaths filled the air and, at one stage, Vaz's base rumble of a laugh carried as far as us. After unsaddling came the splash of water as the horses were hosed down, and then the clatter of doors as they were taken back to their boxes for a breakfast top-up. Maybe it was wishful thinking on my part, but it seemed that Bailey was listening attentively as well. I was about to say something else but there was a loud interruption. Patrician was demanding his grub and making plenty of noise about it. It was enough to provoke another small chuckle from next to me.

"As Eamon says, we'll be dug out of that horse."